Torrian

The Highland Clan
BOOK TWO

KEIRA MONTCLAIR

THE GRANTS AND RAMSAYS IN 1280S

Grants

1. Laird Alexander Grant, and wife, Maddie (Book #1)
   a.   Twin lads-James (Jamie) and John (Jake)
   b.   Kyla
   c.   Connor
   d.   Elizabeth

2. Brenna Grant and husband, Quade Ramsay (Book #2)
   a.   Torrian (Quade's son from first marriage)
   b.   Lily (Quade's daughter from first marriage)
   c.   Bethia
   d.   Gregor
   e.   Jennet

3. Robbie Grant and wife, Caralyn (Book #4)
   a.   Ashlyn
         (Caralyn's daughter from a previous relationship)
   b.   Gracie
         (Caralyn's daughter from a previous relationship)
   c.   Rodric (Roddy)
   d.   Padraig

4. Brodie Grant and wife, Celestina (Book #3)
   a.   Loki (adopted) and Arabella-son, Lucas
         (Book One of The Highland Clan)
   b.   Braden
   c.   Catriona
   d.   Alison

5. Jennie Grant and husband, Aedan Cameron(Book #7)
a. Riley
b. Tara
c. Brin

Ramsays

1. Quade Ramsay and wife, Brenna Grant (see above)
2. Logan Ramsay and wife, Gwyneth (Book #5)
   a. Molly (adopted)
   b. Maggie (adopted)
   c. Sorcha
   d. Gavin
   e. Brigid

3. Micheil Ramsay and wife, Diana (Book #6)
   a. David
   b. Daniel

4. Avelina Ramsay and Drew Menzie (Book #8)
   a. Elyse
   b. Tad
   c. Tomag
   d. Maitland

CHAPTER ONE

Early spring 1280s, Scotland

Heather of Preston jolted up as soon as she was able to clear the sleep from her brain. Nellie, wee Nellie, where was she? She crawled across the cold stone floor until she found her daughter of four summers. Gathering the lassie into her arms, she pressed her cheek to her forehead, her heart hopeful. The heat from her wee one's tender skin shattered that hope in an instant. Still, she crooned to the lassie and shook her ever so slightly to see if she could wake her.

She could not. After three days, her daughter's fever had not abated. Heather carried her out of the hidden cave, hoping the early dawn light would rouse her. Nellie's fair locks, normally shining from the sun, hung limp around her face, and the skin across her cheekbones was dry and dusky. Her eyes had not opened in two days, and her breathing was even shallower than it had been the day before.

Heather had to do something. Afraid to move Nellie and even more afraid she would be unable to carry her far, she took the lassie back into the cave they had lived in for the past three summers, covered her with a warm plaid, kissed her cheek, and struggled to keep the tears from running down her face. "Mama loves you, sweeting. I must go for help. 'Tis time to go to the greatest healer in the Highlands. You know we've watched her for many moons. She'll know what to do."

A sickening feeling welled in her gut at the thought of leaving Nellie, but there was no choice. After strapping her bow and quiver to her back, she tied on her boots and set off toward the Ramsay clan.

Just move one foot in front of the other and you will get there.

She continued her mantra as she raced through the forest, thankful it was early spring so she did not have to run through heavy snow. In her heart, she feared she would not be successful. It was a trek, especially since she hadn't eaten much of late for fear of leaving Nellie to hunt, but her daughter meant more to her than aught in the world. Neither beast nor man would impede her effort to reach Brenna of the Ramsays. She would not allow her fears to get the best of her.

When she finally reached the meadow, her ragged breathing was audible above the sounds of the morning birds. *Please God, please God, save my daughter, she is everything to me.*

She'd watched the Ramsays from afar for many moons, admiring the clan's tenacity and hard work. There was one lass who was an amazing archer, and Heather had watched and listened as she trained the youngest members of the clan. Using the lass's lessons as a guide, she had crafted her own bow. It had taken her a long time, but it was worth it to have another weapon besides her dagger.

Why hadn't she hunted for food before leaving? The grumbling deep in her belly reminded her how long it had been since she'd eaten. She could feel her legs weakening beneath her, but her will would prevail. Of that, she was certain.

She had to save her daughter, she just had to.

⚬⚬

Torrian Ramsay, first son of the Ramsay chieftain, stood near the gate of the Ramsay curtain wall, conversing with two of the guards and his friend and age-mate, Kyle.

"Aye, Torrian," Kyle said, "'tis time for you to marry. Your sire wishes it, Brenna wishes it, just pick one. Why not that saucy wench who was clinging to you the other eve? She had plenty of...attributes." The guards laughed right along with Kyle, but Torrian took it in stride.

"When I find the right lass, I'll marry. Until then, worry about the lasses in your own beds." His sire and his uncle told him it was the way of men to tease each other about their sexual exploits, and Uncle Logan had taught him how to spar with words. No one needed to know that he preferred not to keep company with promiscuous women.

The sound of heavy, ragged breathing reached his ears, and he turned his head just in time to see a frenzied lass running straight for them, coming from the meadow, not the village. Though she was fleet of foot, she seemed weak.

One of the guards started to make a quip, but Torrian cut him off. "Is your tongue so busy you have forgotten to do your duty?" He pointed to the lass and then launched himself in her direction, Kyle fast behind him. He made it to the meadow behind the row of cottages just in time to catch her before her head hit the ground.

He scooped her into his arms and headed back to the castle, intent on finding his stepmother, Brenna, the Ramsay clan's healer, but her eyes flew open and she shoved her wee fists against Torrian's large chest.

To his bafflement, he realized he'd seen her before on Ramsay land. He'd tried to speak to her, but she had run from him as soon as their eyes met. There was no mistaking her, for she had one blue eye and one green eye. The only other person he'd ever seen with eyes like that was his cousin, Loki Grant. The Grant family had adopted Loki after he was found living behind an inn at the royal burgh. Did the shared eye color mean they were related? He had no idea, but he would be sure to ask his cousin the next time they met.

"Nay, the healer," the lass shouted, breaking him out of his daze. "Find the healer. I need her."

"I can see that, lass. I'm taking you to our healer, Lady Brenna." Torrian could tell the lass searched for his stepmother, the person who'd healed him and married his sire. He used to call her mama, but now, he called her by name. Lily, his sister, still used both depending on the occasion.

"Nay, not for me." She gasped for breath, but managed to continue. "Not for me. I need the healer for my daughter. Please. My daughter. She's dying. Help me." Her eyes closed, and her head fell back against Torrian.

Kyle ran ahead, yelling back over his shoulder. "I'll find Lady Brenna and bring her to you."

At the sound of his voice, the lass's eyes flew open again, and she said, "Stop, please stop!"

Torrian found a nearby bench and set her down. Her eyes were so full of worry, he would have done aught to comfort her. "We'll wait here until the healer arrives."

"Aye, please, the mistress of the castle, Lady Brenna. I need her. She can save my daughter." She paused to catch her breath, her fingers still gripping Torrian's tunic.

"What is your name?

"Heather. Please, my daughter, my Nellie, is dying."

"Where is Nellie?"

"In my cave. We live in a cave." Her breathing became more labored. "Not far. She is dying."

"What happened to her?" He brushed her golden locks back from her eyes, the wind having almost completely undone her plait. Not only were her eyes unique, her entire countenance was different from most of the lasses he knew. Dressed more like a lad than a lass, with a bow strapped to her back, she reminded Torrian a little of fierce Aunt Gwyneth, Uncle Logan's wife.

Brenna came running toward them from the gate, Kyle following at her side. "What is it, Torrian? What's wrong with her?" Lily was directly behind her.

Both he and the lass turned toward Brenna and Lily at the same time. Mindful of her ragged breathing, Torrian answered for her. "She says she's not hurt. She came to seek help for her daughter, who has taken ill. The lassie is in a cave not far from here."

"Please come with me?" Heather's hopeful gaze locked on Brenna just as the older woman nodded her head.

"Of course, I'll come with you. Help me decide what to bring. What kind of problem is your daughter having?"

"Fever. She's had a fever for several days," Heather gasped out. "Now she won't stir at all. I cannot get her to drink or eat aught." She still held a tight grip on Torrian's forearms, as if she were afraid he would run away, and for some odd reason, Torrian found that he quite liked her touch. Her scent was fresh—the wind, the trees, everything outdoors. Heather was the perfect name for her, for she looked like a wildflower in the meadow. Her skin was lightly bronzed from spending time in the sun, but it was flawless and beautiful.

Brenna issued instructions and everyone headed off to do as they were bid. "Torrian, get the lass on a horse with you and have another one saddled for me. Kyle, tell my husband what we are doing and find a few more guards to travel with us. Lily, I'm glad you're here. Please run to Cook and find some oatcakes and fruit we can take along. The lass looks as if she hasn't eaten in days. We'll meet at the stables."

As soon as she moved away, Heather locked gazes with Torrian. "Is she the one?"

"The one?"

"Is she the healer? The one who's healed so many?"

Torrian lifted her into his arms and started toward the stables to do his part. Brenna was right, she did not weigh much at all. "Aye, she and her sister Jennie, who lives near the abbey, are the best healers in the land."

"Are you sure? Nellie needs the best."

"I'm sure. I wouldn't be here if not for her skills." Torrian had a flashback of the many days he'd spent hidden in a distant cottage, so ill he couldn't get off his pallet. As a bairn, he had spent many days piled atop mounds of furs because of the painful blisters all over his body. His life had started again after Brenna cured him, and for that he would be ever grateful.

"Are you the laird's son?"

"Aye."

"She saved you, did she not?"

"Aye, she did. Me and Lily, my sister. She'll help your daughter. How do you know me?"

"Only from afar. I saw you in the forest many moons ago. But please, we must not tarry. Please hurry." She reached up and cupped his cheek.

Torrian almost jerked at her touch, so surprised by it, yet he found he did not wish for her to move. Though he knew she had heard Brenna, he found himself stammering, "We...we're at the stables. We'll ride so we don't waste time." One of the stable lads brought Torrian's horse out, then helped Torrian get Heather settled on the horse.

There was the sound of approaching footsteps, and moments later, Torrian's sire Quade appeared beside him. "Who's on the horse, Torrian," he said gruffly, "and where are you taking her?"

"Brenna is getting her healer's satchel and we're heading out into the meadow in search of a cave. This is Heather. She says her daughter is dying and needs Brenna's help. How old is your daughter?"

"Nellie is four summers."

Quade yelled for six of his guards. "Mount up, you'll go with my wife and son. Remember, Torrian, you and Brenna must ride on separate horses."

Torrian nodded, used to this command of his father's. After all Quade Ramsay had been through, the laird insisted that his wife and heir ride separately for fear of losing two loved ones at once.

CHAPTER TWO

Heather leaned back against the Ramsay lad, letting his heat envelop her in a warm embrace. The nights had been a bit cool of late, and she usually gave Nellie the heat of her body. It felt good to lean on someone, and Torrian had a rock-hard chest that supported her. Besides, he seemed to be sincere and kind, unlike another man she knew…

Having never known her parents, Heather had grown up with her grandmama, whom she'd lost in the year before Nellie was born, and her grandpapa, who'd died just after Nellie's birth. She'd chosen Nellie's name because it reminded her of her grandmother, Nellie.

Things had not gone well for her after her grandmama's death. Though her grandsire loved her, he knew naught about raising a lass. It had been a difficult time for her, but he'd trained her to hunt and shoot, the most valuable skills he could have taught her. Her daughter had given her a reason to live, a reason to care, a reason to wake up each morn. How such a beautiful thing could come from such a horrid act, she would never understand.

She'd devoted herself, heart and soul, to Nellie's well-being for the past four years. Tears stung her lids at the thought of losing her and going back to her old life.

She believed in the Ramsay healer. She had to.

Torrian's warm breath sent a shiver down her spine. "Is it just the two of you, or do you have a husband?"

"Nay," she whispered, staring at her hands. "There's just the two of us."

"How long have you lived in that cave?"

"Three summers now. 'Tis a wonderful life because 'tis just my Nellie and me, with naught to bother us."

For some reason, Torrian tucked her closer to him at that. How she wished she could have faith in a man, but experience had taught her they could not be trusted.

Somehow, she knew Torrian was unusual. Nay, this man would not harm her. Having watched him enough times over the years, she knew he was not the sort. Aye, he was trustworthy, unlike the other man in her life.

Stop thinking horrid thoughts.

The bouncing of the horse kept her from sleeping, which was good. She needed to give them directions. Steering them toward a well-hidden path, she led them through the twists and turns to the cave. As soon as the purple wildflowers came into view telling her they were close, she leaped down from the horse.

Her cave was well hidden, and she took off in its direction without him, trusting he would follow her. Before she could spare a thought for the others, she needed to know Nellie still breathed. Racing up the narrow path, swiping the tree branches away from her face, she hurried into the cave, only stopping when she fell to her knees beside her daughter. "Nellie?"

Nothing. She lifted the bairn into her arms and spoke into her ear. "Nellie. Wake up. Please, you must speak to Mama." Still, the wee lassie did not answer. Heather spun around to carry her out of the cave, but a soothing voice stopped her in her tracks.

"Set her down there," Brenna said. "I'll come to her, or you may settle her on your lap if you'd rather."

Heather glanced into Brenna's warm gaze. "Many thanks for coming. I do not know what I would do if..." Her voice cracked, so she stopped.

"I understand, I have three daughters," Brenna said, squeezing her shoulder. "I'll do my best for her, I promise."

Torrian came in behind Brenna after he delivered instructions to his guards. Torrian acted as if he'd been in charge his entire life, something unusual for one so young. But then again, she had little to compare him to.

Heather did Brenna's bidding, and soon she was sitting with Nellie's head cradled in her lap. She watched as Brenna gave Torrian a jug. "See if the guards can find fresh water."

"To the north. There's a creek there," Heather choked out.

When Torrian left to send the guards out for water, she found herself watching him. A brief tug inside her was persistent enough to cause her to stare at him before she remembered where her focus belonged.

Brenna worked on Nellie for almost an hour, washing her body with the cool liquid from the stream, doing her best to get her to drink, and rubbing a salve on her chest. Heather prayed over and over that her daughter would awaken, but she did not.

"Heather, I know this is probably against your wishes, but I think you should bring her to our keep so I can spend more time with her. This cave is fine for the two of you when she is well, but now that she's sick, I suspect you haven't been able to spend much time searching for food. Our keep is quite large. Why not bring wee Nellie to stay in a chamber with a soft bed and pillows—somewhere she can be warm until she heals? We can place you and Nellie in your own chamber so you can care for her, and we have maids to assist you."

"You will not try to make us stay, will you? You'll not try to keep her against my will?"

"Nay, I promise." Brenna patted her hand, then arranged her supplies and returned them to her satchel.

Torrian returned and strode over to her. "Here's an oatcake for you," he said, staring into her eyes as he reached out and handed it to her. "My guess is you have not been eating much."

Heather reached for the oatcake, her mouth watering at the mere thought of food, let alone the sight of it. "My thanks. I have not eaten."

Torrian added, "I remember what my sire was like when I fell ill. He barely left my side for years. You must take care of yourself, as well. 'Tis probably in your best interest to return to the keep with us for a short time."

Heather paused for a moment to consider their offer. Torrian was right—she'd stayed by Nellie's side ever since the fever struck, and she hadn't given food much thought. She'd barely had the strength to run to the Ramsay keep today.

"You've left the cave unguarded, lass." Torrian tipped his head toward the two spears she kept nearby in case any animal came inside the cave, along with a pile of rope and strings she usually tied across it to keep the smaller birds and animals at bay.

She gasped at the realization that she'd left without placing any ropes across the opening. Nellie had been in the cave without any protection. Tears flooded her eyes at her poor judgment. "We'll come along. Many thanks."

Torrian reached down to help her to her feet. "You're overtired, too. Brenna will watch over her so you can get some sleep. You wouldn't have forgotten the rope when you left if you'd been rested."

Her gaze locked on his as she stood with his help, and his green eyes offered her something she hadn't experienced in over five summers—comfort and support. And for the second time that day, Heather let herself lean on someone.

Quade, Torrian, Logan, and Gwyneth sat gathered in the laird's solar. Two of Quade's top guards, stood to the side. Torrian's da had asked them to his solar to remind them of the importance of always being aware of what took place outside the keep.

Quade sat behind his desk, rubbing the leg that had been bothering him lately, then waved his hand toward the door. "You may go, Seamus. I know you and Mungo will make sure the guards are doing their jobs as always. Just do not allow them to get distracted by idle chatter."

Unfortunately for the Ramsay guards, Quade had been in the lists with his men when the lass almost ran through their small village without any of his guards at the gate noticing. He was aware of everything.

"Chief, we'll make certain they understand. My apologies for failing you," Seamus bowed and turned to leave, Mungo trailing behind him.

As soon as they left, Quade added, "Not that a lass of her size was truly a threat…"

Logan barked, "Her size is of no import. What matters is she almost made it past four of our guards. Torrian was the first to notice her, and he had his back to her. There are many different ways to start an attack, and distracting our guards could be one of them. We must not lose our vigilance."

"All right, Logan. You've made your point, and 'tis a good one. Now, since the lass is here, what else do we know of her? What clan is she from?"

Torrian filled them in. "We know only what little she's told us.

She lives in a cave on the edge of our land, and she does not identify with any clan. She's been staying there with her daughter of four summers. I suspect she ran away from some situation. Nellie is four and she's been in the cave for three years. She must have gone to the cave soon after giving birth to her. She says there is no husband, and she's happy there. Though she's agreed to stay here until the wee lassie is better, she does not wish to stay permanently."

Quade thought for a moment, his fingers steepled in front of him. "'Tis all you've discovered about her?"

"Aye, there is one more thing, but I'd prefer if you do not mention it to the lass. She has the same eye color as Loki."

"Two different colors?" Quade asked.

"Aye, 'tis quite rare."

"They are exactly the same as Loki's." Gwyneth agreed with Torrian. "I agree that we not discuss it with her until we speak to Loki. But for now, she's verra worried about her daughter. Once Nellie begins to heal, I'll question her further."

"I hear she dresses as you do, Gwyneth," Quade said with a smile. "I'd love to know more about her."

"And in time, you will," Gwyneth promised.

"Accepted, 'tis no reason to rush this. She's welcome to stay, and I hope my wife can help her daughter. There are more pressing matters for us to discuss."

"Continue." Logan stared at Torrian. From the nature of his attention, it was clear Torrian was to be the next topic of discussion. The thought came with a fair portion of foreboding.

"Torrian, after much thought, your stepmother and I have decided 'tis time for you to marry."

Torrian almost toppled off his stool. So Kyle had spoken true. He had no response at all. None. Everyone in the solar stared at him, waiting for his response, so after a long pause, he decided to give them what they wanted. "Why must I marry? I have no interest in any lass here at all." Though he wouldn't admit it, Heather suddenly came to mind unbidden. Of course, she would not be considered a good match since she lived in the wild, but there was something about the lass that was difficult to forget.

There was a smirk at the edges of Quade's mouth, which only infuriated Torrian more. It was an unusual reaction for him.

Torrian prided himself on having a steady demeanor like his father, on being a peacemaker who rarely turned to anger to solve problems. He didn't get angry.

Until now.

"Well? Why throw that command at me without saying aught else? Da? Uncle Logan? Aunt Gwyneth? Who wants to speak? 'Tis clear you're all here to see how this ill news settles on me."

Quade started to speak, but stopped, his hand hovering in front of his mouth.

"Da. This is not funny! When have you started barking orders at me? Or am I not entitled to choose my own mate as the rest of my family has done? I'll call Grandmama down to haunt all of you if you continue with this ridiculous notion." What he wouldn't give to have his beautiful grandmother at his side this moment. They'd lost Lady Arlene Ramsay almost five years ago, and Torrian still missed her dearly. She would never have encouraged her son to press this issue.

Logan held his hand out before he stood. "Now, hold your tongue, lad. I know this upsets you, but do not start throwing out accusations before you hear who we have in mind. You know as well as the next one that a chieftain's heir must have his own heirs, and 'tis near time for you to be started on it."

"I'm only five and twenty."

"You're six and twenty, and your cousin Loki is already married with a bairn on the way."

Torrian got up out of his seat to pace. Six and twenty? When had that happened? He halted for a second to face his sire. "I know full well what my responsibilities are as your son, Da. Or have you not noticed? But I had thought I would have the right to choose a wife of my own liking."

"Torrian, calm yourself," Quade said. "I have mentioned this to you before, yet you still have not courted any lasses. King Alexander mentioned to Logan when he last saw him that he thought he had a good match for you. 'Tis only fair for you to meet the lass."

His king had found a match for him? Torrian fell into a chair. This was too much to take in all at once. "All right. I'll listen. Tell me what you know."

Logan folded his hands together and waited for Torrian to give him his attention. "Are you ready to hear me out?" Uncle Logan and Aunt Gwyneth had both worked for the crown many times over the years, sometimes as spies. They were very familiar with King Alexander, though they had another contact, Hamilton, with whom they worked more frequently.

"Aye. I said I'd listen."

"True, but are you open to this suggestion, or are you already rejecting it as a possibility?"

Torrian closed his eyes for a moment before taking a deep breath. "I shall listen to what you have to say. You have my undivided attention."

Logan nodded and said, "The king has asked if you would consider marrying Davina of Buchan in Perthshire. She is a lovely lass of ten and nine summers. I've seen her myself, so I can attest to her beauty. The Buchans have been having some issues with their neighboring clans, so they do not wish to marry her to anyone nearby. They are interested in an alliance with the Ramsays. You are the eldest male, and they are requesting a betrothal to the laird's son. Gregor is near ten years younger than you, so he does not suit. Now, do you have aught you'd like to ask me?"

"I'm highly suspicious of a clan who cannot get along with any of their neighbors enough to arrange a marriage," Torrian grumbled. "Have you any more to say on the matter?"

"I have. The Buchans are becoming more aggressive. That's not to say Davina is aggressive, but her cousin, brother, and sire are stirring up trouble in the Highlands. The king is hoping this alliance will help satisfy them and prevent them from causing trouble."

"In other words, if I marry Davina, you and Da will be more aware of the Buchan's movements, so you can let the king know if trouble is brewing before it happens. I'm to be the pawn in his game."

Logan smirked a little and glanced first at Gwyneth and then at Quade. Though not pleased with the situation, Torrian felt gratified that he'd read it correctly. He sat back in his chair and crossed his arms in front of him, awaiting the others' response.

Aunt Gwyneth said, "I told you he was quick. Well done, nephew." She nodded and then walked from the room, patting

Torrian's shoulder on her way out.

Logan caught Quade's gaze and nodded. "He's all yours, Quade." But he stayed in the solar with them, watching with his hawk-like eyes that saw everything.

Quade played with one of the carvings that decorated his desk. "You are correct in your assessment. But you're not interested in any of the lasses on our land, are you, Torrian?"

"Nay, but you advised me not to bed any of the lasses from our clan unless I was serious and interested in marriage. I have not found that lass yet." He paused, then decided to be honest. "'Tis true I have not searched verra hard."

"I will support your final decision, as I know how your grandmother felt about forced marriages, but I would like you to at least meet Davina to see if you would make a match. She would be a smart match, and I believe 'tis always wise to expand your allies. 'Tis also best to keep watch of your enemies. Davina of Buchan is not our enemy, but her brother, sire, or cousin—the MacNivens—could be."

Torrian mulled this over for a moment without speaking.

"I see your keen mind whirring," Logan added, "so allow me to add that it would be highly insulting for you to refuse the match without meeting the lass, both to her sire and to the king, and I would not recommend it. We're asking you to do a favor for your clan, lad."

Shite, his uncle had just made the one plea he would never be able to refuse.

Do a favor for your clan. He'd been raised to believe that his clan was more important than aught. That guaranteed his answer.

"And if you do not suit," his sire added, "I'm sure she'll feel the same, and the betrothal will never take place."

"I'll agree to meet her, but only for the clan."

"That's all we ask, lad." His sire stood and clasped his shoulder. "If she be ill natured or uncomely, there will be no match. Logan will send word to the king. We will travel to the Buchans together. Be ready to travel soon, possibly on the morrow."

How he hoped his father was telling the truth. He had a very bad feeling about this.

CHAPTER THREE

When Torrian stepped outside the solar, his faithful Scottish Deerhound stood there waiting for him, her tail already wagging.

"Och, Gertie. 'Tis true I must leave you for a while." He patted her head and walked over to the corner of the great hall where he'd set out a mound of furs for her and her pups. She'd had a fresh litter of pups several weeks ago, and they were growing stronger every day. He'd already given one away to a sickly lad in the clan. The last litter he'd given away because Gertie was due for this new litter, though he gave the pups only to families he trusted.

The new litter of pups slept in his chamber at night, but during the day they stayed in the stables or the great hall where they could play with the wee ones. The bairns loved the pups.

Torrian sat down on the floor, allowing the pups to clamor into his lap while Gertie rested her head on his lower leg. "I swear, Gertie, you always seem to know what's to happen before I do."

Gertie grunted and Torrian snorted. "I agree, 'tis not a good thing for a future laird."

Torrian would never be without a Deerhound companion—Gertie's grandsire had saved him from a life of immobility, and he would always be grateful.

After his stepmother had discovered the cause of his childhood illness—an unusual response to the ingestion of most grains—Torrian's health drastically improved, but he was still too weak to walk and his father and uncles needed to carry him around the keep. The memory of how thin his legs had been was fresh in his mind, as was the number of times he'd fallen while trying to walk. Though his new food choices had soothed his stomach and cured the painful blisters that had once covered his skin, he'd gathered his fair share of sore bruises from falls.

Then Brenna Grant did something wonderful for him. He would never forget the day she'd appeared at the door to the great hall with a giant Scottish Deerhound named Growley at her side. She'd arranged for someone to train the large dog to walk strong by his side to support him.

And that one act had transformed Torrian's life. The big lumbering Deerhound had licked his face in greeting and then arranged himself at his side, where he'd stayed for the rest of his short life. Torrian had gripped the fur on the dog's back and taken his first successful steps in years. Once his father had married his stepmother, he'd called Brenna "Mama" for years for two reasons—because his sister Lily had wanted him to, but more importantly because of all Brenna had done for him in such a short time.

Growley had helped him learn how to walk, but his faith and faithfulness had also taught Torrian to believe in himself. When he fell for the first time on Growley's watch, the dog nuzzled him with his cold nose until he giggled and stood up again. Aye, his first dog had taught him patience, too.

Torrian sighed, wishing his faithful friend was here beside him again, because he wasn't thinking patient thoughts after the meeting with his sire.

The littlest pup stared up at him.

"What is it, Bretta? What do you think I should do?" He reached down to rub behind her ears, her favorite place. Her brothers, Bram and Birk, were both scuttling to get their noses into his sporran.

"Och, you lads think you deserve a treat?" His hand touched his sporran and the two pups sat down in a hurry, almost knocking each other over in their excitement, their wee tails cleaning the floor behind them they were wagging so hard. He gave them each a treat and they ran off to the side to devour them. Gertie lifted her head to stare at him. "Aye, Gertie. Growley would tell me the same. Trust my sire. So I shall."

He stood and gave his dog a farewell treat and headed to the stairs. At the moment, he only wanted to see Heather. The lass had a pull on him he'd never experienced before. She was pleasing to the eye, of course, but it was not just that. There was a steadfastness to her that he admired—she was not some foolish lass who thought only of kissing lads. Even though he hadn't talked with her much, he sensed her shrewd intelligence. Her strength. This lass had kept her daughter alive in that cave for years, and that in itself was no small feat.

Normally Torrian was not the kind of man who gave in to impulse. But soon he would leave for the Buchans' land, and he was no longer content to set aside his wants and desires. He'd do as he wished for a change.

Torrian climbed the stairs and noticed Brenna emerging from the chamber where Nellie was being treated. "Brenna, how is she doing?"

"Better. I think she'll wake up soon. Heather has not left her side. I worry about her, yet I would have done the same for all of my bairns." She stopped in the passageway and looked at him, her eyes seeing beyond his calm façade. "You are finished in the solar with your da?"

Torrian nodded.

"And how are you feeling about what they suggested?" She angled her head to the side, the same way she often did—her way of letting you know she was willing to listen. How he adored his stepmother, the woman who had helped pull him out of the hell he'd been forced into as a child. He had been so ill, abed for years, his own family had pretended he was dead, not wanting the clan to know the true state of the Ramsay heir's health. Brenna, whose shrewd mind could understand and interpret matters few others could, would always hold a special place in his heart.

"Better now than I was at first."

"They convinced you to meet Davina?"

"You did not think they would be able to?"

"Torrian, it was a difficult decision for your father to make. He believes in love matches as much as his mother did, but since the edict came from our king, 'tis difficult to refuse."

"I understand. I agreed to meet her, but that's all at this point." He conceded that his sire was probably in a difficult position. From his point of view, he was probably doing what was necessary in order to remain in the good graces of the King of the Scots, Alexander.

"You are being more than fair. I do not think your father

expected aught else from you."

"Will you travel with us? I'd appreciate your input." His father and his uncle were so supportive of each other. He wanted, nay, needed someone who was more objective. He knew Brenna would tell him her mind.

"I'll talk with the others. Everyone in the clan must be hale and hearty for me to travel, and I believe you'll be leaving soon, possibly within two days. But I would enjoy visiting for a bit. I'll do my best to make it happen if you'd like me to come along."

"I would." He paused before changing the subject, pushing against the wall he was leaning against so he'd be ready to move. "I'd like to stop in to see Nellie. Do you think Heather would mind?"

"Nay. She's awake and would probably appreciate a different face than mine." She chuckled, her eyes dancing, and turned to head toward the staircase.

It was a comfort to know Brenna might be joining them for the trip. He moved to the door of Nellie's sick chamber and gave it a gentle rap.

"Aye?"

Torrian opened the door far enough to peek his head through the opening. "Do you mind if I enter? I'd like to visit with you and Nellie, see how she fares."

Heather said, "Aye, please come in."

Torrian entered the chamber, but before he could close the door behind him, a wee lass brushed in past him, followed by another. His sister and his cousin—the lassies went everywhere together, and they were as fast as rabbits running from Aunt Gwyneth's bow. He thought about sending the two lassies away, but they were about the same age as Nellie. Mayhap they could encourage her to get better.

His sister squared her shoulders and approached Heather. "Good morn to you. My name is Jennet, and I'm the healer's helper. Lady Brenna is my mother. She teaches me how to heal, so I thought I could help you with your daughter. She's only been here since yesterday, aye?"

Heather cast Jennet a skeptical look, but didn't send her away. "Aye."

"Has she awakened yet?" Jennet gave Heather an intent look

that would not be out of place on a lass of twenty summers. Brenna was often teased that Jennet was a miniature form of her, and her brown eyes and brown hair helped to complete the image.

"Nay." Still hesitant, Heather sat atop the furs on the bed, Nellie cuddled on her lap asleep.

"I brought my helper. This is Brigid, and mayhap we can convince her to awaken. We could play healer with our dolls later if she'd like."

Torrian suppressed his urge to laugh. Brigid, Logan and Gwyneth's youngest, stepped out from behind his sister and lifted her gaze to meet Heather's. People were not used to seeing such forthright girls, but they were being raised by two of the strongest women in the land. Together, they were quite persuasive. Each had been a surprise to her parents, but also a delight, especially since they were so close in age. They were of an age with Alison, the youngest child of Brenna's brother, Brodie Grant, and whenever the three lassies were together, they could maneuver and trick their way into getting most anything they wanted.

Torrian leaned toward Brigid, tickling her neck with a few strands of hair that had freed themselves from her plait. "They enjoy helping my stepmother," he said to Heather. "They're quite harmless, and only wish to be helpful."

Brigid nodded emphatically and linked her hands behind her back, waiting for permission.

Heather glanced at Torrian before she answered the lassies. He caught a slight twitch in her jaw, but then she became quite serious and said, "Your mother just left after bathing her and rubbing fresh salve on her chest. What would you like to do to help her?"

"First, I would like to listen to her heart," Jennet said. "Then we could give her a backrub to make her feel better. We could sing to her if you'd like."

"That sounds nice," Heather said. She glanced at Torrian, and from the look on her face, he could tell the two girls were charming her. "Nellie does not have much experience with others her age."

"Mayhap 'twill be good for her," Torrian said.

Heather set Nellie down, moved to a chair by the bed and kept careful watch as Jennet climbed up on the bed and then helped her cousin up behind her. She leaned close to Nellie and placed her ear next to her chest. "It would help if you were quiet for a moment," she said, and Torrian could not help the small smile that tipped up his lips. They all watched her until she lifted her head and spoke to Heather in a reassuring tone, just like her mother. "She has a verra strong heartbeat. I do believe she will get better."

She motioned to Brigid to help her. "May we lift her gown to give her a backrub?"

As the two lassies continued their task, they began to sing a song Torrian recognized from his younger days. Brenna had sung it to him whenever she bathed him. He recalled how soothing her soft ministrations had been.

"Why, 'tis a most lovely song," Heather said, tears misting her eyes. "Is it from your mother, Torrian?"

"Aye."

"Your family is quite special. You are a fortunate lad."

"Aye, I know that more than anyone." He paused, then said the words that had been longing to leave his lips, "If at any time you change your mind, you will always be welcome here at Clan Ramsay."

∽∾

Heather lifted her gaze to the broad expanse of chest not far from her. When had she ever been so drawn to a lad? And yet she could not deny that his soft voice, warm green eyes that reminded her of a summer breeze, and his handsome face drew her in. She thought it must be due to her exhaustion over worrying about Nellie. Her inner voice screamed at her—*you do not need another man! You need no one's help but your own.*

"My thanks. I'm not making any decisions now. I'm just hopeful she will get well." Tears flooded her cheeks, and Torrian reached over to squeeze her hand, a gesture meant to comfort her, she was certain, not some move to try to get into her bed. Unfortunately, her limited experience with men had taught her they often had ulterior motives.

Torrian took a seat in the chair next to her while the girls continued their song, caressing Nellie's skin lightly, both using the lightest of touches. It gave her the opportunity to take a longer look at him. Torrian was tall and muscular, but not as broad as his sire and his uncle. He walked with the proud air of a leader, which made him seem older than his years, but he was quite handsome.

His skin had a golden glow from the sun, his long hair was a light shade of brown with strands of yellow interspersed, and she noticed he was always freshly shaven. His eyes were green, the color of a spruce tree in the winter. But what she liked best about him was his aura: calm, confident, supportive, and trustworthy. He was unlike any other man she had ever met, and she found herself staring at his lips, wondering what it would feel like to be kissed by him. She'd never been a fan of kissing, with all the spittle involved. But this man inspired something different. How she wished she could try—just once.

She blushed when he caught her staring, but he raised his eyebrows as if to say he approved, then smiled the most gorgeous smile she'd ever seen.

The girls finished their song, so Torrian moved over to the bed to hoist them up and set them down. "I think you did a fine job, lassies, but let's allow Nellie to rest again."

Jennet and Brigid said goodbye to Nellie, then each gave Heather a quick hug before they ran back out of the room.

Torrian moved his chair closer to hers, so close she could reach out and touch his face. While she found it odd that he would come this close to her, she decided to allow it. Perhaps she'd been away from others for too long. She was enjoying every minute with the man, and she would not rush him.

"They were so sweet. How I wish Nellie would awaken so she could meet her new friends." Her voice came out in a nervous whisper.

Torrian rested his hand on the bed and leaned toward her. "I think 'twill happen soon. She looks much better to me. Her color has improved, and I think staying warm is important for wee ones."

She locked gazes with him, but her gaze kept returning to one thing—Torrian's lips.

⮾

Hell, but the woman was enticing. Why had she come into his life at the exact wrong time?

As soon as he sat beside her, he almost groaned as her womanly scent reached him. Though she'd been inside for a day, she still smelled like a summer forest. Pine and wildflowers came from every pore of her body. The lass was probably way more experienced, which embarrassed him a touch, but he still wanted to taste her sweet lips. The encouraging thing was that she seemed to want it as much as he did.

Just as he was admiring her rosy lips, she brought her gaze up to meet his. He could suddenly see the desire there, so he leaned toward her.

The moment ended as quickly as it started when a little voice called out, "Mama?"

"Nellie? Oh my Nellie? How do you feel?" Heather jumped up from her chair to lift her daughter into her arms.

Torrian could hear in her voice that this was the proof she needed to believe her daughter would get better. She glanced at him, a small moment, but enough to make him feel it was a wee intimacy.

"Mama, I dreamed I had two friends. They were helping me get better and sang a song to me."

"Och, wee one, 'twas not a dream. There were two lassies here who would like to be your friends, Jennet and Brigid. They were trying to help you get better. Mayhap they'll return later." She gave Nellie a fierce hug before letting her go. "I'll get you something to drink."

Torrian held his hand up to stop her. "Allow me." He moved to the chest and poured water for her into a small cup.

"Mama, I'm hungry. Is there aught to eat here? Where are we? This is the softest bed I've ever been on."

Torrian said, "Why don't I go find Lady Brenna, and I'll see what I can find in the kitchens. Mayhap some porridge?"

"Aye, that would be wonderful. My thanks, Torrian." She gave him a look that said whatever they'd shared was gone, long gone. But he'd find a way to bring it back.

Torrian wanted Heather of Preston. And after what his sire had told him, he was not going to let her go easily without pursuing his feelings. He'd only agreed to meet Davina of Buchan, not marry her. Heather was the first lass who'd affected him this strongly. He had to follow his instincts. He wanted no regrets.

After the last meal of the day, Torrian joined his father in front of the hearth, where Logan and Gwyneth sat as well. Brenna had brought dinner up to Heather, and the wee ones were off playing with their dolls. Jennet was directing the other lassies on how to heal their "sick" dolls, and the poor fabric creations were already beset with multiple carefully placed stitches to fix their wounds. The older children were arguing over at the table, Gregor and Gavin verbally sparring with Bethia, Sorcha, Molly, and Maggie.

Lily had stayed in her room, claiming an upset belly. She had the same issue Torrian did—for both of them, a wicked belly was the immediate response to the ingestion of most grains. Oats were the only ones they could eat. Torrian understood that some foods did not set right with them, though they had no idea why, other than their bellies were extra sensitive.

Sometimes their bellies hurt because they gave in to their cravings and paid the price, which is what he suspected had happened with Lily. They were both old enough to understand. He did not think he would see Lily until the morrow, but all of a sudden, she flew down the stairs, headed directly for him. He and Lily had lost their mother before Brenna came along and married their sire. Though the whole family was close, the two of them had a special bond.

She landed on a stool that she pushed into the center of the group with a huff, her expression one of deep concern.

"I hope there is a solid reason for your rudeness, daughter," Quade said, silencing the rest of the group with his words. He never raised his voice, but they all understood when to heed his words.

Lily peered at her father, her face crumpling with emotion. "Please tell me that what I've heard about my brother is wrong."

Quade quirked his brow at her, waiting for her to continue. "Explain, Lily. I know not what you've heard." He rested his hands on the arms of the chair in which he sat, leaning back.

"About Torrian."

"What about Torrian?" Quade asked, his calm gaze on Lily.

Torrian thought about intervening, but he decided he'd first wait to see what this was about.

"You're betrothing my brother to someone in a foreign land? Someone who belongs to a questionable clan? Someone whose clan is threatening to attack many other clans without provocation?"

Quade leaned forward and placed his elbows on his knees to

answer Lily. "Nay, I have not betrothed Torrian to anyone yet. Aye, we are visiting a clan not far from here, but it is not in a foreign land, nor is this a clan that has attacked others. Where do you get your information, Lily?"

Tears filled Lily's eyes. Torrian wished to reach out to her in comfort, but he knew he could not, not with this audience, not with his da sitting so close.

"You're taking my dearest brother, my dearest friend, away from me. How could you, Papa?" Lily was just over twenty summers, but at present, she appeared closer to ten summers.

"Lily, I have not met Davina yet," Torrian said softly. "We are not betrothed, but I will meet her. Our king has requested it, and he's a difficult man to refuse. And agreeing to meet with the lass does not mean that I leave for more than a visit. This is my clan and I'm still heir to the chief. That does not change."

Her lower lip quivered as she fought back tears. Och, he hated this. Lily was his best friend. Aye, when Loki was around he enjoyed spending time with him, and his other cousins were good company too, but Lily was the one he turned to when he needed to talk with someone. In turn, Lily came to him with any questions she had. She was strong, supportive, and always positive, unlike the traumatized lass in front of him. Her golden curls, usually beautiful, were disheveled.

Once her lip stopped quivering, she swallowed and looked from her aunt to her uncle and then back to her sire. All had silenced in the hall; none of them were used to seeing Lily in such a state. Lily had been the wee lassie with the smile that always lit up the darkest rooms, the giggles that set everyone's heart to rights. It pained Torrian to see her so upset, and he could tell the others felt the same.

She stared at Uncle Logan. "If you did not work for the crown, this would not be happening. 'Tis your fault, Uncle, and I will never forgive you for sending my dear brother away."

The shock on Logan's face spoke as loud as words. Lily had never spoken to him in such a way.

Then she turned to Aunt Gwyneth. "And I would have expected you to talk him out of this ridiculous idea."

Gwyneth's eyes grew wide with shock, but she said naught.

"And you, Papa? You know better than anyone what Torrian

means to me. You know how we only survived our illnesses by relying on each other. And you wish to send him away? Anyone who is fortunate enough to be chosen to wed my brother should come *here*. He belongs with us, not in some foolish court, not in some unknown castle, not as a representative of our king who's meant to smooth things over. He's an intelligent man who can make his own choices."

Quade never said a word.

"Grandmama is following every bit of this. I believe she's watching us from heaven. And I know she does not like what she sees."

Sobs burst from her as she stood from her stool and ran to the stairway, only to stumble directly into Heather.

The sister he loved stared at the woman for whom he was beginning to form feelings, then made her way around her and raced up the stairs to her chamber.

No one said a word.

CHAPTER FOUR

Heather realized it was an uncomfortable moment for the Ramsays—one she'd intruded upon—so she needed to make a quick decision. Stay or run like the wind?

Without pausing, she headed out the front door of the hall, having the sudden need for fresh air. As she pushed against the heavy oak door, the presence of a warm body invaded her senses, and she knew without looking that it was Torrian. She waited until the door closed behind them before she spoke to him over her shoulder. "My apologies if I interrupted something I should not have."

When she turned around to look at him, Torrian was giving her his usual lazy smile. "You did naught wrong. Have you met my sister before?"

Heather shook her head. "Is she usually this easily upset?"

"Nay, Lily is known for her exuberance, and her behavior is rarely like that. 'Tis why there was no response to her outburst. If any of my other siblings or cousins had lashed out in such a manner, they would have been advised to hold their tongue, but Lily never complains."

"I…I heard a bit of what was said. You are leaving?" The night had cooled down a touch, so she pulled her shawl over her shoulders. Torrian moved closer to her, managing to block the cool breeze and warm her from the massive amount of heat that always seemed to surround him. Rather than move away, she leaned into him, close enough for him to nuzzle her hair.

"I do what our king has asked me to do. I am to meet with a lass of another clan to see if we suit."

"Have you met her before?"

"Nay." He led her toward a bench, a secluded area under the

trees in the outer edge of the courtyard. "I have not. I told my father I would honor the king's request to meet with her clan, but I have not committed to the betrothal."

She sighed and stared off into the night, the stars just now visible after the sun had dropped. Somehow, she was not surprised. How foolish of her to think she could form a relationship with a lad who was destined to become chieftain of his clan. Even so, she could not push him away. For the short time they had together, she would enjoy his company in whatever form it took.

"'Tis terrible the way the nobility and the court forces marriages today. I wish they would not. Would it bother you if you were forced, even if she was nice? I mean, some people you can grow to like, others you get along with from the start, but mayhap you would be missing that spark."

"I know naught about that spark. I have never experienced it."

She hadn't either, but she'd heard of it. How she wished there was truth to the statement. She shivered, so Torrian wrapped his arm around her shoulders to pull her to him. The oddest thing was she did not mind at all. This man was someone she trusted, without a doubt. She knew little about him, but of that much she was certain.

He continued. "Have you been in love? Did you love Nellie's sire? Forgive me if I pry too much."

She shrugged. "I do not mind your questions. I have never been in love. At one time, I thought I might be, but nay. Everything changed. 'Tis why I fear for you. Sometimes you think you know someone, but it turns out you do not know them at all. I think women especially can put on pretenses to get what they want. Mayhap your sister has that same fear."

"You need not fear for me. I can handle myself, and I simply need to assure Lily I will always be here for her. I do not plan on leaving my clan for anyone. If that is what this girl wishes, she's come to the wrong man. I was brought up believing that I would be the one to lead Clan Ramsay one day when my sire is unable. That has not changed, and I am excited about facing that challenge someday. Aye, I will travel to meet her, but then she will be expected to come here. I will lead my clan someday."

She peeked up at him only to find an intense pair of green eyes locked on hers. This man was so handsome it took her breath away, though she knew better than to base her opinion of someone on looks alone. This was different. Torrian was different. Anyone that had that much compassion for his sister had to be a good person. She enjoyed the fact that he was always calm and steady, not prone to fits of anger. She didn't look away, instead choosing to stare at his lips, wondering…

His lips met hers—warm, soft, persistent. He pulled back as if to see if she would push him away, but instead she parted her lips to invite him back for more. She wanted to see how different this felt with him—with a man she truly wanted. Did that make her a bad person?

He leaned down and devoured her lips, teasing her with his tongue. He tasted of ale, but warm and delicious. She dueled with him as he angled his mouth over hers. Wanting him closer, she wrapped her arms around his neck, tugging him to her to absorb his heat and everything about him.

But it ended as quickly as it started, leaving her in a daze. He stood and spoke to two guards who'd just come upon them, but she didn't pay attention to what was said.

"How did you know? I never heard them approach." She stared at the departing guards as if they were apparitions.

He sat down next to her again, wrapping his arms around her and pulling her back against him so he could whisper in her ear. "Is it not my job to protect you? To make sure I know of aught that goes on around us? I'd be a failure as a Highlander if I did not. At least, 'tis what my sire and my uncles have taught me."

She had to admit she liked everything he'd just said. Satisfied with her instincts, she replied, "Aye, you did a fine job."

He chuckled, bringing his lips close to her ear. "Did I, lass? Do you approve?"

She giggled, astounded at the sound that came from her own lips, having not giggled in a very long time. "Aye, I do approve."

He held his hand out to her and said, "Come with me. I have something special I'd love to share with you."

She hesitated for a moment before placing her hand in his.

"I was worried for a moment. I thought you were about to turn me down." He grinned as he clasped her hand. "You trust me, do you not?"

She glanced up at the tall Highlander next to her, her gaze locking on his. The smile on his face, so genuine and handsome, warmed her. "Aye, I trust you."

He squeezed her hand and they walked in a comfortable silence toward the stables. Once there, he opened the door and stood back for her to enter ahead of him. "Gus? You have visitors for the pups."

Not long after, the Ramsays' stable master limped into view. "Aye? Well, the pups will be happy to see you." Gus pivoted and led them back to a stall that appeared to be empty but for a soft mound of straw in the corner and a crate.

Then she noticed the Scottish Deerhound who dragged herself out from behind the crate to lumber over to Torrian. Pups? Had he said pups? How she'd wanted for a dog to protect them out in the wilderness. Her gaze darted around the room until she settled on the corner near the crate.

"Come along, no one will harm you." Torrian leaned over and held his hand out toward the small, fuzzy dogs. As they scampered toward him, he explained, "These two wild ones are Bram and Birk, and the one quivering behind them is my wee lassie, Bretta. Do you like dogs?"

"Oh, I love dogs, especially puppies. May I pet them? Will their mama allow me?"

"Of course she will." Torrian found a spot in the straw for Heather, helped her to sit, then sat on the stone and leaned against the wall. Gertie settled her head on his lap while he rubbed her behind the ear. "Gertie is getting older, aren't you, Gertie?" The dog glanced up at him, clearly entranced by her master.

"Have you always loved dogs?" Heather reached down to pet Birk and Bram, who were swatting at each other with their paws, competing for her attention. "These two are characters, aren't they?" She giggled as Birk leaped onto her lap, then turned around to face his brother as if to boast of an achievement. "They are so cute, Torrian. How could you not love them?"

Staring down at Gertie's head, almost as if embarrassed, he said, "When I was young, Gertie's grandsire helped me learn how to walk."

She had been petting Birk, but her hand stopped mid-stroke. It was the last thing she had expected him to say to her. What man liked to admit to a weakness? And yet Torrian had not hesitated. "You needed help walking?"

"Aye. 'Twas a childhood illness. Once I was healed, Growley, Gertie's grandsire, helped restore me to a normal life. He was the perfect height for me to hang onto his fur so he could right me whenever I started to topple. I loved that dog like no other."

Heather watched him as he continued to pet Gertie, his affection for the dog apparent in the way he handled her. His gentleness and his honesty were weaving a snare around her heart. She knew it might not be safe to care for him, but she felt powerless to stop herself. "Part of me aches for what you endured, but I am glad that you had such a powerful friend as a child. Nellie has not been so lucky. Mayhap 'tis time for us to leave the cave."

"You are the only one who can make that decision. Do not feel sorry for me. The trials I've endured have only made me stronger."

She continued to lavish attention on Bram and Birk while wee Bretta made her way over to Torrian. The pup plopped down next to his leg, almost as if waiting for something. Heather was amazed when Torrian reached for Bretta and tucked her into the elbow of his arm, much as a woman would do with a wee bairn.

"Bretta was the runt of the litter, but I refused to give up on her. She just needs my warmth. She hasn't grown as fast as her brothers."

The wee pup closed her eyes with a sigh, content to be cuddled in her master's arms.

"Who taught you how to train the dogs?"

"No one. My stepmother often offers advice, but it does not take much to train them."

"Nay?" She was surprised that he didn't seem to consider it a chore.

"All it takes is love and a little patience." He rubbed Gertie's ear as he continued to cuddle wee Bretta. "Dogs love you unconditionally and do not expect much. They are also great listeners, or so I've found." He winked and gave her a lopsided grin.

And that was all it took for Heather to lose an even bigger piece of her heart to Torrian Ramsay. It was too early to know, but somehow she did anyway. If there was ever going to be another man in her world, she wanted it to be *him*.

But did she stand a chance against a lass of noble blood?

"Torrian, may I ask you a question?"

"Of course, I'll answer if I can."

She knew she had no business asking, but she had to ask. "Who is the lady you are visiting?"

"Davina of Buchan. Do you know aught about her?"

Heather's stomach plummeted at the name she'd dreaded hearing. Her past threatened to rear its ugly head, for sure. "Nay, I've never met her, but I've heard she is a beauty." How could she compete with a beautiful lass of noble blood?

"Heather," he said, staring into her eyes. "Beauty is in the heart, not in the face. I've known many stunning women who are cold as a winter loch on the inside. I am only making this trip to satisfy my sire and my king. I will meet her, but I do not expect we shall suit. I will fight for the right to choose my own wife."

But experience had taught Heather how difficult the nobility could be—they expected their every desire to be met. Could Torrian stand up to the Buchans?

Only time would tell.

Torrian couldn't deny the irony of his situation. He had finally found someone who lived with his clan—almost—and he was leaving to consider marriage to another.

"I probably should get back, Torrian," Heather said. "I'd like to check on Nellie."

Torrian said, "Of course. I'll help you." He returned Bretta to her crate and held his hand out for Heather. He couldn't resist pulling her close after he tugged her up. He just wanted to catch her enticing scent one more time.

"May I ask you a question?" He nuzzled her golden hair as he spoke.

"Aye, though I do not promise to answer."

Torrian considered several questions, but decided she would tell him what he needed to know about her past when she was ready. So he asked the most important question, because if her answer was nay, he would not be able to pursue her. This was the irrevocable question. "Would you consider living somewhere other than the cave, permanently? With your daughter, of course."

She turned to gaze up at him, taking a moment to think about her response, and then said, "Aye, for the right person and the right reasons, I would. With my daughter, of course."

The door opened and Brenna's voice echoed through the night air. "Heather?"

Heather rushed over to Brenna. "Nellie? Is she all right?"

"Aye. She's just awakened and is looking for you. I thought she would sleep through the night, but this proves she's getting better." Having delivered her missive, Brenna spun around and left, almost as if she wished to give them more time together.

Torrian knew his stepmother well—she had done that intentionally.

"Sorry, but I must go."

"Please, go to your daughter. I'll see you back to the keep." Torrian rubbed her arm as he escorted her through the bailey and to the door. Right before they went up the steps to the great hall, he stopped her. "My thanks, Heather."

She turned to him, a perplexed expression on her face. "For what?"

"For giving me a reason to rush home. We may leave on the morrow."

"I'll pray for a safe journey for you and your clan."

He opened the door and she rushed inside. Rather than follow her into the great hall, Torrian remained in the courtyard and made his way out to the portcullis, wanting to catch one last look at their castle bathed in the torches of the evening. Once there, he leaned against the curtain wall and glanced up at the keep. His ancestors had built a mighty fortress for them, and he was proud to be a part of Clan Ramsay, and even prouder he would be its leader someday. Those many days he'd spent sick and unmoving on his pallet, he'd dreamed of the day he would work by his sire's side to lead Clan Ramsay into greatness in the land of the Scots. The day was here, and he would make his sire proud of him—his ancestors, too.

A sweet voice cut through the night. "Torrian?"

Lily. His golden-haired sister, usually so full of life and laughter, ran toward him and threw herself into his arms. "Torrian, what will I do without you? Please do not leave. I have a bad feeling about this."

"My sweet Lily." He kissed her forehead and set her away from him. "Lily, I must leave, but I shall return, you can count on that. I must do what our king has asked, but I only promised to meet her, not marry her."

She clutched both of his hands in hers. "You must find someone here, Torrian. If you do not, then while you're gone, I'll find her for you. Then the elders will not argue." She dropped her voice to a whisper after scoping the area for any who might overhear them. "Torrian, is there not someone here who interests you? If you start courting someone before you leave, I believe Papa will be more reasonable. You know he'd prefer us to be with someone in the clan than to go outside, even if 'tis for someone of noble blood. You must find someone before you go."

"As it happens, there is someone who interests me, but 'tis difficult to court someone in one or two days. Please have faith in your brother, lass. You'll be fine without me for a sennight or two. Lairds must leave to go to court sometimes."

He could see the hope bloom in her gaze at his declaration. "Who is it? Heather? It must be Heather. I thought it the moment I saw her. The verra moment I saw her on the horse with you, I thought there was something there. 'Tis perfect. I like her. Even though we have not officially met, I hear wonderful things about her."

"I'm glad you do, though I'm not sure Da would be pleased to see me interested in someone without a clan."

"Papa will not care. Uncle Logan and Aunt Gwyneth adopted Molly and Megan, and Brenna is our adoptive mother. He'll just want you happy."

"I hope you're right. We'll see when we get to Perthshire. I believe we will leave on the morrow."

"Do not trust this woman. They say she is spoiled and manipulative. She's to be like a sister to me, and the thought of such a person being the mistress of the castle frightens me. Please be wary and alert. Promise me, Torrian. Promise me you will not fall in love while you're away."

"I cannot promise that, Lily. But I can promise you I shall return."

"Mayhap I should go with you."

"Nay, you should not. Focus instead on finding a lad for

yourself. You cannot do everything for me."

"What are you talking about? I do not try to do everything for you." She slapped his arm playfully to make her point.

"So, you do not recall all the times you would hide your precious stones when we were small? You would ask me to find them, but you would always find them on your own."

"Nay, I did no such thing. Why, 'tis silly, what you suggest." She gave him her shoulder to show him the seriousness of her denial.

Torrian couldn't help but grin. Och, he remembered it well, but she had been very young at the time, so perhaps she did not. "Aye, you did. Though I think you knew, in some small way, that I would not be able to find the stones because I wasn't strong enough to walk on my own. I did not have Growley yet. Either way, you would hide them for me, then find them for me. You've never stopped."

"Fine, then. I will not help you again."

Her pursed lips told him he'd hurt her pride, and he did not want to leave her on such terms. He adored his sister.

Torrian headed back toward the keep, dragging Lily behind him. "You can help me whenever you want, sister, but you cannot help me find a lass to marry. 'Tis something I'll do on my own."

She slapped his arm again. "Torrian, stop being so crude."

"I'm being crude? You suggested it," he drawled.

"I'll leave you to find your own wife, but if you do not find one within a moon, I'll start searching." With that statement, she huffed and yanked her hand free from him so she could flounce back to the keep.

"Am I not your favorite brother?" Lily spun around to cast one last glare at him. He hated to admit it, but Lily was right. He had to find someone, and soon, particularly if he did not want his marriage arranged for him.

Could Heather be the one?

CHAPTER FIVE

Heather awoke just before the sun was up, roused by all the commotion outside their window. Nellie had improved, but she wasn't back to her usual self yet. She crept over to the window and pulled back the furs.

Numerous lads ran about in the courtyard, shouting back and forth about the preparations for the journey to the Buchans' land. Their voices carried both excitement and trepidation. She identified with the latter—her belly rumbled with the fear that Torrian might leave and never return.

A soft rap sounded at the door. Since Nellie was still asleep, Heather hurried to the door and opened it a crack to peer out. She was surprised to see Torrian standing there holding one of the pups.

"Forgive me for bothering you, but may I come in?"

Heather nodded and pulled her threadbare night rail tighter around her, wondering what she looked like so early in the morn. Fortunately, she had only lit one small tallow in the room.

Torrian entered and closed the door behind him. As soon as he came into the chamber, Nellie sat up in bed and rubbed the sleep from her eyes.

"Mama? What is he holding?" Her gaze had settled on the wee pup in the crook of Torrian's elbow.

Torrian whispered, "While I'm gone, I thought Bretta could help Nellie through her sickness, and Nellie could keep Bretta warm. Is this agreeable to you?"

Heather's heart melted again. "Aye, I think 'tis a lovely idea, but why do you not ask Nellie yourself?"

Nellie's eyes lit up with excitement as Torrian approached her with the pup. "Nellie, this is Bretta. She's a wee Deerhound puppy, and I need someone to help keep her warm while I'm gone. Would you like to help her and feed her for a few days?"

Heather was delighted by her daughter's reaction. Nellie clapped her hands and held them out to Torrian. He sat on the edge of the bed and showed her how to hold her arms, then settled Bretta in her lap. The pup glanced between Torrian and Nellie, dancing around a little.

"Here, you can pet her head or her back. And when she gets really tired, she loves to have her belly rubbed."

Oh, how dear of him to do this for Nellie. Heather felt her heart swell as she watched Nellie pet Bretta's head. The pup reached up and licked the wee lassie's hand, making her squeal and burst into giggles.

"May I, Mama?" Nellie asked, looking up at Heather with wide eyes full of hope. "May I help him keep her warm?"

Heather, with a lump in her throat, just nodded and whispered to Torrian, "My thanks."

"If she becomes too much for you, just find Lily and she'll help." Turning back to Nellie, Torrian said, "Your mama will return in a moment, lass. Bretta will keep you company." Relief swept over Heather—she had hoped they'd have the opportunity to say a private farewell. She offered her hand to him, and he tugged her out of the chamber and led her to an alcove down the passageway. Once they were hidden, he cupped her face and kissed her hard on the lips, angling his mouth over hers, sweeping his tongue inside her parted lips. He nibbled on her lower lip, then ran his hands down either side of her body, cupping her breasts and tweaking her nipples until they were taut, threatening to bust out of her night rail.

His hands roamed even further until they cupped her bottom, lifting her off the floor. The hard length of him was pressed against her belly and he groaned, his hands caressing her soft skin through the thin material, setting a fire in her. As he lowered her back to her feet, a small moan escaped her lips. She tingled in places she'd hardly ever felt before, and she clutched his plaid, not wanting to let go.

"Lass," he whispered. "I just wanted to let you know that I will miss you. I hope you know how much."

Heather stuttered, "You're leaving now?"

"Aye, but I look forward to getting to know you better upon my return." He kissed her again, a soft, sensual assault that left her breathless. The man knew how to kiss, how to touch, and what to say. "You are beautiful, Heather Preston, and I would love naught more than to kiss every inch of you."

Her legs threatened to buckle, but he caught her and led her back to her chamber. "I only wish I dared to have you escort me out, but 'tis probably not something my clan is ready for yet."

Heather's eyes widened and she shook her head vehemently. "What is it?"

"Nay, I could not."

"What?"

"Go down with you. The crowd, I could not handle it. I have a fear of large gatherings."

"Well," he said gently, "we have something to work on then. I'll help you to manage that fear. I felt the same way after I became healthy again. I was not used to being around more than one or two people at once. It does take time, but I believe I can help you."

Heather sighed. Could the man be more perfect?

Once he was gone, her eyes misted with tears. He would not be perfect if he came back betrothed to Davina of Buchan. Her entire world teetered on the edge of something she did not like.

How she hoped it would tip in the right direction.

❧

Two days later, the line of Ramsay guards finally drew near the Buchan castle. The castle had a dark air about it, even in daylight. The Buchans and two of their neighbors, the Russells and the MacNivens, oft joined together to threaten other clans. Up until now, they had rarely done more than steal sheep or battle over the land, but Torrian's father and uncle both expected more unrest would be forthcoming. Torrian's aunts and uncles, Drew and Avelina Menzie, and Michael and Diana of Drummond, were not far. Menzie held borders with the MacNivens, and the Drummonds shared a border with the Buchans.

Just as Aunt Avelina had predicted long ago, the Highlands had been mostly peaceful for a decade, with an occasional skirmish or two, but that would always be the case. Now, though, something was brewing—even Torrian could feel it. Unfortunately, he didn't have the experience to interpret his gut or follow it.

Five guards led the way down the valley toward the castle, his sire and Uncle Logan followed, then Brenna riding between Quade and Logan. Torrian came up behind them, Kyle at his side, with another fifty guards in the rear. He and Kyle had carried on many discussions along the way, but always careful about who was listening.

Gwyneth had stayed behind to protect the castle. There were no direct threats, so Torrian's sire had not been concerned about any attacks. He had another hundred and fifty guards at the Ramsay castle, and they would protect his clan if need be.

Torrian noticed plenty of guards set at various distances, even some archers, which didn't bode well, but his sire did not seem to be concerned. This was a friendly visit, by order of the King of the Scots, so any threats visited upon them would be akin to threats against the Scottish crown. He prayed his feelings were unfounded, and yet the premonition would not leave him.

As they drew closer to the gates, a line of horses moved out to greet them.

Torrian rode up to his sire's side. He'd do everything possible to make his sire proud, his goal since he'd been abed with his illness. Yet the turmoil in his belly belied his outer countenance. He feared he would not get along with Davina, and that he would therefore disappoint both his father and his king.

This day could be one of the most important days in his life, the kind of event that determined his future, his happiness, even his direction. Not realizing he was holding his breath, he let it out slowly when their horses were almost nose to nose with the Buchan horses.

"Greetings. We welcome you to Buchan Castle." The man in the center, who also appeared to be the eldest of the group, was the one who addressed them. "I am Glenn, chieftain of the Buchans." He nodded to the rest of the group before continuing. "To my right is my eldest son, Dugald, and to my left is a neighbor, Ranulf, chieftain of the MacNivens. My daughter Davina rides behind me. Hugh, my second, rides next to Dugald. My youngest son, Cormag, rides next to him."

Torrian arranged himself so he could see past the Buchan to Davina behind him. Dark-haired and beautiful, she sat tall, her shoulders back and a beautiful smile directed at different men in their line.

Quade responded with a nod. "I am Quade, chieftain of Clan Ramsay. My son Torrian is to my right, my wife Brenna is to my left, my brother, Logan Ramsay, rides next to my wife. My second Seamus is far left, my son's second, Kyle, is far right."

There was a slight, nearly imperceptible twitch of the Buchan's eyebrow. "Your wife rides *next* to you?"

Quade squared his shoulders and sat taller on his horse. "Aye, as she always does unless we are under attack. I need not concern myself with such during a visit for the king, do I?"

The chief of Clan Buchan chuckled. "Of course not. You are our esteemed guests, as it should be. Allow me to lead the way."

The chief turned his horse around so quickly he unsettled a couple of the beasts near him, but they calmed as the group headed toward the castle. Torrian caught Davina glancing over her shoulder at him, giving him a coy look and a smile before she lowered her eyelashes and followed her sire.

Torrian had to admit his uncle was correct about one thing. Davina was a beauty. He couldn't tell the color of her eyes from this distance, but her hair was almost dark enough to be black, something he'd rarely seen before except on his Uncle Alex, though he noticed the Buchan brothers had the same coloring.

He immediately thought of the blonde locks in total disarray around Heather's face, somehow more entrancing because they weren't all tidied up. He chastised himself for the thought; he needed to give Davina a fair chance. He owed as much to his sire and his king. While he had every intention of returning to Heather, he knew the importance of treating Davina with respect and acting as though he was a willing participant. He and Kyle had discussed that Torrian needed sound reasons for rejecting the betrothal or relations could turn to violence with a clan like the Buchans.

He vowed to draw out as much information as possible, learning all he could about the Buchans and the MacNivens.

The Buchan castle was well-made, surrounded by a strong curtain wall.

Once they had dismounted and were headed toward the keep, Logan said, "Such a fine curtain wall I have not seen. 'Tis new?"

"The old wall was crumbling, so our chief replaced it,"

Buchan's second, Hugh, replied. "We have added two towers with more chambers."

"Surely not as fine as the Ramsay Castle or the Grant keep we've heard so much about." Glenn turned to gauge their reaction to his comment.

Quade was quick to reply, "We've added to our keep, as well. The clan continues to grow. However, we cannot compare to the Grant estate. 'Tis my name for the creation built by Alexander Grant for his sisters, brothers, and their bairns. He wishes for them all to stay nearby."

Logan smiled sweetly. "I do not think I've seen any castle finer than the Grant's. Poor choice of words. The royal castle is certainly finer, but no other castle boasts the number of warriors in the Grant lists. Aye, 'tis an impenetrable fortress high in the mountains."

Torrian knew Logan's goal was to make sure the Buchan understood who they would be up against if they decided to cause any trouble with the Ramsays. Once inside, they settled at the dais as the chieftain directed his staff to bring food and ale out for the guests. Torrian was assigned a seat between Davina and MacNiven.

The Buchan great hall lacked a woman's touch. The rushes on the floor needed changing and the trestle tables could have been cleaned better. He thanked his stepmother for the cleanliness in their keep, something she'd learned from her mother. The walls were covered with various weapons of all shapes and sizes. While not unusual, rarely did weapons cover all four walls, and Torrian assumed it was meant as an intimidation tactic.

It did not work on the Ramsays.

The Buchans continued their quest to wheedle more information from them in a manner meant to be non-threatening. Still, the aggressive undertone to the conversation was unmistakable. "I hear Alexander Grant is getting on in age," said Dugald, Davina's older brother. "Mayhap he was the finest swordsman at one time, but he must not be any longer."

Logan quirked his brow at Dugald. "Have you not heard of Grant's nephew, Loki? I watched him drive his sword through two attackers at Cliffnock not long ago. And anyone would be a fool to doubt Alex Grant. I just watched him toss someone only a bit smaller than him through the air as if the lad weighed the same as a feather. Only a fool would go against him, unless his numbers were stacked."

Torrian stifled a grin at his uncle's colorful language.

Glenn of Buchan raised his goblet. "Here's to a fine visit, and to young lovers." He pointed toward his daughter and Torrian. Everyone lifted their goblets in a toast, though Torrian could not put much spirit behind it.

Davina leaned toward him, exposing a bit of her breasts. "Are you not in favor of this marriage, my lord?"

Torrian gave her a surprised look. "I'm for certes not against it, but we've only just met, my lady."

"Aye, but since most marriages are arranged, we shall suit as well as anyone. I look forward to our union." She cast him a glance that was anything but shy.

Torrian hesitated, but then chose honesty. "My grandmama believed in allowing her bairns to choose their partners. My aunts and uncles married for love, and they are all quite happy. There's a good chance you and I will suit, but I wish to get to know you a wee bit more before carrying on with the arrangement."

Fury flashed in her eyes, but it disappeared just as quickly. "Of course, whatever you say, my lord."

She was trying to play the demure lass, but Torrian was quite sure it was feigned. What was her game? He recalled what Heather had said just before he'd left about people pretending to be what they're not. Davina of Buchan could be an example of just that type of person.

Ranulf MacNiven spoke up, drawing Torrian's attention away from Davina. "Tell me more about the Grants. Surely, they must be weakening. I agree with the Buchan. Alex Grant is quite old."

"Aye, he is older," Logan said, "but he still works daily in the lists. His size has not changed. He delights in challenging his three sons and his brothers and their sons. Swordplay is their entertainment. His nephew, Loki, is just a wee bit shy of his height and was given the lairdship of the old Comming land. He's forming a reputation for himself as the strongest swordsman in the land, second only to the Grant. I was there when he fought Blackett."

"Being a good swordsman does not mean you are the best

leader," MacNiven pointed out.

"Loki Grant also managed to get himself free of manacles when he was chained in Blackett's dungeon," Logan continued, "*and* he walked past all of the man's guards with his knife to Blackett's throat. None of them dared to go against him. He's almost as tall and easily as broad as Alex Grant. Do not doubt him."

"With the right number of warriors, anyone can be defeated," MacNiven said.

Torrian pursed his lips in thought. A moment later, he said, "You sound as though you plan to go on the offense. Who exactly is it you wish to defeat?"

MacNiven covered quickly. "Nay, not me. Do not be ridiculous. I'm happy leading my clan."

Torrian had a difficult time believing Ranulf MacNiven. He sounded more like a man intent on getting as much information as possible on the people he planned to attack. He'd backed off too quickly for Torrian to accept his explanation. He doubted he would be happy leading his clan for long. He made a mental note to speak to his uncle later about the MacNiven. Was he top of their list of those suspected of stirring up trouble?

Davina leaned against Torrian again, this time rubbing her breast against his arm. "Must we talk of fighting? Is there not something else I can interest you in, my lord?"

Torrian stared back at Davina. Aye, she was a beauty, her long dark hair hanging loosely in waves over her shoulders, her brown eyes glittering with something that looked a lot like mischief. And he knew her breasts were full since she'd not only shown him, but given him the feel of one as well.

Torrian found himself thinking more and more about blonde hair and blue eyes—or to be exact, one blue and one green.

❧

Heather had finally decided that Nellie had healed enough for them to return to their cave. Certain that Torrian would be betrothed when they returned, she thought it best for them to leave. The Ramsays had been very generous, and she did not wish to take advantage of their kindness.

Outside the Ramsay stables, Heather mounted the horse and then reached down to take Nellie from Gwyneth's raised arms.

Gwyneth's daughters Brigid and Sorcha were riding together, as were Jennet and Bethia, Brenna and Quade's two daughters. The wee ones were not allowed to ride on their own, though Gwyneth preferred to ride alone in case she needed to use her bow and arrow. Her daughters had strict instructions to run into the forest if aught happened. Three Ramsay guards led the way, and five followed them.

"You are verra kind to travel with us, my lady," Heather said to Gwyneth as they left the gates.

"Please, do not call me any kind of lady. Do you not see what I'm wearing?" She glanced down at her tunic and leggings, at the warm plaid wrapped around her. "Call me Gwyneth."

Heather laughed. "Many thanks for the new tunic and leggings, Gwyneth. You are more than generous."

"And now I can look just like my mama in my new tunic," Nellie added brightly. Both were now dressed in matching green tunics and brown leggings—a vast improvement over their ragged clothes. She patted her mother's arm as they cantered through the meadow, and once again, Heather allowed herself to bask in the relief that she was hale.

Heather had stayed two more days at the Ramsay keep to make sure Nellie was well, but it was time to move on. They could not still be there when Torrian returned from the Buchans. It had been a big mistake to kiss that man—not because it did not feel right, but because it did…and she wanted much, much more of it.

She knew they could never marry. Torrian was to be laird someday, so he must wed someone of equal station, a lass of noble blood. The Buchan lass would probably suit him perfectly. Mayhap the stories she'd heard about her were false. Heather knew that the only way to forget him and heal would be to leave the castle and return to her solitary life. She was not in any position to make any claims on the heir to a chieftain.

Clearly noticing her change in temperament, Gwyneth said, "You seem disappointed to be leaving the castle. You are welcome to stay, but I'm sure you know that."

"Aye." Heather's stared up at the gray sky, trying not to think of what could have been. "You all have been wonderful. Torrian and Lady Brenna both asked us to stay, but 'tis best for us to return to our home. We love the outdoors and summer is upon us. I prefer the time when the bluebells and heather decorate the fields with color. 'Tis my favorite time of year."

Nellie peered up at her mother with her big eyes. "But Mama, may I not keep my new friends? I like having friends."

Gwyneth slowed her horse so she could draw closer to Heather and Nellie. "Of course, Jennet and Brigid will always be your friends. You may come visit whenever you would like, and the lassies and I often travel through the woods to practice hunting and archery."

"Then mayhap you would come visit us sometime. We would love to see you," Heather added, hoping to placate her daughter. She understood how much her newfound friends meant to her. Their present circumstances were definitely lonely at times. Heather had to admit that she'd enjoyed the company of the Ramsays and was grateful to find other kind people.

"May we, Mama? Please?" Brigid pleaded.

"Aye, we'd like to visit again, Aunt Gwyneth." Wee Jennet sat tall on her horse in front of her elder sister.

"Of course, you may," Gwyneth said. "We'll visit again."

They increased their speed since they were at the beginning of a meadow. The girls giggled as they galloped across the flat field, the guards rounding out the periphery of the group.

They slowed their horses as they neared the patch of forest around the cave. There was only room for one horse at a time down the path, so the guards once again split between the front and the rear.

"Are we close to your home?" Gwyneth asked.

"Aye," Heather answered. "We can dismount in that small clearing up ahead." She pointed out the area decorated with purple flowers.

Once they arrived, they helped all the lassies dismount. Gwyneth gave the guards instructions on where she wanted them to wait, and Heather told them, "There's a stream just to the north if you'd like fresh water."

One of the guards said, "My lady, we'll take jugs and fill them for you, if you'd like."

Heather smiled at the lad, then led the way to the cave. Some containers sat just inside the stone lip while others were positioned to catch rainwater. "That would be much appreciated." She stood just outside the cave as the girls ran ahead, already chattering up a storm.

Gwyneth held back, waiting until the wee ones were out of earshot. "Why, 'tis quite beautiful with all the shades of purple in the area. But I must be serious for a moment. Heather, I sense there could have been something between you and Torrian. Brenna thought the same." She paused to see if she would respond.

Heather did not know quite how to answer, but she felt heat rise to her cheeks. "I...I...do not know for sure..."

Gwyneth reached over to pat her hand. "My apologies. I did not mean to make you uncomfortable, and mayhap 'tis none of my concern, but his mother and I would both support the match. Torrian has not shown much interest in any particular lass up until now."

"But he'll be chieftain one day, and I..."

"It does not matter where you live or who your people are. If you two have feelings for each other, it might be worth pursuing them. His grandmama supported all of her descendants choosing their own partner. She was unconcerned with matters such as blood ties."

"But the Buchans..." Though Heather was shocked and pleased to hear that the Ramsay women would be willing to accept her, she did not wish to get her hopes up for something that could never be. And she still suspected that such happiness might be beyond her.

"Both Brenna and I suspect that the matter will not work out the way our king hopes. But we'll see. I just wanted you to know that we support you, should Torrian choose to pursue you. I respect a woman that prefers independence, as I was much like you before I met Logan. I stayed a distance away from everyone due to a personal issue, but I never realized what I had been missing. 'Tis beneficial to allow others close to you."

Having said her piece, Gwyneth headed into the cave after the bairns. "What are my wee lassies doing in here? Are you cleaning since Heather and Nellie have not been here in a while?"

Jennet, Brigid, and Nellie came running toward her, hands linked. "Mama," Brigid said, "will you kill a rabbit for us so we may examine its insides? Nellie said she would look with us."

Gwyneth rolled her eyes. "Nay. No surgery without Aunt Brenna. You know the rules."

Sorcha and Bethia stood behind the wee ones. "But could we not help them hunt for their dinner? Surely, we may practice our shooting."

Heather noticed they each had their own bow and quiver.

"Aye, I'll take you two hunting for a wee bit before we return to the castle."

Heather wished she had enough confidence to ask for lessons from Gwyneth, especially after all she'd learned from Torrian. She decided to stay back and watched as the younger girls started to play a game with sticks and stones, aiming at a target outside. Nellie's face was bright with excitement at having so many friends, a completely new experience for her.

It was enough to make Heather feel guilty for having deprived Nellie of the experience of being around others her age. Heather could not help but wonder how different their lives would be if they lived with the Ramsays.

CHAPTER SIX

After the evening meal, Torrian got up from his seat by the hearth and made his way over to Davina. He held his hand out to her and said, "Would you care for an evening stroll in the bailey, my lady?"

Davina gave him a demure smile, her lashes downcast, as she set her hand in his. "That would be lovely, my lord."

Torrian kept his eyes off his sire and the other men around the hearth. He'd already decided at dinner that he was not interested in Davina, but he couldn't yet put his dislike into words. His best strategy would be to talk to her as much as possible to try and uncover exactly what it was he didn't trust about the lass. Then he could decide what to do moving forward.

Torrian helped her on with her mantle and then escorted her out the door of the great hall. One of the most unusual things about the Buchan great hall was the apparent lack of females. "You have only brothers, Davina? No sisters?"

They made their way through the center of the courtyard. He was pleased to see there weren't many about, which gave them the freedom to talk more openly.

"Aye, just two brothers. My mother died when she was birthing her fourth bairn, and the bairn died as well. I was between five and six summers when she passed, so I have few memories of her. Do you have sisters?"

"Aye, I am close with my sister Lily, and we have two younger sisters, Bethia and Jennet, who is only six summers." He watched her as she sauntered down the path. There was plenty of room, but she made a point of bumping her hip into him as they traveled.

"I wish I had a sister. I have naught but men around me." She sighed, a deep heavy sigh that told him she was searching for sympathy.

"Surely, you must have friends."

"Not many." Her eyes widened and she pointed at a star shooting across the sky. "Look.

'Tis a magical sign. Let's move out from the trees to see it."

Torrian squelched his own sigh over that. It was hardly a magical sign. He was certain if he checked with Aedan Cameron or his wife Jennie that they would agree with him. Nonetheless, he went along with her, following as she moved close to the curtain wall and a small copse of trees beside a bench.

They stared at the sky a few moments longer, until the star disappeared, and then she peered up at him with a hopeful look on her face. Torrian knew what that look meant. She was hoping for a kiss. He decided to accommodate her wish just to see if there were any stars shooting about afterwards. After all, he'd pledged to see if it was a good match. What better way to tell if there was a spark?

His lips descended on hers. As soon as their lips met, she wrapped her arms around his neck, grinding her pelvis into him. She parted her lips and immediately crushed her tongue against his in a most unappetizing way. It only reminded him of a different kiss, of honeyed lips and a lass who smelled like a forest.

Davina ended the kiss and stared at him, as if expecting something. Her eyebrows rose in a question, as if she were quite dissatisfied with his response.

"You did not like my kiss, Torrian?"

"Aye, 'twas nice." He pondered her question, unsure of what she wanted from him.

Then she stared at the front of his plaid as if she were expecting something. That was when it dawned on him. She had expected to feel his hardness against her, and it had surprised her that he was not excited. Trying to hide his surprise, he turned his head to the sky. "No more stars performing their magic?"

Truth was, she did nothing for him. But how could a lad say that without insulting a lass?

"Och, you are different, are you not?" She gave him a sideways glance, then cupped his cheeks and pulled his lips down to hers. She kissed him, sweeping her tongue to force his lips open, and then bit his lower lip.

Torrian pulled back and stared at her in shock. "You bit me? 'Tis your way to entice me?" The lass had him so confused, he knew not what to say. But if she hoped to excite a reaction from him, she was surely going about it in the wrong way. He rubbed his bottom lip, felt the blood trickling from it. "I think 'tis time to return to the keep."

Davina glowered at him and murmured, "You are different, quite." She stalked back to the keep one step ahead of him, never looking back, her hips swaying enough to collide with aught within a few feet of her.

It was going to be a long trip.

Later that night, heavy footsteps paced, stomping through the hay. He had told her to meet him in the stables to be sure they were not overheard. Shite, but he was mad as hell. How could he look at someone so beautiful and want to rip out her hair one strand at a time? He paced back over to her and spoke in as deep and threatening a voice as he could muster. "How could you fail to make him interested in you? You have the beauty, must I do everything?"

Davina whispered, "Ranulf, time will fix this."

Ranulf MacNiven replied, "Time will not fix aught if he's not interested in you. Are you sure he had no response to you?"

Davina replied, "I think I know by now what a man's response should be. He had none."

"Then you must have done something wrong. You must seduce him. He has to want this marriage. 'Tis part of the plan. We need him to be so besotted with you, he'll make poor decisions. This is a long-range plan, but it all begins with your marriage to the Ramsay's son."

"I know." She cast her eyes downward.

Ranulf loomed over her. "You have the breasts every man wants. Now use them. You teased him, but you must be bolder. If you must, you will use trickery to get him into your bed before he leaves. Is that clear?"

"I tell you it takes more than one night with some men."

He grabbed her hair and yanked her so her face was inches from his.

"Ouch, Ranulf. You're hurting me. Let go of my hair."

"I'll let go when I'm ready. You need to do whatever it takes to entice him. Do you understand?" The woman was so tempting, was the lad blind? With her this close, he had to fight the urge to toss up her skirts and...

"Aye, but stop hurting me or I'll go to my father. He'll not allow you to...ow...."

"You must...you will...you know how important this is to me. This is everything. Do you wish to please me or not?"

"Aye. I love you, Ranulf. You know that."

"Then prove it. Make him fall in love with you." And with that, he gave in to the temptation in front of him. Releasing her hair, he grabbed her bottom and pulled her close. He sealed her lips with his and ravaged her mouth with his tongue as he reached down to the bodice of her gown, snapping ribbons as he pulled the flimsy material down and back.

He massaged her breasts until she moaned, then flicked her nipples with his nails before pinching them hard. She pulled away, gasping with desire. He'd have her begging in a few moments, he knew. She was a passionate one, so passionate that he could control her completely. Unfortunately, sounds outside the stables forced him to cut their tryst short.

He didn't love her, but he did love it when she begged him to swive her. More curves than any man could ever want...aye, in truth, while he did not love her, she did have a wee bit of control over him.

He could never let her know that. Never.

At the end of the night, Torrian made his way back through the courtyard at a slow pace, made slower by his desire not to run into Davina again. It was late, but he hadn't been able to sleep so searched out his friend. He and Kyle had spoken at great length about his betrothal, and his mind was no more settled than it had been before. The woman seemed to be everywhere, and Torrian wanted naught more to do with her. He opened the door to the keep as softly as possible, closing it just as carefully so he could creep up the stairs without being seen.

He'd walked outside for quite a while, hoping to clear his mind and think about his options logically and methodically, leaving his emotions aside, if that were possible. He had no answers, other than his heart leaned toward another.

His father and Uncle Logan had not given up on the idea of the marriage, though they both accepted that the Buchans and MacNivens needed to be watched. The three of them had discussed the possibility that their hosts were planning something other—and much darker—than a wedding, but there was little evidence. They would need to be patient to ferret out the goals of the Buchan and his followers. So the charade continued, much to Torrian's dissatisfaction. It gave him a headache the likes of which he had never experienced before.

Uncle Logan and Brenna had been strategizing and analyzing ever since they'd arrived, keeping his sire busy. His father had not asked him once how he felt, and considered it part of his duty to continue on.

He wanted naught *more* than to tell his father exactly how he felt.

But to do that, he would risk losing his father's respect, something he had dreaded his entire life. He moved down the passageway to his chamber, not running into anyone, thankfully. He grabbed the torch from the bracket outside of his door to light the one just inside it, but when he pushed his way in, he was surprised to see the room was already illuminated by torchlight.

There on the bed, wearing naught but a smile, lay Davina of Buchan. Torrian froze—from shock rather than temptation—and then acted swiftly.

"You will not entrap me this way, my lady." He stepped back into the corridor, closed the door behind him, and headed straight to his sire's room. Once there, he rapped harshly on the old wooden door.

The door flew open and Brenna stood there with a surprised look. "Torrian? Is something wrong?"

"May I come in?" When it took her a moment to respond, he added, "Please, Brenna. I must come in." She could not know how much he needed to get away from the madness of the Buchan keep.

Brenna stood aside and said, "Of course."

He left his torch in a holder by the door and stepped into the room, closing the door behind him.

His father sat in one of the chairs arranged by the hearth. "What is it, son?"

"You look as though you've just encountered a ghost," Brenna added. "Sit, Torrian, before you collapse. You're terribly pale."

Torrian sat in a chair near his father, leaned his elbows onto his knees, and allowed his head to fall into his hands.

"Torrian?" Quade asked. "What is it?"

After a long pause, he lifted his gaze to his sire, saw his concern, and spoke. "She's trying to entrap me."

"What? Please be more specific. Who?" Quade glanced from Torrian to Brenna, and back again.

What stood out most to Torrian was not the shock or disbelief on his sire's face, but the knowing look his stepmother now wore. Torrian turned back to face his father. "I went for a walk alone, to consider what is best for me. I returned to my room to find Davina lying on my bed without a stitch of clothing."

His father stared at him in disbelief.

Brenna asked, "And what was your response?" Brenna seemed quite calm, as though he'd told her something she'd known for years.

"I closed the door and came here."

"Did you say aught to her?"

"Aye, I told her she would not entrap me."

"Did she respond?" Brenna asked. His sire just continued to stare at him in apparent disbelief.

"Nay. I left. I was afraid to stay. What if someone else had come along? Had her sire found me in that position, I would have been forced to marry her."

His father finally spoke. "Are you telling me that Davina of Buchan was lying nude on your bed, as if waiting for you?"

"Aye. Da, 'tis the truth. I would not lie about such a thing."

"I can hardly believe it. She does not seem mischievous to me."

"Conniving is the word I would use, husband, and you need to take this verra seriously. This one move shows me she wishes to become Torrian's wife at any cost." Brenna started to pace the room as she spoke.

"Had I not walked away, I could have been forced to marry her before we leave." The thought sent a thrill of fear through him. He could not imagine spending his life joined in a marriage to such a woman.

"Torrian," Brenna said in a calm voice he knew all too well, "you must consider the possibility that she will lie and say it happened whether it did or not."

Quade bolted out of his chair. "You're suggesting she'd lie about it just to entrap my son?"

"Aye, I am. You must consider the possibility, and I think we need to decide what we shall say if she does try to accuse him of impropriety." Brenna stared Quade in the eye as she spoke. "That tells me we need to leave on the morrow before she has the opportunity to plan something more devious."

"You think she will? You think she would dare to carry out such an atrocity?" His father limped a little due to his sore knee, but it did not stop him from pacing.

"Aye, I do. If she's capable of trying to seduce him, she is capable of much, much more. We need to minimize the target by removing him. The two have met. Either send him home or stay fast by his side. That lass has plans for your son, and we cannot allow her to run his life or ruin it, as the case may be." She tilted her head to await her husband's response, but then added, "And you need more salve on your knee."

Torrian's misgivings blossomed into frightening possibilities. "I'm not sleeping in there tonight. I'll stay on the floor in here. What if she returns and brings a witness? I do not wish to become the victim of her craftiness."

"We'll not run away. 'Twould be rude. If we go, I'll tell the Buchan why." Quade addressed both of them, one hand on his hip and the other stroking his jaw.

"Husband, I would not advise anyone of our plans. If everyone knows when we are leaving, you may force the lass to act quickly. We must not give her the chance."

"You have a good point, Brenna. Sleep in here tonight, Torrian, and we'll leave at first light. I wished to speak with you before we left, so this will give us a moment to discuss your thoughts on the betrothal. Glenn of Buchan wishes the match to go forward, and until this moment, I saw no reason to deny him. But, after the discussions I've had with your uncle, I worry about this. If this is her plan, then she is not the lass for you, nor would I welcome her into the clan. However, we must deal with our king. I'm afraid he will still support the marriage. 'Struth is any trouble by the

Buchans may make the match more desirable. Alexander is keen on the idea that this marriage will allow us to maintain a modicum of control. What were your thoughts before this happened?"

Quade returned to his seat by the fire and waited for Torrian's response. He thought of many different answers he might make, but he expected most of them would bring disappointment into his father's gaze. He decided to plunge forward.

"Da, I do not think our personalities are a good match. Davina is lovely, but she is a forward lass, the verra opposite of my own nature."

Quade said, "You make a fine-looking couple. She will give you handsome bairns, and a strong-willed woman is preferable to one with a weak, shy personality. Someday, you'll be chieftain, and your wife must be able to run the keep should you leave for battle or head to court. She must be strong and independent. Those were my thoughts before this new development."

"I will not disagree with you, Da, but I still do not think we suit. The thought of living with such a deceitful lass does not settle well with me. What kind of life could we have together if I had to question all she did, all she said?"

Quade ran his hands through his hair, still thick after many years. "I cannot argue with your reasoning, Torrian. You realize the king may decree this match. If so, it could be considered treason to refuse, or at the verra least, a cause for the Buchans to attack us to retain their dignity. 'Tis an embarrassment to refuse a betrothal ordered by the king."

"I would like to speak to our king before I agree."

"I wish to speak with our king as much as you do, but he is not here. And despite how you feel today, you must not refuse Davina on the morrow before we leave. The Buchan talks as if the king has promised him that this marriage will happen. If you sever the connection now, you could bring repercussions down on me and the rest of your clan. After all we've seen and heard, mayhap the king does need our help to maintain peace. Your uncle believes the king may order the marriage in an attempt to control these clans, although I am not convinced it will work as he wishes. Logan believes this to be the case, and he finds conditions here less than favorable."

Torrian wrung his hands as the words settled on him. Marry

her or anger their king, cause embarrassment to his clan. In other words, he had no choice in the matter.

Brenna did her best to soften the blow. "I agree with your father that this is not the time to refuse, nor is it the place to refuse. We are in their castle, surrounded by Buchan guards. The safest response is to agree to the match and then postpone the marriage for as long as we can. We all need to take a closer look at the implications of refusing before you make that decision. Mayhap Uncle Logan can speak to the king on your behalf. Or mayhap he will escort you to Edinburgh to talk with the king directly."

Torrian let his breath out between pursed lips.

It seems he would be officially betrothed on the morrow.

CHAPTER SEVEN

Torrian descended the staircase just before dawn, his sire and stepmother directly behind him. Logan met them at the base of the stairs.

Kyle waited not far from the door. "Are we truly set to leave soon?" he asked. "All the guards were informed of the change in plans just now. Word has already passed through the Buchan guards that we are rushing home and they are ready to pass bad judgment on us. What say you? Why has this been decided so quickly?"

He glanced at his parents before whispering to his friend. "I'll explain later, but suffice it to say that I feared the lass would entrap me. Do not tell another soul."

Kyle's eyes widened, but he did not speak except for one whispered word. "Truly?"

Torrian only had time to nod as a booming voice carried across the balcony.

Glenn's voice echoed through the hall. "Good morn to you all. Are you not pleased with this pending betrothal? Is this a meeting I should have been invited to attend?" The Buchan met his daughter at the top of the staircase, and they descended the steps together.

Quade squeezed Torrian's elbow and moved him off to the side of the door, a tactic to encourage him to keep quiet, he was sure. Kyle stepped aside to make room for him, and they stood to the back as the two chieftains squared off, Brenna at her husband's side and Logan at Torrian's side.

Glenn of Buchan said, "You leave so soon? Before we have made our decision?"

He crossed his arms in front of his chest, a move Torrian did not think boded well for them.

His sire acted completely unperturbed. How Torrian envied the way his father could hide his thoughts and feelings. He paused before he spoke, a power move for certain. "My wife has been called home, a personal issue she must attend to as our healer, and we shall all escort her. As far as we are concerned, the betrothal will continue if you are agreeable."

Glenn of Buchan grinned and squeezed his daughter's shoulder at the same time. She gave Torrian a sweet, almost modest smile. "Verra well. Then we shall plan the wedding to take place at your castle. When is your preference?"

Torrian was amazed by how quickly the Buchans had agreed. He'd wanted to argue and cast as much doubt as possible on the betrothal, but his parents' way was wiser. Leaving was their top priority, and agreeing to the betrothal would speed their departure. The rest could be sorted out later.

"A fortnight?" Quade posed the question to Brenna. Torrian held his breath, giving his sire a pointed look, but both of his parents ignored him.

Brenna gasped. "A fortnight? We could never prepare for such a grand affair so quickly. Mayhap two moons?"

"Two moons?" the Buchan chieftain barked. "'Tis way too long. I say one moon."

Brenna thought for a moment, then said, "Aye, I am agreeable to that."

They all looked at Torrian, so he nodded, then Davina added, "That sounds wonderful."

Torrian nodded to his betrothed and said, "I look forward to that day, my lady." He almost choked on his words, as he did not care to lie, but he had planned his phrasing intentionally. In his mind, that day would mark the end of this fiasco.

He would see to it.

When Heather awakened a few days after returning to her cave, there was a sinking feeling in her gut. It did not take long for her to realize why. Nellie was burning up again. She could feel the fever her wee body fought through her clothing, and Nellie had cuddled close to her in the middle of the night. The sun was just peeking out over the horizon, so she gathered her daughter and carried her out to her horse that Gwyneth had left with her. She had no choice but to bring her back to Brenna Ramsay. Before positioning the ropes across the mouth of the cave to deter birds and animals, she decided to bring a few more belongings than she had the last time, not wishing to be a burden to the generous clan.

When she arrived this time, she had to stand at the gate for a few minutes before she was allowed to enter. Gwyneth came out to greet her, yelling at the guards to open the gate.

"Sick again, is she?" Gwyneth asked, her concern evident as she rushed toward them, accepting Nellie into her arms before she leaned down to press her cheek to the wee one's forehead. "Poor lass is burning again."

"Aye, and she will not awaken. I do not understand what could be wrong. Has Mistress Brenna returned yet?"

"Just last night. Head to the stables and once you've dismounted, I'll give her back and carry your satchel for you."

Heather did as Gwyneth asked, and the two made their way toward the keep as quickly as possible. They were nearing the great hall, making haste to find Brenna, when a familiar voice called out from behind her. "Heather, may I assist with aught?"

She swung around, only to be hit by her body's quick response to Torrian Ramsay. His essence washed over her, giving her unexpected comfort.

"Here, I'll carry her while you get your things. I'll take her directly to Brenna. Does that suit you?" Only then realizing she had frozen in response to his presence, she readily relinquished Nellie to his strong arms. Surprised by that telling move, she glanced up at Torrian, comforted by his strength. Even if Nellie awakened in his arms, she would accept him, something that was amazing given Nellie's inexperience with men.

"Aye." All she could do was gaze into his green eyes as he took Nellie from her. Gwyneth handed her satchel back to her, and once she was able to collect her thoughts, she hurried to follow Torrian's long strides. "I'm so sorry to bother you, my lord."

Torrian glanced over his shoulder. "'Tis no bother. I'm here to help."

The moment they stepped inside, Brenna rose to greet them from the hearth. "Och, nay. The lassie is sick again?"

"Do you want her in the same chamber?" Torrian asked his

stepmother.

She nodded. "Aye, we'll follow you in a moment. Heather," she said as she wrapped her arm around her waist. "Does it appear to be the same or something different?"

Strangely comforted by just the presence of Lady Brenna and the compassion on her face, she leaned into her, almost collapsing. "The same." The tears that had threatened to spill onto her cheeks finally overflowed. Heather had the odd trait of not crying until after the imminent danger had passed. "She is the same as before. I cannot awaken her. She went to sleep without a fever last night, but this morn she was burning with it and she cuddled close to me in the middle of the night. I probably overheated her."

"Nay, when bairns have fevers, they seek more warmth. I'm sure you did naught to cause further harm. Let's bathe her again, then I'll place the salve on her chest. I also managed to find some tuberous comfrey, which may help her."

At the mention of her special herbs, Heather rummaged through her satchel and then handed Brenna a small sack. "Here, I've been foraging in the woods near us to find some of the herbs you taught me about. I wanted to make sure you had plenty to help with the illnesses in your clan. It's the least I could do."

Brenna peeked into the bag and smiled, "You did well. Mint leaves, coriander for fever, licorice, basil, and yarrow. My thanks, Heather. I will make great use of these."

"How was your trip, my lady?"

Brenna hesitated before answering. "The trip went as expected. Torrian is betrothed, but I will tell you in confidence that I intend to do all I can to release him from his betrothal. She is a beautiful lass, but I do not trust her, and neither does Torrian. In fact, I will do all I can to see him with another. They do not make a good pair."

"Oh, I am sorry your trip was not a good one."

"Aye, 'twas good enough to help us understand why the king pushes this match. Something goes on there that does not seem right. We will forge ahead with the intent of finding Torrian a more suitable lass, but try to do it without offending anyone."

She locked gazes with Heather, who did not begin to know how to respond to her.

"Heather," she took a step back to gather some linen squares from a chest near the hearth, "I do hope you will consider Torrian as a possible match for you. I know Gwyneth spoke to you about my stepson. If you have any interest in him at all, I beg you to consider accepting his suit, if he feels the same way. We will have to find a way to handle this situation delicately so as not to offend anyone, but my wish is for my stepson to be happy."

Heather stared at Brenna, unsure of how to answer her. "I think 'tis best to see how Torrian feels. Of course, I would be willing to speak with him."

They headed upstairs together, and followed Torrian into the chamber that had become Nellie's sick room. Just as they reached the door, he left the room, giving her a nod and a serious look before he slipped past them. Heather couldn't think clearly enough to wonder what he felt for her. She couldn't deny her body's response to him, but right now she could only focus on making her daughter well.

Once inside the small chamber, Brenna placed the bag of herbs on the chest and motioned for Heather to sit in the chair that was still positioned next to the bedside. The chamber was also furnished with a small table and two stools arranged along the opposite wall. But as Brenna busied herself with filling a basin with water and herbs, Heather sat on the bed directly beside her daughter and tugged Nellie onto her lap to undress her, tears misting her eyes as she felt the frailness of the wee one's body. She'd lost too much weight during her last bout of sickness. What would this one do to her?

Together, they bathed Nellie, but she still did not awaken. Brenna fiddled with her vials, carefully covering the wee one's chest with a paste smelling of potent herbs, and then left Heather and Nellie to rest together. She did not know how much time had passed when she was awakened by a knock on the door. No light came in through the furs, so she must have slept for a while.

"Enter, if you please." Heather rubbed her eyes and released her daughter since her fever had abated a bit, moving to the chair next to the bed. Torrian entered the chamber, carrying a trencher of pottage that he set on the chest next to her. "My lord, you do not need to wait on me."

He leaned down to kiss her cheek. "That's to remind you that we know each other well enough for you to call me by my name, not my lord."

She couldn't stop the blush from heating her cheeks as she stared at him. Hell, but he was enough to take her breath away. "My thanks, Torrian."

"You must eat to stay strong for your daughter. Is there any improvement?"

"Her fever seems to have improved, but she still sleeps." She glanced at Nellie. "She looks so innocent and peaceful, does she not?" She swiped a tear away from her eye.

"Aye, she's a beauty like her mama." Torrian pulled a stool over to the bed. "Does Brenna have any idea what is causing her illness?"

"Nay. She thinks it's related to the blood and phlegm, but I'm grateful she doesn't believe in bleeding. She has a cough, and when we were here before, Brenna gave her something to help her breathe."

"I'm going to say something that may upset you, but only because I'm trying to help. Do you think it would be better for your daughter to stay here where she could sleep inside instead of out in the cold? I know 'tis summer, but the nights can still be cool. 'Twas chilly last night. Mayhap she feels it more keenly since she's been so ill recently."

"I've considered the possibility. 'Tis why I brought more of our belongings. I may decide to stay longer…for Nellie."

Neither of them spoke for a few moments. Heather enjoyed the small comfort of having him there by her side.

"I was sick for a verra long time as a bairn, Heather, and I was kept hidden in a cottage away from all but my closest family. I can tell you from experience that part of my improvement came from being around others. I do not mean to judge you as a mother, as I know you would do aught for your daughter, but living alone is hard for a child. I had no idea what friends were when I was a laddie. Besides my mother and sire, I only knew my sister, and we were often kept apart. Mayhap in a small way, Nellie's mind wished to be back with her friends."

"Are you suggesting that she is making herself ill?" Heather was shocked at his words, but mayhap he spoke the truth. After sharing so much with the Ramsays, even she had missed their presence once they had returned to the cave.

"Nay, not at all. I'm suggesting that she'll heal faster around friends, and in truth, she may be happier to live in a larger group now that she knows the difference. I know from my own experience how much happiness and friendship can improve everything about your life. She's too young to question what you do, but she could have the hidden desire to be with her new friends. I could be wrong, of course. I speak from my own experience."

Heather didn't know what to say, but mayhap he had a point about Nellie's wee body wishing to be near her friends. Besides, it made practical sense to keep Nellie at the keep for the time being; the caves were cold, though she wrapped them both in furs each night.

Lily came in later that evening and pulled a stool up close to Heather.

"I'm sorry to bother you when your daughter is so ill, but I must speak with you."

Heather said, "Of course, Lily. I welcome you. Thank you for helping my daughter with the pup, Bretta."

Lily had a beauty that lit up the room around her. Her hair fell in golden waves over her shoulders, her enchanting emerald eyes were much like her brother's, and her smile was the type that could lighten even the foulest mood. Today she was dressed in a light green dress with long sleeves.

"My brother is betrothed to Davina of Buchan. My sire feels he must do as his king decrees until something comes to light about the family's ill intentions, so agreed to the betrothal. But they do not suit at all, everyone agrees, and I worry that he will be pulled away from our home. I love my brother—he and I have helped each other through many difficult times."

"How can I help?"

"Do you have any feelings for him?" Lily's hopeful gaze broke Heather's heart.

"Lily, 'tis too soon to tell. We've only just met."

Lily sighed, a deep sigh that told Heather how helpless she felt. "I understand, but please be open to the possibility. I know my brother. If the king expects him to marry the lass, he will, even if he hates her. He'll do what's expected of him. I need you to spur deeper feelings in him, the kind he cannot fight."

"I doubt that I can fight Torrian's feelings of loyalty to his king and his clan. He is not the sort."

"If he loves you more than aught in this world, he will fight for you. We just need to find a way to make him fall deeply in love with you."

Heather gave a very unladylike snort. "That, my dear, is almost asking the impossible."

"Why?" Lily tipped her head, obviously having no experience with what she was about to say.

"Because lads do not fall in love like lasses do."

Lily considered this before she stood from her chair. "I must disagree with you. I'm sorry you believe that, but naught could be further from the truth. My sire adores my stepmother, and Uncle Logan would easily die many times over for his wife. All of the Grants love their wives. But most of all, I know my brother. He has feelings for you." She gave her a swift hug. "The wee lassies wish to come sing to Nellie as they did before. They like to play healers like Brenna. Would you like them to come in?"

Heather said, "Certainly. Allow them inside."

Lily opened the door to Jennet and Brigid. Jennet entered first, direct as usual. "My lady, my mother gave us this special ointment that we can rub on her back. There's a hint of mint in it, and we hope the tingling will awaken Nellie. We'd also like to sing to her as before."

Heather helped wee Brigid up onto the tall bed since she was a year younger than Jennet and quite a bit shorter. Jennet had her father's height. "Aye, I'm sure Nellie would love to hear her friends sing to her again."

Jennet and Brigid sat on either side of the wee lassie while Heather sat back down in her chair.

Lily turned to leave, but before she could go, Heather whispered, "I'll do my best, Lily."

"Many thanks." Lily closed the door as the girls began to sing.

Heather watched the two wee healers. Jennet did most of the work on Nellie's back, her light brown hair weaving a path down her back as she rubbed in the salve. Her wee friend's lighter temperament was evident in the way her head bounced back and forth as she sang two different songs to Nellie. What a gift their parents had given them. They both genuinely wished to help and soothe others, something you did not often see in bairns so young.

Her own youth had been very different from that of the bairns in the Ramsay clan. The only thing she knew for certes about her mother was that she'd died birthing her. Her sire had never been mentioned, other than the fact that her grandmother had not liked him. Her grandmama had loved her, aye, but her grandsire was a quiet man, probably because he was deaf in one ear. She vaguely recalled meeting an aunt, but she had lived a distance away, and she'd only seen her a few times. Either way, she hadn't heard much singing...or even many kind words. That lack of warmth was also the reason she had run into the arms of the first person to speak sweetly to her.

The snake. How she hated him...

A few moments later, Nellie opened her eyes and said, "Look, Mama, my friends are back."

Heather bolted out of her chair to hug her daughter. She was so happy to hear her sweet voice again that she hugged Jennet and Brigid, also. "My thanks, lassies, for helping with my daughter." She kissed each of them on the tops of their heads before she was able to release them. So grateful that Nellie had come back to her again, she vowed to allow her daughter to spend more time with her new friends. She would make it work, for Nellie's sake.

Mayhap Torrian was right about staying at the keep. For her daughter's sake, she'd ask to remain for a while. She'd just have to stay out of the way of the wedding plans.

She did her best to convince herself this was not about Torrian at all.

CHAPTER EIGHT

Kyle clapped Torrian on the shoulder as they headed into the keep from the lists. "Nice workout today. Did it help you release some of your anger?"

Torrian shrugged his shoulder, his hand still flexing on the hilt of his sword. "It did feel good to let it all out. I decided 'twould help me before I walk into the solar. There I'll be attacked for sure, but I'll have no sword to defend myself." He had been directed to the meeting on his betrothal and found he dreaded every moment of it. He just wanted to be free to get to know Heather Preston better.

"You've been fighting and practicing like a lad who's about to fight the world," his friend said with a thoughtful look. "'Tis how you feel?"

"Sometimes. Mostly I fight to improve my abilities. After watching Loki fight, I strive to be better. As Loki said, any fight can be the most important—or the last—in your life."

"Surely, you can convince them you do not suit without resorting to swordplay."

"My sire is more concerned with whether the *king* thinks we suit. The fact that he saw the lady's comeliness with his own eyes only makes matters worse. Mayhap I would have a better chance of escaping the arrangement if she were as ugly as a warty hedgehog with a nose like a beak."

Kyle spat out the water he'd just drank from his skin. "I feel better that she's lovely. At least your bairns will be handsome. 'Twould be easier to get her with child than if you had no choice but to lay with the hedgehog."

They both laughed as they climbed the hill, but Torrian shook his head. "I feel as though I'm attending my execution."

"Hardly. You know your sire has your best interests at heart. Plus, did you not say your Uncle Logan will be there? You know how much he cares for you. You're the reason he spent so many seasons away from home. He could not handle to see you so sickly."

Once they were inside the keep, Torrian turned to Kyle. "I hope you're right. I hope Uncle Logan is on my side and not the king's. I'll let you know how it all turns out later. And Uncle Logan may have acted that way when I was young, but lately, all he wants to do is kick my arse. He was the same way with Loki."

"He's just acting in your best interest."

Torrian laughed. "Make sure I ask cousin Loki if he thought it was in his best interest when Logan watched him battle a daft man unarmed."

"I thought you said 'twas your uncle who gave him the sword to use against the fool?"

"Aye, 'tis true, then he leaned back to watch the whole thing with his arms crossed. I thought Loki was about to have his head sliced clean off while three of his uncles watched."

"I'll be waiting to hear about the meeting. Come get me when you've finished. I'm headed to the kitchens to sweet talk Cook into something good."

Torrian nodded and turned toward the solar at the end of the great hall. He was about to open the door when Heather descended the stairs. He watched her in silence, wondering why he could not be left alone to explore the connection he felt with this woman. To him, her beauty far surpassed Davina's. Davina never had a hair out of place, while Heather's tresses were always in tousled disarray. But the most arresting difference between the two? Their eyes. Davina's were cold and calculating. The two lasses could hardly be more different.

"Good eve to you, my lord," Heather said.

"How is your daughter?"

"Much better. She awakened to the soft songs of Jennet and Brigid. Mayhap you were correct about her needing her friends."

"Glad to know she is doing better. Please excuse me, I am expected inside."

"Of course," Heather replied, blushing a little.

Torrian paused for a moment, just long enough to watch her

sweet backside as she moved through the great hall. If he did not stop staring, he'd probably walk into the solar with an embarrassed flush of his own.

Torrian stepped into the solar and four sets of eyes immediately fell on him. Both of his parents were there, along with Uncle Logan and Aunt Gwyneth. He sauntered into the room, not wishing to hurry this inquisition. His father motioned for him to take a seat in front of his desk, so he did as he was told. In this room sat the four people he feared most, but not in the usual sense of the word. Nay, he lived in fear of disappointing them. As a wee bairn, he had dreaded the pain in his father's eyes more than the continued symptoms of his illness.

And Uncle Logan? Logan had spent much of his youth away from home. He'd always assumed his uncle did not care for him. It was his grandmama who had informed him of the truth of the matter. Uncle Logan had stayed away from the Ramsay keep because it had pained him to watch his nephew and niece suffer. Torrian's grandmama had told him about the day she'd found Logan crying over Torrian's bed, one of the days they had given him something to make him sleep. After that, Logan had told his mother that he could not bear to stay at home until his niece and nephew were healthy, although he'd returned many times to check on their progress. And as far as his uncle was concerned, his stepmother could do no wrong. In fact, Torrian had often wondered what would bring the worst repercussions from Logan Ramsay, an attack on his wife or an attack on Brenna.

Torrian took a seat and forced himself to control his expression. His sire had taught him a laird had to learn to hide his emotions unless in battle.

Logan spoke first. "The king has decreed that you are to marry Davina of Buchan in one moon."

Torrian bolted from his chair to argue, but his uncle held his hand up to signal for him to wait.

"The king has agreed to visit with both you and Davina to judge the matter for himself. He does wish to speak with you. He will be here in three days, along with Davina and her sire. They will bring a small contingent with them at the king's request. Prepare yourself for his visit."

Torrian wanted to shout and curse, but he managed to hold his temper in check. After allowing himself a few moments to fume, he said, "Does it matter at all what I want?"

Quade gave him a resigned look. "Unfortunately, nay, it does not. Anyone can see her beauty, and she is of noble blood, so it is considered a good match. I'm sorry, Torrian. I know you do not wish to wed the lass, but mayhap you will be of a different mind once you get to know her better."

Logan strode over and rested his hand on Torrian's shoulder. "Now, lad. I know you believe this to be a death sentence, but I was not idle while at the Buchans. They are bent on stirring up trouble in the Highlands. I overheard a few discussions about becoming the finest and largest clan in all of the land of the Scots. What we need to do is go along with this farce until we can determine their true plans. You happen to be the only way for us to get near to them at the moment. And if we uncover any information, the king will be eternally grateful. Patience, lad, patience."

He stood. "Since it matters not what I say, I'll take my leave...unless there's something else you would order me to do?"

Gwyneth said, "Torrian, do not fret just yet. The wedding has not taken place, and there are many who are on your side."

Logan added, "We all must tread carefully. Whether we like it or not, the king has made his decision. To go against it would be an act of treason. He could be put any of us in chains, if he so chooses."

Torrian turned to leave. Over his shoulder, he mumbled, "Seems I'm bound for chains no matter what I do."

❧

Heather paced and paced inside the small hut that sat at the edge of the village. It looked as though it hadn't been inhabited in a couple of years. It was a distance away from the other cottages, so it was no surprise that it sat empty. When Lily had approached her with this scheme, her head had told her to refuse, but her heart had whispered otherwise. Her heart had told her it was time for her to take a chance on opening herself to another man. Torrian Ramsay, to be specific.

She didn't have many experiences to base her desires on, only one. But the memories of the night her daughter was conceived were bitter enough to make her wish to swear off men for a lifetime. But something had changed inside her, and Torrian Ramsay was the cause.

Suddenly, the urge to feel wanted, loved, and special dominated her. Was she expecting too much? She had a beautiful daughter who meant more to her than anything, yet she felt as though her life was missing something. Could that something be Torrian?

The door flew open and she jumped, though she had no reason to be surprised. Torrian filled the doorway, casting a questioning glance her way before he closed the door behind him and came toward her. "Heather, 'tis lovely to see you. I suspected you'd be here. This is one of my sister's tricks to get us together. If you'd like to leave, just say so. I'll escort you back to the keep."

She shook her head vehemently. "Nay."

He glanced over his shoulder, as if expecting to see someone standing there, but they were alone. Torrian's fair locks were ruffled from the wind. His skin was bronzed, a beautiful glow that made Heather wish to touch him everywhere.

A smile crept across his face, making his green eyes dance. "I think my friend's words suddenly make more sense."

"And what words are those?"

"Kyle, my best friend, brought me here, but this also screams of my sister. I'm quite sure she and Kyle are plotting against us. Actually, I guess they would be plotting for us. He also told me he couldn't stand by while everyone else tells me what to do with my life. My guess is he prefers you to Davina, or mayhap he just knows that I do."

Heather rubbed her hands, not knowing what to say to that. She was about to speak when the door popped open again and Lily strode it, Kyle following fast behind her.

Torrian stepped forward to stand at Heather's side, as if declaring they were on the same side of an argument, and crossed his arms over his chest. Lily did not make them wait too long before stating her purpose.

"Forgive me for being a wee bit sneaky, but I do not want our elders to know what we've done." She cleared her throat and glanced at Kyle before continuing. "Torrian, you do not belong with Davina, you belong with Heather. You only have three days left before that woman arrives here, though I do *so* look forward to meeting her." Her chin lifted a notch, telling him exactly what kind of welcome Davina could expect. "After all the tales I've heard of the crude woman, I shall enjoy meeting her."

Kyle said, "Lily, I cannot wait for you to meet her either. 'Twill be most enjoyable." A grin covered his face, but Lily was clearly in no buoyant mood, and she narrowed her gaze at him.

"Never mind, Kyle." She returned her attention to Heather and Torrian. "We have arranged for the two of you to have some time alone. As you can see—" she waved her hand toward the small table in the corner, "—we have brought food for you, Kyle has started a fire in the hearth, and there is wine and ale. The rest is up to you. Heather, Nellie is excited about sleeping in the same bed as Jennet and Brigid tonight. She'll be fine, and Brenna promises to check on her frequently."

Torrian's grin left his face. "Brenna is in on this?"

Lily stared up at the rafters in the ceiling. "Brenna agreed to visit Nellie to ensure she continues to improve. I did not tell her exactly why I requested this favor."

Torrian turned to glance at Heather. "Seems we have the support of more than just these two." He turned back to Lily. "And my father?"

"Brenna and Aunt Gwyneth have worked up some story for him and Uncle Logan. Torrian, I cannot allow you to marry that witch."

Torrian crossed the hut in a few big steps and pulled Lily into an embrace. "My thanks, Lily. Heather and I shall spend some time together, enjoying the fire and the food you've brought for us."

"Aye, Lily." Heather's gaze searched the small hut. While deserted, she could tell that someone had spent some time cleaning it up and making it more than presentable. Two cushioned chairs sat in front of the fire, a small table between covered with flowers and a basket of food and wine. "The cottage is verra nice with the dried flowers and the fresh rushes." Heather peeked at her from around Torrian's shoulder and noticed the misting in Lily's eyes. She loved her brother—there was no doubt of that.

Kyle grabbed Lily's shoulder and gave her a gentle push toward the doorway. "Let's leave them be, Lily." He winked at

Torrian, then closed the door behind them.

Torrian ran a hand through his hair, as if nervous. "I apologize for my sister if she has tricked you into doing something you did not wish to do." He waited for her answer, unmoving.

Her gaze shot up to meet his, and to her relief, he was smiling.

When it became clear she did not intend to answer him, he put his arm around her shoulder and ushered her over to the table. "I think we better eat something. If not, she'll never let me forget it."

Heather glanced in the basket. Her mouth watered as soon as she saw the fresh loaf of bread and chunk of cheese next to the fruit and the wine skin. "Aye, the food looks wonderful. I will admit I am hungry."

"Have you been ignoring yourself again because your daughter is ill?" They both sat, and Torrian pulled out two goblets, filling each with wine. Then he prepared some bread and cheese for Heather and cheese for himself.

"Aye, I must admit 'tis true. I am so overcome with worry for her that I sometimes forget my needs."

"Then I'm glad Lily brought this for us to share."

She leaned back in her chair, keeping a chunk of bread in one hand while she broke pieces off of it to chew on. "What did your sister mean by three days?"

"According to my uncle, the king has decreed that my marriage to Davina Buchan will take place within a moon, and he has decided to visit with the Buchans in less than a sennight to assure himself of his plan."

Heather's hand froze. "Why would Lily plan this if you are to marry so soon? I do not understand."

"Lily planned this because she believes in the two of us, and she probably hopes that if I have feelings for you, I'll fight harder against the wedding. If something does exist between you and me, she wants us to discover it before the wedding rather than after. I know my sister well. When she makes her mind up about something, there is no changing it. She thinks we belong together, and Lily is verra skilled at getting what she wants."

"But if you are to marry, what chance do we have? I might feel something for you, but I do not wish to have my feelings hurt again if 'tis hopeless." She set her bread back onto the table. Never again would she subject herself to the torture Nellie's father had put her through.

"Do you wish to tell me about it?"

Heather thought for a long moment, staring at the food in front of them. "Nay, not yet. If there is something between us, then I will tell you all. But this is too new for me to share the worst experience of my life with you."

Torrian reached for her hand and tugged her onto his lap. "Tell me what brings you here. Why did you go along with Lily's plan?"

Heather did not know what to say—only one thing came to mind. "I'm here because of you, naught else."

Torrian brushed the back of his hand across her cheek. "Lily did not trick you into coming, did she?"

The warmth of his hand caused a tingling in her that started in her core and moved deep into her womanly place. She did not know exactly how to explain why she was here, but lately she had begun to wonder what she had been missing in all the time she'd spent alone with Nellie. And after picking up on bits and pieces of different conversations among the maids in the kitchens and in the keep, she wanted to know what was so wonderful about coupling. She had no fond memories of it, and yet one glance from the man in front of her made her wish for things she did not altogether understand.

"Nay, she did not use trickery. Lily was honest and sweet. I'm here because I want to know if there's more."

"More?"

"Aye. More. It seems that there could be more, much more, but I am confused." She stared at him, taking in the strong jaw line, the straight nose, the long, light-colored hair. He hadn't shaved in a couple of days and had rough stubble along his chin, and on him, she liked it. Then her eyes found his lips, and she could not help but wonder if she could will him to kiss her, to desire her.

His lips found hers and melded to her. With a sigh, she parted her lips, allowing him inside. She wrapped her arms around his neck and leaned close to him, wanting even more from him. His tongue dueled with hers, teasing her, pushing her for more. He pulled back and kissed her cheek and trailed a line of kisses down to just below her ear, where the heat of his breath caused her to shiver.

"Are you cold, lass?"

"Nay." She leaned into him, wishing to savor his scent and his warmth, yet somehow it felt wrong. He could be marrying another woman soon. She shoved herself away from his chest. "I'm sorry, I'm not ready for this." She leaned her head toward the pallet and whispered, "I know this is what they had planned, but I cannot agree to it yet. We do not know each other well enough. Does that upset you?"

Torrian lifted her from his lap and set her away from him. Then he stood up and held his hand out to her. "Nay, naught about you could upset me, lass. Mayhap we could ride to the archery field. I noticed your bow when we first met. We could practice together."

She stared at his outstretched arm for a moment before she tucked her hand in his and followed him. The man was too wonderful. She swore he understood her feelings better than she did.

CHAPTER NINE

Torrian helped her onto his horse, then climbed up behind her. "Now I can take you to the popular Ramsay archery field."

"I only now remembered that I do not have my arrow and quiver," she said softly, looking back at him with big eyes. "Do you?"

He chuckled. "Do not worry, there are plenty at the field."

"Why do you call it popular?"

"We created it for our Ramsay Festival. My sire invented the festival years ago as an event we run whenever the Grants come to visit. We usually have an archery contest, a horse riding contest that seems to change every year, and an obstacle course for the bairns to run. 'Tis great fun. My aunt Gwyneth is one of the best archers in all of the land of the Scots, mayhap all of England, so she took charge of the archery field. We even have cases full of equipment just for the festival, and there are several fields set up with different distances marked off. You'll see."

"I've watched your aunt in action before. In fact, I must confess I stole behind her a few times when she was hunting and training the lassies so I could learn. If I ever get the courage, I'll tell her and ask her to teach me more. I was always afraid she would see me."

"Och, I'm sure she knew you were there. Aunt Gwyneth is aware of everything around her, sometimes at distances way beyond what you would expect. She also believes in women choosing their own destiny, so mayhap she trusted you and allowed you to follow along. I would be willing to wager she did everything at a slower pace to allow you to learn."

"Hmmm. Now that you mention it, you may be right. She was slower than I was expecting."

"Trust me, my aunt is aware of everything around her. She knew you were there."

Torrian loved having Heather cradled in front of him on the saddle. She had soft curves in all the right places, but she was as slender and willowy as a graceful swan, unlike the woman who'd splayed herself on his bed the other night. Even though Heather had a daughter, he sensed an innocence about her. They fit each other in a way he and Davina never could.

"Your festival sounds like such a joyful gathering, but I do not know if I could ever attend." She peeked over her shoulder at him.

He rubbed his free hand up and down her arm. "Would you like to tell me why you have this fear? You do not need to talk about it, but sometimes it helps."

"I fear it will not," she said, looking down.

He kissed her neck. "It would help me understand you better. But I can start. Once I became sickly, I was moved to a cottage away from the village, hidden in a copse of trees. I was cared for by a clan family who had been chosen because they had a son about my age, so at first I did not mind it. But they lost him, and then I was alone. Eventually, my weakness overtook my body and I was confined to bed. I just could not get any strength from my food because it would not settle in my belly. I only saw the close members of my family—my da, my grandmama, my uncles, and my sister. She developed the same sickness, but 'twas never as bad as mine.

"I became so accustomed to living in the cottage that when I finally healed, I felt lost in the real world. Of course, I had to learn to walk again, but people still stared at me. Everywhere I went, I felt uncomfortable."

"Torrian, 'tis hard to believe since you are so tall and strong now. Why did it bother *you* to be around others?" She squeezed his hand, and he ran his thumb across the tender skin of her wrist.

"Because I was used to being alone. I learned to entertain myself, mostly by reading. My da taught me how to read. I often practiced my letters and numbers, always hoping that I would be by my sire's side one day, helping him with the stores and the crops. I'm comfortable alone. Lily needs to be around people, but I am completely the opposite."

"My situation was different."

He caressed her hip, hoping to give her encouragement.

She took a deep breath and continued. "My grandparents took me to the fair once a year. I loved to go. The colorful tents and banners were beautiful, and I loved to watch the jousting. But I was always entranced with the jewelry. One day, I sneaked over to the jewelry tent without telling my grandparents. It began to rain as soon as I got inside the tent. The vendor pushed me back out, sending me home because the winds had come up. I stood in the middle of the field as the trees bent in the wind, loose flags blowing everywhere, the wind howling in my ears. I had no idea which way to go. There were so many banners and branches blowing in the wind that I lost my bearings. Everyone tore through the area, yelling and crying, pushing and shoving, but I could not move.

"I screamed and screamed, the rain pelting my face. I knew not where to go, and no one would help me. It seemed like forever before my grandsire finally wrapped me in his arms and took me back to our tent that we slept in, which was still erect. I still carry that fear of being alone in the middle of a crowd of people." She leaned her head back on his shoulder. "Seems I go back and forth between fear of crowds, then fear of being alone. Even that has overtaken me at times in our cave."

"I'll help you conquer that fear. I promise to stay by your side whenever we go into a crowd together." He'd been impressed at the fact that she'd raised her daughter in a cave alone, but now to hear of her fears, fears that he was able to identify with, he had even more respect for what she'd been able to do on her own. Could he have done the same?

"I hope I can make you proud, but I'm not sure. It has been a verra long time."

He pulled the reins of the horse and stopped, turning her toward him. His fingers nudged her chin up so his gaze caught hers. "I understand, but I *will* help you with this fear. I promise." His lips settled on hers and he groaned. She tasted so sweet, and she clung to him, allowing him to set the pace. His tongue mated with hers briefly before he ended the kiss. The dazed expression on her face made him cup her face and kiss her again. "We're here. I'll help you down before we both tumble off together."

She laughed and he jumped down, then set his hands on her

waist and lifted her off the horse. She set her hands on his shoulders, sending a bolt of warmth through him. He stared at her, wondering if she'd felt it too. "Here, follow me. We'll try the first field, so we can find out what feels best to you."

Torrian clasped her hand in his and led her across fields to where the wooden chests filled with equipment were kept. While Torrian busied himself with one of the chests, he noticed Heather was staring at the field with something like wonder on her face. Though it was a sporting field, there was a woman's touch in the neatness and the exactness of everything.

"Here, see if this works for you."

Heather took the bow and settled the arrows and quiver where she wanted them. Then she nocked her first arrow and let it loose, missing her target completely. Her shoulders slumped. "Mayhap 'tis why I have better luck spearing fish than I do hunting for meat."

Torrian came over and stood directly behind her, close enough that she could feel the warmth of his body. "Take your stance."

She did what he instructed.

"Nock your arrow but do not shoot it."

Again, she did as he had asked. This time, he came close enough that their bodies touched.

"Adjust your stance just a bit, line everything up better." He moved her arm just a touch, then said, "Fire away."

She loosed the arrow and it swished through the air, and caught the outer edge of the target.

"Better," he said. "Do you trust me?"

She peered up at his tall frame, his gorgeous lips, and his bronzed skin. "Aye. What am I doing wrong?"

"If you trust me, I'll help you line up the next one even more. Grab another arrow."

A bit suspicious, she grabbed another arrow and nodded to him. "I'm ready."

His body came directly behind her this time, his arms covering her arms, showing her exactly how to draw and nock the arrow, then line up with the target. The only problem was all she could feel was his rock-hard abdomen, the heat and calluses of his hands, and the warmth of his breath.

Everything changed in that instant. She could not deny to herself how much she wanted this man. She let the arrow loose and just missed the center of the target. Her face lit up at how much better she'd done with his help.

"Go ahead, try it on your own." He placed his hands on his hips and watched her, giving her pointers as she progressed.

As they practiced, Heather could not help but notice that every time she made a good shot, Torrian's face brightened with satisfaction and delight. And she discovered something else—she wanted to make him proud. Never would she have guessed that a man would take such interest in her and her talents. A feeling was building inside her that she hadn't experienced in a long time—pride.

"Are you not going to shoot?" she asked.

"I will if you'd like, but I do not wish to get in your way."

"Nay, please do. I learn from watching others."

He cast her a sideways glance of doubt, but grabbed a bow and took aim. She stood back and watched him shoot arrow after arrow. He hit the center every time.

She stared at the target in shock, then turned to stare into his blazing green eyes. Both of them stood unmoving for a moment, and then he dropped his bow and remaining arrows into the grass and reached for her. Tossing her own bow down, she tugged him closer as his lips claimed hers. She moaned at his taste and wrapped her arms around his neck, throwing herself into kissing him more than she'd ever done before.

The man tasted delicious. She parted her lips, wishing to taste more of him, and melded her body against his. His hands cupped her cheeks with such tenderness that she wanted to do the same for him, but instead she gripped his hips. She wasn't ready for all of him yet, but that didn't mean she couldn't enjoy some of him, did it?

He caressed her back and ran his hands down her sides, finally moving them to her bottom and tugging her close. He angled his mouth to take the kiss deeper, making her want to drop her clothes to the ground and allow him to taste every inch of her body. She vowed to allow herself the pleasure of enjoying this lad, this man, this warrior she clung to with every fiber in her being, simply because she trusted him, simply because he stirred a fire in her like no other.

Torrian continued to caress and tease her with his tongue, making her moan with the most unwomanly sounds she'd ever heard, but she did not wish to stop. She wanted him to go further, touch her, tempt her more. Though she did not want to risk the act that could get her with child, she wished to experience more of womanhood, more of passion.

Her heart thudded against her chest, even more so when he lowered his head to her chest and released her ribbons to free her breast. He cupped her with such tenderness that she could do naught else but watch in awe as he took her nipple in his mouth and suckled her. She moaned and ran her hands down his arms, then continued to stroke his chest and belly. "More, Torrian, more."

He obliged and tugged the other side of her gown down, flicking his tongue over her taut peak, then drawing on her nipple until she ran her hands through his hair to get him even closer. His hands skimmed down her thigh, pulling on her skirts until it found its way to her bare skin, tantalizing her. He found the vee of her curls and softly caressed her bud, then slid his finger into her slick passage, moving in and out in a suggestive way, the way she needed.

"Nay," she panted.

Torrian stopped and gazed into her eyes. "Did I hurt you?" His ragged breathing was no different from hers.

"Nay, I just…I know where this is going. I cannot risk another bairn. I'm sorry."

Torrian said naught, but he helped her tie the ribbons on her gown.

She peeked at the tense line of his jaw, wondering if it meant he was angry. "Torrian. Forgive me."

He kissed her soundly and caressed her hair. "You've done naught wrong. Forgive me. I have gone too far, especially for a lad betrothed."

Torrian helped her onto his horse and then mounted behind her. As they headed back to the keep in the lowering sun, all she could think of was what she could be losing. Thinking about what they'd just done, she couldn't believe she had stopped him and he had done what she'd asked. There had been no judgment or censure on his part, just assistance in righting her clothes. He'd accepted her request and honored it, treating her with the respect she deserved.

This situation was so different from her previous experience. Respect, honor, trust, all terms new to her. Dare she think love? She wanted him desperately, but was there any possibility of a chieftain wedding a lass who lived in a cave? Nay, not when the king wanted him to marry a lass of noble blood.

CHAPTER TEN

The next day, Heather brought Nellie to the special healer's building where Brenna did much of her work for the clan. She was eager for Brenna to take another look at the bairn, and to confirm what Heather felt in her heart—that she was getting better. And there was another issue she wished to discuss with Brenna…one that embarrassed her more than she would like.

"I have never heard of a healer having a separate building," she said in wonder as Brenna emerged from the front door. The building was made of stone, but she could see Lady Brenna's warm touches on the outside. There was a small stone path to the door and around to the side with flowers edging the borders. On the right side of the building sat a carefully tended rock garden with herbs and flowers flourishing amongst the stones, a stone bench off to the side.

"My husband had it built for me," Brenna replied. "Would you like to come inside?" In response to Heather's nod, she ushered them in through the front door. "I often take up too much space in the keep, so he thought it best to give me my own area. This way—" she swept her arm around the large chamber, "—I can see as many patients as necessary. I have room for five pallets and can squeeze more if necessary."

"Aye, 'twas a wise decision. 'Tis quite clean here. That must be comforting to those who are ill. I know 'twould be to me, Lady Brenna." There was a small chamber in the center with several stools, probably for a waiting area. A doorway to the back led to a chamber full of supplies and on each side sat a doorway to chambers with multiple pallets.

"My mother insisted on cleanliness, though every other healer says it matters naught. She raised us to believe otherwise. Even if it does not make a difference in a sick one's care, I always feel better when 'tis clean."

"Why did you have Nellie stay inside the keep?" She held her daughter's hand as they followed Brenna toward a chamber off the supply room.

"The bairns can be frightened out here, particularly if anyone else is recovering in the building with them. I prefer to treat them inside. She was more comfortable there, and I believe 'twas better for you, also."

Heather nodded, deep in thought. Brenna was a gifted person indeed. Only someone with a keen, sharp mind could heal people, let alone design this space. She followed Brenna to the chamber off the back.

"I have two chambers in the back, one for supplies, and one for my surgeries. Are you squeamish?"

"I am not," Heather replied, "but I'm not sure about Nellie." As they neared the doorway, Heather caught a strong odor. She glanced at Nellie's furrowed brow, guessing she was noticing the same.

Brenna stood in the doorway, hesitating, and then shoved against it. "I was doing a wee bit of surgery for Jennet. She is verra curious, so occasionally I practice after the men slaughter an animal, before they butcher it for meat. It helps me understand our bodies when I must cut inside, and she loves to observe. You're welcome to come in and see, if you'd like."

Heather glanced at Nellie, who nodded, her face eager. "Aye, Mama. I'd like to go inside the chamber where Jennet is."

"But there will be blood from an animal."

"Do not worry. I'd like to see it." Nellie squeezed her mother's hand to convince her, but Heather believed her true purpose was to see Jennet.

She hesitated, but Brenna added, "Jennet loves it, but sometimes 'tis too much for Brigid. I cannot decide for you."

"We'll try it. She has seen me gut fish and hunt before."

They stepped inside, and were immediately hit by the wave of the odor of blood. Jennet stood on a stool, peering over the lamb carcass, a tool in her hand as she pushed into an open wound. "Mama, I think this is where the blood comes from." She pointed to a section, her eyes bright with excitement.

Heather's belly turned squeamish at the same time Nellie said, "Mama, it smells in here. Must we stay?"

"Nay." Heather spun her daughter around and pushed open the door.

Brenna followed them out. "Do not feel bad. I understand. Verra few people comprehend our curiosity. Jennet follows in our family's inclination for healing. My sister Jennie and I were the same way, and we always liked to watch whenever our grandsire and our mother did surgery. I miss Jennie dearly and named Jennet after her. It seems appropriate she has the same curiosity."

Heather coughed twice and leaned against the wall, getting her bearings.

"Are you hale?"

"Aye. I will be fine. Nellie?" She checked her daughter. "Better now?"

Nellie scrunched her face together. "Aye, but I do not like it in there. 'Tis much better here."

Brenna laughed and ran her hand through Nellie's thick yellow locks. "I am happy to see the wee one doing so well, but is there a particular reason for your visit?"

"Aye." Heather cleared her throat again and looked pointedly at her daughter, who was leaning against her and clutching her skirts. "She seems better to you? Should I restrict her from aught?"

"Nay. Let her do as she wishes, just make sure she drinks often. Goat's milk is fine. Are you eating well, Nellie?" she said, crouching down to speak to her.

"Aye, Cook has made me baked apples and porridge with honey. I like the warm food on my throat."

"Good. I'm glad." Brenna straightened and looked Heather in the eye, waiting for her to share her true purpose for the visit.

Heather's eyes teared up. She thought about Torrian and how sweet he'd been, but her heart broke in two whenever she thought of him marrying another. It seemed like a situation with no graceful conclusion. "What should I do?"

"I think you need to stay here. Nellie is out of danger now, but since she has had this sickness twice, I would advise you to keep her where she can stay warm at night. I did not like the sound of her cough this time. I would advise you to stay until the air warms again. The nights are too cool for her."

"But with the wedding and all…"

Jennet came barreling out of the surgery. "Mama? May I play with Nellie? I can put her on the pallet and we can pretend, can we not?"

Brenna crossed her arms in front of her chest. "Of course, if 'tis what Nellie and her mama would like."

Nellie nodded, peering up at her mother with an expectant gaze.

"Of course, you may. Go play with Jennet."

"Jennet, wash your hands first, lass," Brenna reminded her. "Sorry, Heather, 'tis a wee issue for me. I must insist."

While the lass set about her task, Brenna waited for Heather to continue.

Heather squeezed her eyes shut to hold back tears. "I do not know if I can watch the wedding. We have spent some time together, and I have discovered what a fine man he is."

Brenna took her hand and cocooned it in her two. "Heather, some of us are doing all we can to stop this foolish marriage. If I were in your place, I would stay for two reasons."

Heather waited, hoping the answers would give her the justification she sought.

Brenna continued, "First, you need to stay to keep your daughter from becoming sick again. A repeated illness can truly drain a bairn's strength. Second, if you have feelings for Torrian, stay and see what happens. He does not wish to marry Davina, and he will do everything he can to stop it from happening. There are many others who will support him. There are other issues that I am not at liberty to discuss, but we agreed to the betrothal because of these issues. Do not give up hope yet. We all still hope for an end to this match."

"I'd like to stay hidden, if 'tis at all possible. I do not wish to be in the great hall to watch her arrival. I do not like crowds and Nellie is unaccustomed to them. Would that be acceptable?"

"Of course. You may stay in Nellie's sick chamber. Your daughter can sleep with you or with the lassies. They all sleep in one huge bed that Quade built for them. I'll have Fiona tend to your needs when the large party arrives. Until then, you may go to the kitchens whenever you'd like sustenance. We have the back staircase."

"If that is agreeable to all, then I accept. I do not wish to risk Nellie's health." She glanced over at the two lassies, now playing on a pallet. Jennet had given Nellie a fabric doll to be her pretend bairn. Nellie watched Jennet's every move with something like worship.

Jennet patted the doll's arm. "You will be fine. I must sew up your wound, then I'll cover it with salve. Once I'm finished, I'll wrap it in linens until it heals."

Nellie leaned down to her doll and whispered, "Do not cry, wee bairn. Jennet will not hurt you and I'll hold you." She kissed her doll's head as Jennet adjusted her needle and thread, preparing to sew the wound.

"I'm glad we're here," Heather whispered, feeling her eyes tear up. "She needed to meet lassies her own age. Look at how much she enjoys Jennet's company."

Brenna smiled fondly at her daughter. "Jennet loves to pretend to be me whenever she is able. Lily tries to get her to play more traditional games, but she is not interested. Brigid will do whatever her friends are doing. They are sweet together." She turned to look at Heather. "So you'll stay?"

"Aye, and many thanks for all you've done for both of us, Lady Brenna." She hugged Brenna, but only one thought echoed in her mind.

Please, Lord, do not let this be a mistake.

⁓

In a clearing halfway between Cameron and Ramsay land, four people sat whispering about their plans. Ranulf, chieftain of the MacNivens conferred with the Buchans—Glenn, Dugald, and Davina. Cormag sat off to the side, but said naught.

Glenn, the current—but not permanent, if Ranulf had any say in it—chief of the Buchans, said, "You are all being foolish. Aye, I'm all for taking land from our neighbors, mayhap stealing some sheep, but you overestimate your power. You'll never conquer them."

Ranulf's eyes narrowed as he glowered at Glenn. "Old man, do you not listen? We'll not do it all at once. 'Twill take time, Dugald and I both know 'tis true. If we gain land from my neighbors the Menzies and the Camerons and acquire some of the wealth of

Lochluin Abbey, we can hire another four score guards to take to battle. Each time we win a battle, we'll add more men to our force."

"'Twill take more than four score to do battle with the Grants and the Ramsays. I know you're not addled enough to believe otherwise. Are you, son?" He stared at Dugald.

Dugald shifted on the log where he sat. "We'll adjust our plans as we go. The first is that we must be insiders at the Ramsay keep. Then we'll have plenty of ways to build our coffers and spread our guards' influence. Davina is key to this plan."

Davina flung her plait over her shoulder. "I'll do my part, you do need not worry. Just none of you forget you've promised me fine gowns and jewels. And many maids to take care of my needs."

Ranulf chuckled. "I know many who'd beg to take care of your needs, lass." He waggled his eyebrows at her, but stopped as soon as her sire interrupted.

"You talk to my daughter like that again, Ranulf, and I'll cut your ballocks off. You'll respect her. She's to be the mistress of the Ramsays once her husband's sire is dead, and it won't be long before that happens. Mind your tongue."

"Your pardon, my lady," Ranulf ground out. How he'd show them all. It would not be long now. If Davina did her part, everything else would fall into place, and he would gain the respect he deserved. All the power he had ever wanted would fall into his lap. The Buchans knew not who they were dealing with. "Just do as you promised."

"She will," barked the Buchan. He moved closer to Ranulf, pointing his finger in the lad's face. "You just do as you're told. Do not allow yourself to be so caught up with our scheme that you try to go off on your own. You'll regret it if you do. You're young and foolish. Ease off."

Ranulf got up from his place and stalked off into the forest. Shite, but he hated it when that bastard shoved a finger in his face. Aye, he needed him at present because he was Davina's sire. But he would not need him for long. In another year, he'd have everything in place, and they'd all be answering to him.

CHAPTER ELEVEN

Torrian rode his horse outside the gates and fell in line between his father and his uncle. They had received a message that the king's contingency had reached their land, so they were traveling to greet them and offer their guards as additional protection.

Quade spoke under his breath as they approached the king's caravan of horses. "You understand what is expected of you, aye?"

"Aye, Da. I'm to be agreeable to everything, and say naught."

His sire narrowed his eyes at him. "I know how you feel. You agreed to be open-minded. Since the king is here, I'm sure you will have the opportunity to speak your mind. I just hope you realize the importance of doing so behind closed doors and not where wagging tongues can overhear your comments."

"I know 'twas different for you. But can you not see my point of view?" He just refused to believe his sire would so willingly relinquish his happiness by insisting he keep this engagement. Quade had been a man of reason for all Torrian's life. Why was he deserting him now? He loved his father more than anything because of all they'd been through together.

"Aye, I do. I loved your mother, but not everyone is so lucky. An heir to a chieftain does not always get to choose their partner. Should you choose to go against our king, you'll pay the consequences of your actions, not me. You are old enough. Trust in me and in your uncle. We will find a way, but we must be diligent and aware. Please do your best to assist us in this endeavor by not angering our king as soon as you greet him. We need time."

They continued on in silence. As they drew near, his sire whispered out of the corner of his mouth, "Try not to look as though you're visiting the dead, would you?"

Once they met the king's men, their guards surrounded the contingency to offer an additional layer of protection and escorted them toward the Ramsay castle. Quade moved his horse up to ride by the king's side.

King Alexander tipped his chin toward the gray sky, a touch of mist in the air. "'Tis a most lovely day. Do you not agree, Ramsay? Your land is glorious, Quade."

"Aye, and 'tis a beautiful spring day, my king. Blue skies are on their way."

"Good afternoon, young Torrian."

"My king." He forced himself to smile.

"Are you looking forward to the upcoming nuptials?"

"Aye." He couldn't expand upon that word though; the small lie had almost killed him. He thought of sweet Heather instead of Davina, of how much he'd prefer for her and her wee lassie to be by his side for the rest of his life. But he knew this was not the time to discuss it with King Alexander. His father let out his breath as though he'd been holding it in fear. But when Torrian glanced at his father, he was surprised to see a smirk on his face.

"What has you smiling?" Torrian said to his sire.

"A good reason for you to hang back."

Torrian glanced at him from the side, puzzled.

His father tipped his head back. "The contingency behind us is flying Grant banners. I'd appreciate it if you would greet the next group. As chief, I will escort the king into the bailey."

Torrian's face lit up as he peered past the huge group traveling with the king. "Aye, 'tis the Grants."

"I suspect you've some support for your wedding. Word travels fast, even in the Highlands. Can you tell who has come? My eyes are failing me at this distance."

"I can just make out Alex's sons Jake and Jamie at the front of the group. Mayhap Brodie and Braden? I think I even see a glimpse of wee Kenzie. But I do not see Loki." He flashed a grin at his sire as he flicked the reins. "I'll find out for you, Da. See, I can do as I'm told sometimes." He rode off without stopping to look at his sire.

He shouted out a greeting to the oncoming group, and they responded with the Grant war whoop, just as he'd expected. The arrival of his cousins changed his entire outlook in regards to the week ahead. He loved the Grants, every one of them. Some more than others, but they felt as much a part of his clan as the family members who lived in the Ramsay keep. His stepmother's clan was the strongest in the Highlands, so when they traveled, everyone around them knew it. Aye, he could enjoy this week even if he was supposed to be married within a sennight. And he would not give up all hope of changing his fate. Having his cousins here gave him a great feeling. For certes, some of them would be on his side, he was sure of that.

Torrian's time with the king would come, and he'd speak his mind.

Heather moved toward the balcony just to gain a quick peek at the guests in the great hall. Under no circumstances would she risk being seen, but her curiosity over the young bride-to-be had gotten the best of her. She had to see her just once.

She glanced down at the dais and managed to catch her from the side. Davina of Buchan was not just pretty, she was a royal beauty. Dark thick waves flowed down her back unplaited, a bit unusual, but she had no doubt the lass got her way about everything.

She could tell from the way Davina laughed, a phony lilt that carried up over the railing and seemed to act as a siren's call to most of the men in the hall. At least half of the male gazes were focused on her. She was dressed in a dark red velvet kirtle, decorated with gold threads and black ribbons. Red ribbons were also woven through her hair, which cascaded almost to her waist. She had the body men dreamed of, ripe with curves everywhere, full red lips parting at just the right times. She could tell even from this distance. Davina leaned her breasts down toward Torrian often, though she did not need to because they were on full display with the deep cut of her bodice. If she'd ever wanted a lesson on seduction, there it was directly in front of her.

Fortunately, the only one immune to this woman's wares was Torrian. Now that she knew him better, she could see all of his smiles were forced. He was most uncomfortable next to Davina.

"Do not be jealous of her. She has none of the fine qualities you possess."

She jerked her head around to find Gwyneth Ramsay off to the side, out of view of everyone.

Heather stepped back to talk to her. "There's no denying her beauty, and she knows how to show off her assets to their best advantage."

"Verra true. It tells me she's quite experienced. I highly doubt Torrian's proposed bride is a virgin, much as she tries to pass herself off as one. Whether that can be used in his favor, we know not. May we chat in your chamber?"

"Aye, but allow me to check on Nellie first. The lassies are playing healer at present in their chamber. There are three of them, which is perfect. When last I checked, Jennet was the healer, Nellie was the helper, and your daughter was the patient."

Gwyneth followed her to the door, and they both peeked inside.

"We must do surgery right away," Jennet said, her serious little voice audible from the doorway. "Nellie, please bring my satchel of tools."

Nellie ran to the side of the room and brought a small satchel to her, her eyes full of eagerness. "Do not worry, you'll be all better and then we'll sing to you."

Brigid moaned as they prepared their tools.

"Nice moan, Brigid," Gwyneth called out. "Sounds true. Now Jennet, you'll not use any real daggers?"

Jennet's eyes grew wide. "Nay. I would never practice on a person with a knife, Aunt Gwyneth. That would hurt her."

"Good. Just be sure you are playing." Gwyneth closed the door and whispered, "That lass is too bright for her own good. I used to worry about Gavin and Gregor spending so much time together. But with those two, you never know what they'll be up to next."

"They are not like the usual lassies, are they? I've never seen them pretend to be mommy or mistress of a keep."

"Nay, but that suits me fine. We raise our lassies the same as we do our lads. They must know how to protect themselves."

"Would you take my Nellie with you when you teach Brigid how to use a bow? I'd like her to know those skills, as well."

"Of course, I'd love to take Nellie along."

Heather held open the door to her chamber while Gwyneth stepped inside. "Why are you not down at the dinner?"

Gwyneth snorted. "Logan knows such grand occasions are not

for me. I've tried to attend feasts like this at the royal burgh, but my tongue oft gets me in trouble. He's happy to leave me here with the bairns. Besides, I serve a better purpose here." She sat next to Heather on the small bench in front of the hearth.

"What do you mean?" Heather smoothed her skirts, hoping her nervousness did not show. She wasn't accustomed to being around this many new people.

"Well, you know Logan and I have worked for the crown many times."

"Aye, you've said."

"I do not trust the Buchans. All of us will be alert while they are here, but sometimes 'tis best to be in the background observing, not in the middle of the festivities. 'Tis where I prefer to be—watching. And now there are others who will help. Many of our Grant cousins are here, and they will assist in our venture. We have some verra talented people here."

"Why did they come?"

"They heard about the upcoming wedding and sent a contingency. 'Tis what we do when we hear about major life events with the Grants. The lads are all close. As soon as Torrian tells them he does not wish to marry Davina, there's no doubt that Jake and Jamie will be watching for aught they can dig up on the Buchans."

"Do you think they'll discover aught?"

"Aye, if aught is wrong, they'll find it. Wee Kenzie is especially wily. He's just like his sire. When Loki was his age, he'd always know exactly what was going on."

"I hope Torrian has the chance to tell them his true feelings soon."

"Logan does not know for sure, but he thinks Torrian told them on the ride in. You just need to be patient."

"I need to be patient, but I wish someone would slow Davina down. She's quick, too. She knows just what she's doing."

"And I know just how to slow her type down." Gwyneth winked at her and left the room.

A wee glimmer of hope started in her heart.

∽⧜∾

Torrian did not know how much longer he could stand talking to the lass. Aye, she was pretty, but was she interested in aught besides jewels and gowns? The urge to roll his eyes at her every word was becoming harder and harder to repress.

His father had said the fiddlers would be in later, along with a couple of minstrels, and he could not wait. It would be rude for Torrian to dance only with Davina, would it not? He desperately hoped it would be an escape from her—at least for the moment.

"Do you know what my most favorite thing of all is, my lord?" Davina asked with glimmering eyes.

Torrian decided he preferred her mode of address to his real name, although he'd never felt that way with anyone else. "I do not. Please share."

"Emeralds. The way they shimmer and shine in the light fascinates me."

"Aye, they are beautiful. I saw the king's jewels not long ago."

"Truly?" Her eyes lit with excitement. "Were there emeralds? How large were they? What shape?"

Torrian forced himself to contain the deep sigh begging to get out. "There were many emeralds, rubies, sapphires, and diamonds."

"Tell me more, please. Where are they now? Do you have aught here I could see?"

"Nay. We returned the gems to the king. They were his."

"But were the emeralds more beautiful or the sapphires?" She leaned closer, her gaze on his lips.

"They looked about the same to me."

"Oh," she tapped his arm with her fingers. "Men. Can you not see how important they are to a lass?"

Torrian said, "Nay. As far as I can tell, they are not important to my stepmother or any of my aunts. Why are they so important to you?"

"Because I love how they reflect the light. I like to wear many gems. Can you imagine…" Davina fluttered her lashes and turned her head away in a practiced move that seemed intended to convey bashfulness.

"What?" He decided to give in to her whim for the moment.

"Picture me in your mind wearing naught but jewels." She closed her eyes. "Picture me with a sapphire ring, an emerald necklace, and mayhap a tiara of diamonds…and naught else but bare skin."

Davina's eyes remained closed for several moments.

Not eager to play her game, Torrian changed the subject. "Would you like to know what my favorite thing is?"

Her eyes flew open, and he caught a quick flash of fury in them before it disappeared, similar to a look he'd seen before. My, how his betrothed was skilled in certain areas. Cunning, spoiled, and vain were the words that popped into his mind.

"Of course. What is your favorite?" She batted her eyelashes at him.

"Puppies."

As cunning as she was, she could not hide her shock. "But puppies are wee dogs, and dogs are wicked scavengers that drool and bite. How could a puppy be your favorite thing?"

"Because when I was young, my best friend was my dog, Growley."

"That is preposterous. How could a dog be your friend?" She almost laughed aloud, but caught herself just in time, turning a bit pink over her near mistake.

Torrian's gaze found hers. How could he possibly convince her of something she was incapable of comprehending? He'd try anyway, just for his own satisfaction. "Because I was verra ill for a long while. I could not walk on my own, and Growley was always there to assist me. That drooling scavenger acted as my legs for many moons. To a young lad, not being able to walk unassisted is devastating, especially when you are the laird's heir and there are certain expectations."

"I still do not understand how you could value an animal so. You grew up, did you not? Look at you now."

"Because he was always there for me, rain or shine, no matter how poorly he felt. 'Tis why I considered him my friend. And he was the best listener in the world. Somehow, I did not expect you would understand." He watched the emotion flit across Davina's face, though he couldn't quite be sure if it was disgust or anger. Mayhap there was a little of both. At the same time, he recalled the expression on Heather's face when she'd come upon the puppies in the stables and when he'd placed Bretta on Nellie's lap. Both were a far cry from the expression on Davina's face. Heather's eyes had misted, Davina's had turned to disbelief. The two lasses could not be more different.

She reached underneath the table and slid her hand up his thigh. "Mayhap I do not comprehend your fascination with dogs, but there's one thing I do understand. I want you and you want me. Why do we not retire to your chamber so I can help you forget about the troubles you suffered when you were young?"

Her hand moved up his thigh, reaching under his plaid to find his flesh, and though he tried to fight it, she did have certain talents. He was rock hard.

Her eyes glittered with triumph, and she continued her ministrations.

"Stop," he whispered.

"What?" The confused expression on her face told him she hadn't been turned down often.

"Release. Me. Now."

If she continued with her ministrations, she'd embarrass him in front of the entire hall. He reached for her wrist when she finally released him.

"I must say I've never met another man like you, my lord. Did your childhood illness leave you lacking in certain areas?"

The cold, calculating look in her eyes told him he needed to be careful. He glanced over her shoulder and just happened to catch the look in Ranulf's gaze. It was clear the man knew exactly what she had done, and equally clear that he was not happy.

He needed to be very careful indeed.

CHAPTER TWELVE

After the music and festivities began, Heather sneaked into the kitchens the back way to get something to eat for Nellie, hoping to avoid being seen. She moved carefully through the herb garden, but stopped in her tracks when she heard female voices around the corner. She recognized one immediately—Lily. The other she guessed was Davina. She waited, hoping they would move on so she could continue on to the kitchens without interruption.

"Why did we need to come out here to talk, Lily? I know you are Torrian's sister, but there's no reason we could not speak in the great hall."

"Actually, I wished to be certain we would not be disturbed. 'Tis too noisy inside, and I wanted to ensure you would hear me."

Heather was surprised to hear the anger in Lily's voice. She was a happy, warm person whom Heather enjoyed immensely. How she wished she could observe them. She also realized she should probably leave, but her feet stayed anchored in place.

"All right. But please be quick about it. I have better things to do."

"I'm sure you do. You are a conniving woman, are you not?"

Heather could almost picture Davina and her outrage.

"How dare you speak to me in such a way." Davina's voice had lowered almost to a growl. "You will treat me with respect. Have you forgotten that I will be mistress of this castle someday and you will answer to me?"

Someone snorted, but Heather could not picture either one of them doing such a thing.

"I will *never* answer to you, my lady," Lily drawled. "I will treat you the way you deserve to be treated. Are you pleasant, or helpful, or a genuinely giving person? Wait, please do not answer as I plan to answer for you. I've seen no evidence to support any of those things. I have observed you and asked many questions, and I do not like the answers I have received. You are spoiled and manipulative. You are a selfish woman who's only interested in marrying the chieftain of a clan so your status will be elevated to mistress."

"Is that so? And you are the expert who deems this to be true?"

Heather could envision Davina crossing her arms in front of her, and she found herself wishing again that she could see them.

"Aye, 'tis true. Anyone can see it in aught you do. I will not allow you to get away with it. My brother is the most wonderful man you will ever meet, and I believe you realize that you two do not suit. I want you to walk away."

"And how shall I do that when this wedding has been ordered by our king? I did not ask for this, and I am doing my best to do as our king ordered me to do."

"Mayhap, but I'm sure you do not have your maidenhead…"

Heather heard the sound of flesh hitting flesh. Had Davina slapped her?

"You should not try to hit me again. I am too fast for you. As I was saying, my brother deserves the best, and you two are not suited. Tell your sire and King Alexander that you pine for another and you do not wish to marry. Say whatever you like, but you must put a stop to this. The request came from your sire. He's the one who can end the arrangement. Mayhap there's another match your king could make for you. There are plenty of lads in the land of the Scots."

"Mayhap I'd like to marry Torrian. 'Tis none of your concern."

"Both of us know that isn't so. But mayhap you're not capable of caring for anyone, so Torrian is as good as the next lad. Well, know this. You may fool everyone else with your beauty and your smiles, but not me. I will not allow this marriage to take place. You will never make my brother happy, and my nieces and nephews will not grow up with a mother like you."

"I'm sure the king cares not what you say. I'll marry him, and you must adjust, as anyone does to a new member of a family. I tire of this conversation. I'm returning to my betrothed and the festivities."

Heather hurried to hide between a group of bushes in the

gardens. Once they left, she let out a breath. Poor Torrian was the only thing she could think of at the moment. Once all was quiet, she ducked out from behind the tree and started down the path.

A deep voice called out behind her, a voice that crawled up her spine and caused her head to ache.

"What a surprise, Miss Heather! What brings your happy, smiling face to the Ramsay keep?"

Heather spun around and clutched her throat. How she'd hoped never to set eyes upon this man again, yet there he stood in front of her, a wide grin on his face. Since his people had arrived, she'd been wary of just this circumstance, choosing to stay in the keep as much as possible on the upper level. Her worst fear had come to pass.

"I can tell by the expression on your face how glad you are to see me, pretty one. Have you not missed me?" He sauntered toward her, his arrogance evident in his swagger.

"Stay away from me. I told you I never wished to see you again." Her heart threatened to break out of her chest it beat so fast.

He grabbed her wrist and tugged her forward. "You do not have the right to tell me what to do. I'll see you whenever I wish to do so. The cave I set up for you is not good enough anymore? You had to seek out the Ramsays?"

"The cave is satisfactory, but Nellie has been sick."

"My wee daughter has been ill? As soon as she's better, you must return to your cave. I do not want you here. What have you told them?"

"Naught, I've told them naught about you. Let me go, you're hurting me." She twisted her arm to get away, but to no avail.

He held on for a moment longer, just to prove he could, and then released her and stepped back. "Is Nellie better?"

"Not completely. Brenna Ramsay is the best healer. You know 'twas why I chose this area."

"But we agreed you were to live in seclusion and not tell the Ramsays aught about us."

"And that is what I've done. As soon as I'm sure of her safety, I'll return to the cave."

He walked over and stroked her cheek. "Do that. You still are a rare beauty, though. Mayhap I'd like another taste of you."

She jerked her cheek away from him. The look in his eyes made her wish to hurl in the bushes. "Nay, you promised to leave me be if I left."

He dropped his hand. "Fortunately for you, I have plenty of other bedmates to choose from. They all want to be in my bed. Just do not hedge from our agreement. You will regret it if you mention my name to anyone here."

Just the thought of him hurting Nellie made her ill. She tried to hide her reaction, but she could not, instead doing her best to stay on her feet and not crumple to the ground at the mere thought of losing Nellie.

"I see you've realized what I could do. 'Tis true, though I'd hate to hurt my own daughter. But I could take her home with me and leave you behind."

Trying her best to hide her fear, she took a step back. "You would not."

"I would."

"But you have no interest in her." She wanted to scratch out his eyes, claw his face, kick him where it would hurt him most.

"Nay, I do not. But any number of women back at the keep would raise her for me. That I would do."

"I've abided by our agreement. Please leave us alone."

He turned to walk back to the keep, but then stopped to address her over his shoulder. "I will, as long as you do not talk. Understood? One word and I'll take her." He strode off, his arrogant walk enough to make her want to chase after him and punch him with all her might.

But what could she do? She had no choice but to do as he said. He had all the power, and she knew she had none. She ran back into the trees and sobbed.

Glenn of Buchan, Ranulf MacNiven, Davina, Cormag, and Dugald met outside in a hidden spot in the woods midway through the night's festivities.

"This is not going well," Ranulf growled.

Davina lifted her chin. "I believe 'tis going as we planned."

"Nay, 'tis not. I can see he does not like you. You must fix this." Her father paced in the small clearing, his hands on his hips.

She crossed her arms in a pout. "Aye, he does. He's just a bit slower than most lads. He'll be mine in another day."

Ranulf gave her a twisted grin. "Truly? You believe that? I saw what transpired at the dais. He refused your advances."

Dugald added, "I saw it, as well, although his failure to react did not surprise me. Use your head and try not to embarrass the lad in front of his clan and his king."

Her father stopped in front of her. "You need to get him in your bed by tomorrow. I'll give you one more day to sway him."

"One day is all I need, Da." Davina relaxed.

Ranulf wished to shake both her and her sire. The man was clearly blinded by his affection for his daughter. "I do not believe 'twill work. Even his sister does not like you."

She spun on her heel to confront him. "And how would you know that?"

"I have my ways, Davina. The success of this entire venture is in your hands. You must come through."

"And I promise I will. I only need one more day." She glared at Ranulf, but when he stepped closer to her, making his threat apparent to her if not to her foolish relatives, she averted her gaze.

"I have a plan," Ranulf said. "'Tis foolish to sit around and see if our original plan will work. This plan is fool proof."

Glenn paused, clearly deciding whether or not to heed him. He had to convince them. It was the best way forward, he was sure of it.

"All right, MacNiven. We'll listen to your plan," Glenn finally said.

They listened to everything Ranulf had to say, then mulled over the proposition.

"I believe 'tis brilliant, Da," Dugald said.

Glenn nodded as a slow smile crept across his face, showing the missing teeth that had been knocked out years ago in a battle with a boar. "At least 'tis a plan. We shall see how well it works. There is naught more beautiful than you, daughter. Work your magic on the lad. See it done."

Davina smiled and tipped her head toward Ranulf.

"Can you do your part, Davina?" Ranulf asked.

"Of course. I will be successful. Do not doubt it. The man will be mine by the morrow's moon."

Ranulf wished he had a bit more confidence in the lass, but

he'd just have to trust her. Her sire and her brother believed in her, so he had little choice but to do the same. Given the opportunity, Ranulf would use different methods to ensure her compliance. Her sire was too soft with her, but he still needed the Buchans so he kept his opinions to himself.

More than anything, he needed Davina. It would not be much longer now.

The following day had not seen any improvement in his circumstance. The king had continued to show favor to the match, and his father had gone along with him. The only event that had given him hope was that both Uncle Logan and Aunt Gwyneth had disappeared for most of the day. The evening meal had passed with Davina saying little to him. In fact, she'd been so agreeable that Torrian wondered if something was afoot.

Later that night, Torrian paced the parapets. The Ramsay keep hadn't had one when he was a wee lad, but they'd built one after his sire married Brenna. He'd come up here in the hopes that the cool night air would help clear his mind and figure out a solution to his problem.

He had no interest in Davina at all, and his heart longed for Heather. He wished to share this with his king, but there hadn't been a good opportunity. Besides, once he spoke to the king, it would be over. His sire had been clear in his expectations. Torrian would do whatever the king ordered him to do.

But could he subject himself to a lifetime with a lass he could hardly tolerate? The more time he spent with Davina, the worse the prospect of the arranged marriage seemed. It loomed over him like a giant thundercloud, threatening to drench him and break into ripping winds, torrential downpours, and violent lightning. Talking to the lass was a chore, something he honestly did not know if he could do every day.

His alternative was to be accused of treason, and face whatever sentence his king deemed appropriate—flaying, imprisonment, or execution. None of those frightened him as much as the one thing that would surely happen if he denied Davina—disappointing his father.

His only hope was to beg his king in private.

He headed down the stairs to his chamber, his shoulders

sagging in defeat. He would take each moment as it came. Moving down the passageway, he opened the door to his chamber and stepped inside.

As soon as he did, a feminine voice purred to him. "Come inside and warm me."

He pivoted toward his bed and found Davina with the covers drawn back, an open invitation to join her. She wore naught, just as before. He should have known better. As fast as he could, he turned back toward the door, but disaster struck before he could open it.

The door flew open, and Davina's sire stood in the doorway.

A booming voice echoed down the passageway, "What have you done to my daughter?"

CHAPTER THIRTEEN

Torrian's world collapsed in an instant. He stood in shock as Davina covered herself back up and started to cry, her father raging and yelling enough to wake up everyone in the keep.

"What goes on here? What have you done?" Glenn of Buchan moved to the side of the bed.

Davina sobbed as loud as any lass Torrian had ever heard. Her father pulled the covers back and threw a plaid at her. "Cover up, daughter, and get out of that bed."

Her breath hitched as she took the plaid and wrapped it around herself, sliding across the sheets. "But Papa…"

"Say naught, or I shall lose my temper for certes." He moved toward her, but rather than try and cover her, he flung the covers off the bed.

First Dugald flew in the door, then Quade and Brenna. Everyone in the room froze at the sight of the bed linens.

Blood. Dark red blood stained the center of the linens on Torrian's bed, clear as the Highland mountains on a sunny day. Every set of eyes focused on him.

He glared at Davina. "You set this up, Davina. Tell them the truth. Tell them naught happened." Though fury sang through his body, he did not know how to handle this. But he was not going to be set up without attempting to set the situation to rights.

Rather than respond to him, she threw herself into her sire's arms sobbing. "Papa, I knew not what he wished me to do until 'twas too late. 'Tis all his fault. Forgive me, Papa. Please." She buried her face in her father's chest.

The king's two guards entered the room, then moved everyone back to allow the king himself to enter. Torrian could see Lily lingering in the passageway behind the king's men, a horrified look on her face.

"Who would like to explain what has happened here?" King Alexander said, standing with his legs planted wide, his hands clenched into fists at his sides.

"Must you ask, my king? 'Tis plain for all to see." Buchan pointed to Torrian. "This lad has taken my lassie's maidenhead. I know they were to marry in a moon, but I will not tolerate waiting until then. Why, she could be carrying his bairn."

The king waved at everyone for silence, then strode over to the bed to assess the situation. "I must say, 'tis definitely blood. What say you, Torrian?"

Davina continued to sob, but Torrian knew it did not matter what he said. The evidence was against him, and Davina had planned it perfectly.

"I wish to speak in private, my king. With you and my sire."

"I accept. I'll meet with you in the laird's solar."

The Buchan barked, "I wish to be there, as well. I have every right to hear what say you about my daughter."

"You will be invited in after I speak to Torrian. Settle your daughter first. Escort her to her chamber and calm her so I may question her later. Ramsays, follow me."

Quade gave Torrian a pointed look as they followed King Alexander down the corridor and down the stairs to the Ramsay solar. Once the door was shut behind them, the king sat behind Quade's desk, and the Ramsays sat in front of him. "Explain yourself," he said to Torrian.

Torrian glanced at his sire, dreading how this would affect him. Quade rubbed his knee, the spot that pained him most as he aged.

"My thanks for seeing me in private, my king," Torrian started. "I swear on all that is holy that this did not happen. I did not take the lass's maidenhead. I had only just stepped into the room when the Buchan barged in behind me. Before that, I was up in the parapets."

King Alexander folded his hands in his lap and leaned back in his chair. "Are you telling me that the Buchan lied to his king in order to gain his daughter a husband?"

"Aye...I mean...I'm not accusing... but I did not have relations with her." He glanced at his father, hoping for support.

The king stroked his chin as he stared at Torrian. "So a man who already had his daughter pledged to you would risk his reputation and the king's censure to move the marriage up by what, a fortnight? This is what you expect me to believe?"

Quade sat in a chair, clutching his knee. "Sire, they attempted the same ruse when we were visiting the Buchan castle. Torrian opened the door to find her lying in his bed, waiting for him, but he managed to flee the chamber before anyone else arrived."

"And young lads are known to be randy, Chief Ramsay. Your son is no different from the rest."

"Aye, 'tis true, but with all due respect, my son is not a liar." The set in Quade's jaw told Torrian his father did believe him. And that belief meant a great deal to him, even if it did not change his fate in regards to Davina.

"I hope you both understand that I have no choice in this matter. Five people caught you with the lass in your chamber in the middle of the night, and there was blood on the linens." The king squared his shoulders and stood, staring at them with a piercing gaze. "My decision is made. You were to marry in less than a moon, and now I must move this marriage forward."

Quade stood, stumbling a bit before he righted himself.

The king declared, "Torrian, you will marry Davina of Buchan in two days' time."

"But I love another, my king." There, he'd admitted it. He glanced from the king to his sire, but he saw no surprise in either man's gaze.

The king's eyes narrowed. "Then you'll start your marriage better than many, with a mistress by your side. Most women of nobility expect you to take a mistress, so do what you must, but I need this alliance to keep my kingdom calm. Be careful of what you do, lest you be accused of treason, *my lord*. You have been ordered to do this by the crown and by your clan. Do I have your support, Chief Ramsay?"

Both of them glanced at Quade, who nodded after a long pause.

Something exploded in Torrian's brain. When the wedding had been a moon away, he'd believed he could stop it—mayhap by convincing Davina they did not suit or angering her sire enough to change his mind. Now he had no alternative.

The king continued. "Verra well. 'Tis settled. I shall stay until mid-day on the morrow and then head to my castle in Edinburgh.

The wedding shall take place without me. I have no desire to be at these nuptials. I will speak to Father Rab before I leave."

He motioned to the guards to open the door and allow Glenn of Buchan entry.

"Chief," the king said to him, "your daughter is requested by the crown to marry Torrian of the Ramsays in two days' time. Prepare your daughter for her wedding."

Torrian watched the Buchan chief as the king announced his edict, and he was glad he did.

Had he not, he would have missed the smug look of satisfaction in the whoreson's gaze.

Heather threw their things into the satchel. She was about to rouse her daughter when she heard all kinds of commotion in the passageway. Though she opened the door a crack to listen, she could not hear well enough to understand what was happening, so she closed the door again to continue with her plan.

They had no choice but to leave. She would never risk losing Nellie to her father, and Heather was well aware that the man was completely capable of carrying out his threat. Once she had everything she needed, she stuck her head into the passageway again, breathing a sigh of relief when she saw everyone had moved below stairs.

Perfect. She hooked the satchel over her shoulder and reached for her daughter, still sound asleep. How much better she slept here than in the cave. But though she felt guilty for removing Nellie from this safe, warm environment, the alternative was unthinkable.

If that man dared to take her daughter from her, she'd cut off his ballocks in his sleep. But she could not involve the Ramsays. They'd been too wonderful to her.

Nay, it was best for her to return to her cave for now. There was much going on here with the king in residence. She'd leave until events returned to normal, then she'd return to explain and thank Brenna, Torrian, and all the others. But would their lives ever return to normal? With what she knew of the Buchans and the MacNivens, she doubted it. The king was here and would get his way, and Heather would have no role in Torrian's life.

She crept into the passageway and tiptoed toward the back

stairway that the servants used to run to the kitchens. It would take her directly outside. From there, she'd head to the stables, find her horse, and leave. It would be safer to travel close to dawn, when the men would be too sotted to notice her.

As soon as they hit the cool night air, Nellie stirred, so Heather stopped and covered her with the fur, urging her back to sleep. She hoped Brenna would not mind that she had borrowed the fur to keep Nellie warm against the cold Scottish winds. There were few people about in the bailey, and those she saw were headed to the keep with intent looks on their faces. Though she did not know the nature of what was unfolding, it was affecting more and more people.

When she reached the stable, she woke one of the lads and said, "Could you help me saddle my horse?"

A deep voice from behind her said, "Nay, I'll help you. I'm heading outside the gates."

She spun around and breathed a sigh of relief to see Torrian standing in front of her. Then she noticed the expression of despair written across his face. "Torrian, is everything all right?"

"Nay, 'tis not, but I'll not speak of it now. I'm more concerned with where you are going at this time of the night. I thought you'd agreed to keep Nellie here until warm winds blow."

She turned her head toward her horse, "I must get away."

"You must? Why? Has someone threatened you?"

"Torrian, forgive me, but I do not wish to discuss it just yet. Will you help me or not?" She leaned down to breathe in the scent of her daughter's hair, hoping the comfort of her sweetness would keep the tears at bay.

"Of course I'll help you. You may explain later."

"And you can explain why you are intent on going for a ride in the middle of the night. Or is that usual for you?"

The side of his mouth twitched, but he just nodded. "Agreed. Hand Nellie to me once I've mounted. I'll keep her warmer than you can."

She did as he asked because she knew he was right. Once they were through the gates and away from the castle, Heather watched as the man she was growing to love cuddled her daughter the same way she would. The thought of his heat warmed her in the cold wind. The man was like an oven—a tender, caring, thoughtful oven—and how she wished things were different. As a husband and a father, no one would be better. Tears stung her eyes in the wind as the thought of what could never be consumed her. One huge mistake, years ago, had put her in this desperate position.

But she'd never change it. Nellie was her everything. Still, she could not deny that the time she'd spent with the Ramsays had made her feel dissatisfied with her life in the cave. She'd fought so long and hard for their survival that she'd lost sight of her own needs.

Torrian was the one who'd made her realize those needs existed. She needed to be loved, to be warmed, to be appreciated and supported. She swiped the burning tears from her cheeks as they galloped over the glade, the beauty and quiet of the night cocooning them in their own world. How she wished things could be different. Why could they not continue to gallop away from the castle and mold a life of their own somewhere far, far away?

Because Torrian was meant to lead. From the strong backbone she saw in front of her to the compassionate grace he demonstrated over and over again, Torrian would be the strong-yet-tender, fierce-but-caring leader who would guide his people to an even better life. She had no doubt he would exceed all his clansmen's expectations, because that's who he was.

If only she could stand beside him.

CHAPTER FOURTEEN

Torrian's mind kept trying to find an escape out of this maze, but there was none. He thought of the advice his sire had given to him when he was younger. *You need to let things settle before you make a major decision, Torrian. That way, your decision is not just an emotional one, but one of reason.*

How true. Every one of his thoughts was ripe with emotion. He was relieved he'd encountered Heather in the stables. At least with her by his side he could not do any of the self-destructive things he'd originally envisioned—fighting, screaming, punching, howling at the moon.

In truth, he no longer *wanted* to do any of those things. As soon as he'd laid eyes on Heather, his blood had slowed from a raging boil to a rolling one. Now it felt completely settled. Instead of relenting to the power of his rage, he was rejoicing in the sweetness of the sleeping bairn in his arms and the nearness of the beautiful woman riding behind him.

Why couldn't things be different? Besides his desire to lead, he was a simple man, but now he was trapped in a spider's web of deceit, and in two days, he was set to marry a woman he despised.

Once they arrived, he handed the sleeping Nellie to her mother, but he insisted on checking the cave for animals before they entered it. He declared it clear, and Heather headed into the deepest part of the cave to settle her daughter down to sleep while Torrian waited near the mouth of the cave.

When Heather returned, she stood a distance away from him, huddled, her arms wrapped around her middle. He wanted her more than anything at this moment. She had none of the jewels or gowns that Davina possessed, and yet she was the one he wanted to touch—standing there in a tunic, leggings, and boots, the moonlight shining inside the cave highlighting her form. He wished to capture the image in front of him forever. Her eyes were a wee bit haunted, just like he felt, when they met his. Her lips parted to speak, but she stopped short.

He would be forthcoming; it was only fair. "I've been ordered to marry Davina Buchan in two days." He waited, shoving his hands behind his back. How would she react to his declaration? "But I'd rather marry you, someone I want to hold, someone I want to share my life with. You, Heather, and no other."

She took three steps forward until she stood in front of him, close enough that he could see the tears misting in her eyes. "I need to know…"

"I want you, lass, more than I've ever wanted anyone. You cause an ache in my chest whenever you are near. But I cannot make any promises."

She took a step closer and held her arms out to him.

Unable to resist her invitation, he wrapped her in his warm embrace and kissed her hard on her lips. Hellfire, but his desire would unman him, for sure. She parted her lips for him, welcoming him with the tease of her own tongue.

She ended the kiss and stood in the light of the moon at the mouth of the cave, her hands trembling as she removed first her tunic, then her leggings, tossing them back into the cave.

His mouth went dry as soon as she'd removed her first piece of clothing. Heather was so beautiful that if she were his, he'd never pine for another. Grateful that she felt the same way he did, he took two steps toward her. She reached for him and started to remove his plaid and tunic while he removed his boots and breeches. He grabbed a pile of furs and arranged them in a pile on the cold stone, then helped her find a comfortable position before covering her with his body.

"I want you more than anything, lass." He ran his gaze from her toes up to the top of her head. "Do you know how beautiful you are?"

She shook her head. "I've never felt beautiful until I met you, Torrian. You make me feel special, a new experience for me."

He kissed her, a long, tender kiss designed to tell her what he could not say in words. He kissed and suckled and teased her until he heard that wee sound in the back of her throat that he loved, a sound that he would strive to hear again and again. He wanted to feel her passion, her desire for him, and he wished to show her what relationships were meant to be like.

But he also needed to know for himself. He'd never felt this way about a lass before. Aye, he'd bedded some, but not a one had ever captured a piece of his heart the way Heather had. He needed to know how good it could be before he was forced into a relationship with a cold-hearted liar.

Hellfire, but he was sure they would be great together.

∽◦∾

Heather wanted him everywhere. He kissed her neck, nuzzled her ear, kissed one breast and then the other, then settled his tongue on one nipple, circling, nibbling, teasing her until she wished to scream. Aroused to a point she'd never experienced before, she writhed underneath him, tilting her pelvis toward him.

A fire began in her woman's place, a fire she wasn't sure how to handle. She rubbed her mound against him, but he ignored her, continuing to kiss and suckle one breast while his hand cupped the other, his thumb teasing the tip of her nipple. When she started to wriggle beneath him, he traced a hand down the line of her hip and across to her core. He touched her lightly and she bucked, shocked at her body's response to his touch.

His gaze caught hers and his smug expression made her do something bold. She reached for his large arousal, wrapping her fingers around his length and moving up and down. Though she was uncertain if she was doing the right thing, his ragged growl encouraged her to continue her teasing.

His finger plunged inside her and she gasped, shocked at the pleasure shooting through her body. Unable to wait any longer, she brought him to her entrance, rubbing his tip back and forth against her pleasure spot, sending a pulsating need she could not deny through her body.

Torrian took over, grabbing her hips and driving into her until his length filled her completely. She moaned again at the sheer pleasure of being one together, unable to believe it could feel this good, and pulsed against him, a short in and out. Groaning, he gripped her buttocks and thrust even deeper, driving into her at a pace that finally forced her over the edge with a scream, waves of pleasure washing through her. She heard his sound of pleasure as he finished, his thrusts hitting her exactly where she wanted him, needed him.

Perfect, they were perfect together. That was the only thought she was capable of having.

As their panting lessened, his gaze locked on hers and he kissed her, a kiss that told her how much he'd enjoyed what they'd shared. She waited to see what he would say before he left. She was not yet capable of putting a coherent thought together.

Though she expected him to pull out and get up to leave, he instead rolled onto his back and pulled her with him, nestling her in the curve of his arm. She could not think of any place she'd rather be.

She waited until their breathing came under control, then said, "Tell me what happened? Please?"

He kissed her forehead, her cheek, and her lips, a soft feathery kiss that left her wanting more. The back of his hand brushed her cheek, a delicate touch that made her feel treasured.

"I spent quite a bit of time in the parapets, trying to think of a way out of my situation, but I could come up with no solution. When I returned to my chamber, Davina was in my bed with naught on. She'd done this before, but her failure led to a change in tactics. When I turned to leave, her sire opened the door, feigning surprise when he saw Davina in my bed. He bellowed loud enough to wake half the Highlands, including my sire, my stepmother, and eventually the king."

"And they did not believe you when you told them 'twas all a lie?" She stroked his arm as he talked.

"Her father checked the linens and found blood. My destiny was sealed. I spoke to my sire and my king, but I was ordered to marry her in two days."

She wrapped her arms around him and rested her head on his chest. "Torrian, I'm so sorry. What a terrible experience for you. Did you tell them the truth of the matter?"

"Aye, but the evidence was against me." He ran his hands through her tousled locks. "As far as Alexander was concerned, we were to marry soon anyway."

They lay wrapped in their embrace, enjoying this intimacy they knew would have to end.

"Will you tell me why you ran?" he whispered, staring into her eyes. "Who has threatened you?"

She took a deep breath before she spoke. "I suppose I can share what I am able, though I promised not to reveal the person's name."

"I accept your conditions. What has frightened you so?" His hands moved to the base of her neck underneath her hair, massaging the tender skin there.

Heather lifted her head to look for any sign that Nellie might be stirring, then nestled it back against his shoulder and began her story. "I was brought up by my grandsire and grandmama. My mother died birthing me. My sire was never mentioned, only that my grandparents never liked him. I knew naught about the ways of men and women. All I can tell you about where I lived is that it was a cottage far away from any clan, deep in the forest. We were well hidden in a glade thick with trees. My grandsire made a clearing in an area lush with growth because we were near a mountain spring.

"One day, I met a lad who was out hunting. He came straight to me. I was ten and five. I ran from him because I rarely saw anyone near our home. He caught me around the waist and whispered sweet phrases in my ear, but I fought him. His hands brushed the undersides of my breast, but when he reached up to cup one, I was so frightened I brought my elbow back and caught him in the nose, causing blood to spurt everywhere. He let go and I rushed off into the trees.

"I ran as fast as I could, but I heard the others in his hunting party come along and tease him. He let me be."

She brushed strands of hair out of her eyes so she could gaze into his warm green eyes, the eyes of the forest, her grandmama would have said.

In a gentle tone, Torrian said, "He returned."

"Aye, a few times. He brought me sweet pastries and a book, which I adored. Once he found out that my grandmama taught me to read, he brought one book after another."

"Until you felt in his debt." Torrian's eyes darkened, but he said naught.

"Aye. He hugged me the first few times, and I began to trust him. When he finally did what he wished to do, I had no idea what he was about until it was too late. I screamed from the pain and he slapped me, which frightened me even more. He threatened to hurt my grandmama if I said aught, so I kept quiet. I also never returned to that particular clearing in the forest where I usually met him. I made sure never to wander alone again. I had three books to read, but I could not touch them because I felt so dirty."

She swiped the tears from her eyes before she continued, intent on telling him her tale all at once because it was too painful to repeat. "I had no idea why my belly grew, but my grandsire explained it to me. He wanted the lad's name so he could kill him, but I did not know his name. I cried and cried because I'd let him down.

"I did not see the bastard again until he saw me ripe with child, but he left me alone. I vowed to get away so I would never have to set eyes upon him again, I hated him so. My grandsire grew sicker and sicker each day, so he hurried and taught me all he knew about hunting and cooking, just so I could run away and take care of my bairn by myself. He was so afraid of what would happen to me once he passed on."

She stopped for a moment to close her eyes and draw strength to tell him the next part, envisioning wee Nellie as her motivation. "My grandsire died shortly after Nellie was born. I was almost ready to leave when *he* came to my door and forced his way in. I recall it well."

As she spoke, the memories of that awful time continued to roll over her.

∽∾

He barged in through the front door, startling her. "And why are you packing, my sweet one?"

"I'm leaving. My grandparents are gone, so I'm leaving." Her hands shook as she stuffed more clothing into her satchel.

"Mayhap I'd like to keep you nearby. Why do you not return with me to my keep?"

"So all will see what I am? Nay, I think not."

"And what are you?" he asked, running his hand down her arm, causing her to shiver in revulsion.

"My grandsire said a woman who's used the way you used me is a whore." How she had hung her head in shame.

Then he shifted his attention to the babe, opening her rags to peer at her.

She shoved at him, wanting to keep him from touching her wee bairn. "Leave her be."

"Her? Just wanting to see if I have any possible heirs. Och, I see you did not lie. 'Tis a lass and you may keep her for all I care. But I might like a taste of you again. I liked you, and I know you liked me."

Her body had turned rigid at his touch. She loathed him. "Please, leave us be. I'll ask you for naught."

His head tipped back. "If that is your wish, I'll find a place for you. I do not want any issues when I marry. You must promise never to ask me for aught. Where do you wish to live?"

The offer came as a surprise. "Somewhere near the Cameron healer, in case I ever need her."

"She is not far enough away. I'll find a place for you near the Ramsay healer. She's the best in the land."

⁂

Heather's gaze locked with Torrian's as she finished telling him about that horrible day. "Believe me, 'twas the only good thing he ever did for me. He helped me find this cave and get settled. Then he left, and until the other eve at your keep, I had not seen him since."

Torrian's eyes had a vibrant intensity in them as he stared back at her. "What's his name, lass?"

CHAPTER FIFTEEN

Heather cupped his face in her hands. "Please do not ask me, Torrian. I promised. He said if I told anyone about him, he'd steal Nellie away and give her to someone at his keep. 'Tis why I returned to the cave. I just cannot risk losing her. The nights are a bit warmer now, and I thought we would be safe here until he leaves. Then mayhap we will return. Please?"

He nodded. "Aye. But someday, you will tell me."

Heather kissed him lightly on his lips. "Aye. Someday. But you and I can never be together."

Torrian caressed her back as she rested her head back on his chest. "Mayhap we can be. If I could, I'd marry you today if you'd have me."

"But what choice do you have? You could be convicted of treason for countermanding the king's will."

"In all those years I spent alone due to my illness, Heather, I learned to use my mind more than my body. I shall have to outthink my opponents. I'll return in the morn and take part in the pre-wedding festivities, set up some contests, and do aught else I can in the hopes I can uncover or overhear something about the Buchans to change the king's mind."

"But when does he leave?"

"The king leaves mid-day on the morrow. I shall not go against my king and my sire just yet, but know this…"

She picked her head up to gaze into his eyes, those glorious green eyes that beckoned to her like a torch in the dark.

He set his fingers underneath her chin and lifted it. "I love you, lass. And I mean to make you mine. If you can be patient, somehow I'll find a way. I will not marry Davina of Buchan. I'm hoping to discover something that helps free me of my obligation." He paused. "Before I go, I must ask you one more question."

"Anything, Torrian." She was suddenly so full of hope she wished to dance under the night moon.

"Will you have me as your husband if I can free myself from this betrothal?"

"Aye, Torrian. I love you, too. I'll help in any way I can, but I must stay here for Nellie's sake."

"I understand. Much as I hate to leave you, I must go. I have much to do since the dawn is here." He helped her sit up, and then did the same. "I'll run for some water. Where's your container?"

She stood and dressed quickly while he covered himself with his plaid. "You do not need to fetch water for me. I am quite able."

He extended his hand for the jug. "I'm quite capable of taking care of the lass I love. Now, would you allow me the pleasure?"

She handed him the jug, loving the way his eyes sparkled as he took it from her. Suddenly, she felt like the most special lass in the world.

She was in love.

Torrian arrived back at the portcullis shortly after the king had left, much earlier than he had expected. He had no regrets.

Kyle met him just inside the gate after he left his horse at the stable. "Your timing is fine. There's a big meeting inside the solar. I think you need to be there."

"Good, I'll head there now."

Kyle winked at him. "And?"

He scowled at his second, "And what?"

"And did you have a good night?"

Torrian picked up a clump of weeds and tossed it back at his second with a grin. "I'll see you later." He marched through the courtyard and headed into the great hall. His uncle stood just outside the doorway of the solar.

"Perfect timing," Brodie said with a grim smile. "We're meeting to discuss your fate, lad. Please join us." He held the door open, and Torrian stepped inside.

The chamber was full. His sire sat behind the desk, rubbing his knee, and Brenna sat on a stool next to him. Uncle Logan, Aunt Gwyneth, and Father Rab sat in chairs while his cousins stood around the outside of the gathering. Jake and Jamie were having a serious discussion with Braden, while wee Kenzie bounced back and forth between all the groups. Lily looked wrapped up in thought.

As soon as the door closed behind him, silence descended on the room and they all turned to stare at him.

"It pleases me that you could find time for us, son," Quade coughed. "Problems we should be aware of?" His sire was not one to waste words.

"Nay, no problems. Please fill me in on what I missed."

His sire gave him a pointed look, but his mind was settled. He could not marry Davina. He simply could not. Waiting for someone to start, he turned an expectant gaze from one relative to another. None of them spoke.

"Suits me fine to start first," Torrian said with a shrug. "I would like to inform everyone that I am not interested in marrying Davina of Buchan. To my mind, I have two days to come up with a solid reason not to follow the king's orders. As I've said, they used trickery to gain what they desired, so 'tis even more of a reason for me not to go through with the marriage. It is a sign of their dishonesty, and if they were dishonest in this, I believe it's a sign of a greater problem. I do not trust any of them, Davina, her sire, her brother, or Ranulf of MacNiven. Would anyone care to assist me in this endeavor?"

Jamie, Jake, Lily, and Braden all shouted, "Aye!"

He couldn't help but chuckle. "Terrific, I have four. Who else? Do any of the elders wish to assist me?"

"I think we'd like to hear your plan before we continue," his sire said, rubbing his knee again. "If there is a solid reason for us to do this, I would like to hear it."

"The solid reason stands before you, Da. I do not want to marry her. I love another."

Lily clapped her hands and raced over to hug him before returning to her spot.

"I'll ask again. Ideas?" Quade added.

"I'd like to have some contests," Gwyneth replied, "archery, sword-fighting. You can tell much about a person's character in a competition. No coin involved, just the glory of being declared the winner."

Logan kissed his wife's cheek. "Great suggestion, wife. Seems you wish to help Torrian instead of following the king's orders?"

"Just because he's king does not mean he is always correct. We shall help him fix his mistake by uncovering the truth."

Several gasps echoed in the chamber. "What?" She glanced around at her kin. Even Father Rab, her brother, quirked his brow at her.

"Be careful where you say such things, wife. I do not care to have to free you from a dungeon." Logan ran his hand across the stubble on his chin.

"I know a few of you have already voiced an opinion, but I'd like to ask again, and I am quite serious about this. Are you willing to risk the clan's relationship with the king?" Quade asked. "I'd like to know if Logan and I are the only ones who believe in following the orders given by our king. Who wishes to assist Torrian by going against our king's decree?" Naught was said.

A few moments later, Lily's hand raised into the air. "I do, Papa."

"I'm not surprised by that, Lily. You are too soft-hearted. And the rest of you?"

Gwyneth's hand raised, followed by Jamie, Jake, and Braden. Brodie's hand went up strong and straight. Then Father Rab raised his hand, but it was the last hand to rise in the air that surprised them all.

Brenna.

"Sorry, husband," she said, "but you know how my mother and your mother both felt about this. 'Twould be best for him to choose his own wife, and the lass is underhanded at the verra least. You cannot deny that."

Logan said, "Aye" and raised his hand into the air.

Quade leaned toward his brother in shock. "You, too, Logan? But you work for the crown."

"Aye, I'll not deny I favored the wedding before the sly trick they played on the lad. There's no doubt that the Buchans and their friends are planning something in the near future, and an alliance would help us control them. But after this last fiasco, my mind is made up. I know the king wishes for us to keep the

Buchans in line, but I no longer think Torrian needs to be sacrificed to that wee bitch to do it. And 'twould be wrong for his reputation to be ruined by this folly."

Silence reigned in the room for a moment, but Torrian noticed a twitch or two around his cousins' lips as they fought to restrain grins. Gwyneth moved over to her husband and plopped down on his lap. "Well said, husband." She kissed him on the lips.

Logan continued, "The king seems to be the only one who doesn't realize Torrian did not defile the girl. 'Tis not in his nature. I'll do my best to convince him of that. In the interim, I'd like to find more reasons for us not to trust the clan. And do not be so glad I've changed my mind. 'Twill make our work for the crown more difficult." He gave his wife's arm a squeeze.

Gwyneth wiggled her nose. "But we can do it." She stood, a satisfied grin on her face, and returned to her chair.

Logan sighed. "Aye, you are correct, wife. Stop looking so smug."

Torrian rushed over and hauled his uncle out of his chair, hugging him tight. "My thanks, Uncle." Hands waved all about the room as his family members pledged their support, and he couldn't help but smile. But the one hand that was *not* raised was the one he needed to see most. Finally, his sire joined the others.

"I'll assist where I can, as long as everyone understands that the wedding will proceed if we turn up naught."

The hands fell, but Torrian's uncle whispered, "Leave it all to Gwynie."

Her eyes sparkled as she tossed her plait over her shoulder. "This is what we'll do…"

They all huddled around her except Torrian.

He was too humbled to move.

∽

The final decision was to start with the archery contest. Jamie, Jake, Braden, and Kenzie were assigned to eavesdropping duty, but Torrian knew Lily would be everywhere today. His sister was so lovable, she could talk everyone out of their best secret.

A little while later, while the contest was being set up, Torrian stood at the side of the archery field watching her. Sweet Lily was no different than she had been at five summers. Her golden hair danced behind her, and her giggles drifted across the meadow.

Aye, she was a beauty now, but to him she'd always be the wee lass who would visit him in his sick hut and talk non-stop. She had always been able to brighten his mood. All the lads in the clan pined for Lily, but she favored none in particular.

He noticed Dugald, Cormag, and Ranulf's gazes oft followed his sister, a sight that sickened him, particularly since he expected one of them to be Nellie's sire. It had to be one who was concerned about an heir. He dismissed Cormag for being too young. Nellie was four summers. That left Ranulf, Dugald, and—though the thought of it made him cringe—Glenn, with two heirs already.

He spent a few moments studying the three men, trying to identify any facial resemblance, but there was none. Nellie favored her mother. Clearing his head, he committed himself to facing one problem at a time. First, they must catch one of the Buchans in their deceitful ways. The more evidence against them, the better his chances would be to have the betrothal dropped. One step at a time.

To his surprise, Davina sauntered over to stand next to him. "My, but you are looking quite fetching this day, my lord."

Torrian gave her a look that probably spoke his feelings better than words ever could. "Get away from me. You've done enough."

Under her breath, she whispered, "Certes you are intelligent enough to comprehend this was not my doing. I've done only what I have been ordered to do."

"Then follow *my* orders and get away. I'll have naught to do with you, *my lady*."

She reached for his hand, but he pulled away. "I do know how to please a lad, husband-to-be. I promise you will not regret our marriage." She gave him her most demure smile as she parted her lips in a suggestive pose.

"Your wiles will never work on me. I know you for what you are."

Her chin lifted and she spun on her heel, her mantle swinging behind her. She gave him one final glare and then stalked off.

The contest was about to begin. There were five on each team, and Kenzie would serve as the runner at the target.

On the Ramsay team were Jamie, Jake, Kyle, Logan, and Torrian. On the Buchan team were Dugald, Ranulf, Glenn,

Cormag, and one of their guards. Unfortunately, lasses were banned from the contest, though the Ramsays and Grants all knew the rule had simply been made to prevent Gwyneth from being on their team. They'd conceded without reservation because Logan and Torrian were almost as strong as Gwyneth.

Of their competitors on the other side, only Ranulf was reputed to be a talented archer. They'd already practiced and the contest was almost ready to start. Torrian scanned the field and noticed Aunt Gwyneth was nowhere to be seen, and Lily had also disappeared.

Kyle stood next to Torrian. "You can do this, Ramsay. You deserve to be with your lass, and your clan believes in you. I wish I'd been at the family meeting earlier."

"I must admit I was humbled and surprised, but I could not be happier that they have chosen to stand with me. Many thanks, Kyle."

Logan came up behind him. "Trust your aunt, lad," he said, clapping him on the back. "She was selected by Hamilton to work for the crown long before we married. 'Twas because of her clever thinking, not her archery skills, though he had to know she could defend herself. She strategizes like no other, and has a way of understanding the male mind that I cannot fathom. And her best comrade in thinking is our daughter Molly. Have faith and focus on your archery. We must push the others to do something sneaky." He clasped Torrian's shoulder and strode off toward the field.

Much later, by process of elimination, there were only two contenders left: Torrian and Ranulf. Quade stood in front of the group and said, "We shall take a short break for a quarter of an hour. The final contenders will compete at that time to determine the winner."

Torrian grabbed a water skin and threw a gulp of water down his throat. Most of the others departed the field for other refreshments were being offered, but he stayed. He needed to focus on the task at hand and not give in to distraction.

Just before the contest was to commence again, Ranulf wandered over to his side. Torrian was facing away from the crowd, and no one was close enough to hear their discussion.

"So a wee bird informed me that you are not interested in

Davina," Ranulf sneered. "Is she not beautiful enough to suit you?"

Torrian wondered what his game was, so he decided to play. He did not trust the man, chief of his clan or not. "Lying wenches are not my type."

Ranulf snickered and stared at his feet. "And what type *does* interest you? The type with a dick between its legs instead of a slit?"

"Nay, but I prefer my lasses not to slither through the grass." Torrian refused to look at the other man, but he could tell from his stiffened posture that the comment had hit home.

"Then allow me to make you an offer. You may have all the wenches you wish in return for allowing me to plow your wife whenever I would like." He tipped his head back to stare at a bird flying overhead.

"Ah. So you are already quite familiar with her fertile fields, are you not?"

A twitch caught in the corner of MacNiven's mouth. "Davina's exquisite tastes can only be satisfied by certain men. I'm quite sure you are not one of them. Besides, the lass fancies herself in that foolish female state of being in love. She'll do whatever you wish if you allow her to continue as my mistress."

"On no day in King Alexander's reign will you be allowed to touch my wife. Bet on that and you'll be a rich man."

"My betting instincts tell me that you still think you will escape marrying Davina of Buchan."

Torrian did not answer.

"Think again, lad. You are too nice to win." Ranulf pivoted and walked back toward the Buchan contingency.

Uncle Logan was beside him in an instant. "You allow him into your head, and he wins, lad. Be strong against the viper."

Visions of blonde hair and one blue eye and one green flashed through his mind.

"Do not worry, Uncle. I'm focused on the end result. He will go down."

CHAPTER SIXTEEN

Heather managed to finish cleaning the inside of their cave before Nellie finally awoke, sitting up on the fur padding and staring at her surroundings with wide eyes.

"Mama?"

"Aye, sweets. Mama's here for you." Heather had relived her moments with Torrian at least five times in her mind. She was so in love with the tawny-haired warrior, it was a struggle to force her mind back to the present.

Wee Nellie rubbed the sleep from her eyes, then stared up at her. "When did we leave the castle? I fell asleep in the big bed in your chamber, did I not?"

The confused look in her daughter's eyes filled her with remorse, but she had to do what was best for her daughter, and right now, it was most important for her to protect Nellie from her sire.

"Sweets, many more people arrived at the castle, so the Ramsays needed our chamber for guests. We shall return someday soon."

Her wee face fell. She stared at the ground and puckered her lips in a pout.

"My apologies, but we had to do what was right." She chided herself for lying to the lassie, but it wasn't a complete lie. And at least it would protect Nellie from her father's need for vengeance.

Vengeance. After spending time at the Ramsay castle, she now understood the true term for what he'd done to her. Rape. He'd done it without her understanding, he hadn't stopped when she'd screamed, and he'd even hit her at one point. The man was a disgusting piece of scum. He would never touch her Nellie.

Nellie lifted her gaze up to meet her mother's. "I understand.

'Tis all right, Mama, as long as I'm with you." Her wee lip trembled as she fought the tears that threatened to fall down her cheeks.

Heather scooped Nellie up into her arms and kissed her forehead. She could tell from the way her precious daughter burrowed her face into her shoulder that the lassie was broken-hearted, but they would go back.

Would they not?

Suddenly, Heather's mind started to churn with bitter, frightened thoughts. She stood at the mouth of the cave and stared up at the gray sky.

What if Torrian did not manage to find evidence implicating the Buchans?

What if he was forced to marry Davina?

What if Heather carried Torrian's bairn in her belly? From the prattle she'd overheard in the kitchens at the Ramsay keep, she knew lasses did not get pregnant every time, but she had carried a child after her first time.

What if she was forced to live in this cave with two bairns?

Nay, that could never be. Torrian would take care of her, would he not? He seemed to love her, for certes. Even if he was forced to marry another, he'd still find a way to care for her.

Then she thought of Davina of Buchan and what she would allow in her keep.

What would happen if Brenna passed and Davina became mistress of the Ramsay keep?

That line of thought was replaced with another. What if Nellie's sire came for her? He knew she lived in this cave. He'd helped her to find it. What if Nellie met him? What if....

Her entire being exploded, or at least it felt as such. Her heart pounded, her hands broke out in a sweat, and her hands trembled.

"What's wrong, Mama?" Nellie whispered. "You will not leave me here alone, will you?"

And she knew what she had to do. Aye, it was the right thing to do. She would stand up for herself. That fool had intimidated her when she was young, but no more. She had let fear rule her life for too long.

She would fight for the man she loved. Two days. They only had two days to set things to rights before both of their worlds crumbled. She could not let that happen without doing something.

Heather brushed the fine strands of her daughter's hair back and kissed her forehead. "Nay, my sweet Nellie. I'll never leave you. We shall return today rather than wait, though we must be extra quiet because of the festivities taking place. Can you do that for Mama? Can you not make a sound until you are with your friends again?"

Nellie smiled and nodded her head a firm two times. "I promise, Mama."

"Good. And you will stay with Jennet and Brigid and their maid while I do a few things?"

"Aye, and I promise to be verra good."

Heather set her daughter down and turned her back on the fur pelts. "Then get dressed in your gown with your leggings underneath. We're heading back. Your mama has something verra important to do. And I will not give up until I accomplish it."

Nellie clapped and ran back to her clothing. "Yay, Mama!"

Yay, indeed.

∞

The contest started.

At the last minute, Ranulf came forward limping. "I've injured my leg. Dugald has agreed to stand in for me."

Glenn of Buchan stood behind his son. "Dugald's clearly not as good as Ranulf or he'd be in his spot, but we have no choice. Ranulf cannot balance well on his leg. 'Tis only fair."

Quade approached the group and listened to their argument before consenting to the substitution. Dugald should be an easy win, so Torrian was puzzled at the switch in contestants. Ranulf was the type to shoot even if near death, so he knew there was an ulterior motive. Still, he knew he needed to focus on his shooting and leave it to his clan to uncover the truth.

The final contest was simple—the best out of five. They'd shoot one arrow each and determine which was the closest to the target, giving one point to the winner. This would happen five times. Whoever had the closest arrow three of five times would win.

All spectators were hushed as the round began. Torrian stepped up to the line and nocked his arrow. He took his time, making sure to be accurate, then let the first arrow fly, hitting the target dead center. Dugald shot second and was way outside the mark.

"First arrow to Ramsay," Quade announced to the gathered crowd.

Dugald would take first shot in the second round. He fired and missed the center again, but this time he came closer. Torrian stepped up and shot his arrow, dead center again. This time, his gaze scanned the crowd and he noticed both Glenn and Ranulf were missing. While he wondered where they were, he was determined not to allow their disappearance to distract him.

Torrian started to pace as he awaited Kenzie's announcement at the target. While he moved back and forth, he noticed Ranulf and Glenn emerging from a group of trees together. What the hell? Had they needed to pish during the tournament? He ignored them and returned his focus to the field.

Quade announced the second round score—two to zero.

Taking him completely by surprise, Glenn came up on one side of him to congratulate him while Ranulf clasped his other shoulder.

Torrian's gut turned sour. He did not know what the two had planned, but he was sure something was amiss. He checked his arm and shoulder to see if they'd done something to him, but there was no sign of tampering.

"Round three. Torrian, you fire first," Quade announced.

Torrian took his time, ignoring the sinking feeling in his gut and doing his best to focus on the task at hand. He nocked his arrow, aimed, and let it sluice through the air.

He missed the target completely.

The crowd gasped in shock. Torrian stared in bafflement, unable to believe he'd completely missed his target. He hadn't done that in years. His gut had been right. Now all he just had to do was figure out what had gone wrong.

He glanced at Ranulf and Glenn, both of whom had smug grins on their faces. Hellfire, they'd cheated somehow, but how?

Logan came up behind him and whispered, "Keep your head focused. Leave the rest to us. Your job is to shoot and stay in it."

Dugald stepped up and shot his arrow, hitting the edge of the target to beat Torrian.

Quade stepped forward. "Score after round three is two to one, Ramsay lead." He gave his son a pointed look before pulling his gaze away from him.

Hellfire, how Torrian hated to be on the receiving end of that disappointed look. Shite, but he had to do better.

Round four, Dugald shot first, hit the target, and stood back.

Torrian stepped up, but this time he found himself battling with his mind. He had to meet his mark to make his father proud. He had to do it for Heather. But what if he missed the target again? What was wrong with him? Was this how a competitor got into your head? By making you so addled you knew not what you were doing?

Sweat broke out across his forehead, but he stepped up to the line. He took his time, doing everything just as Logan and Gwyneth had taught him, and let the arrow fly.

He missed the target again.

Torrian thought his chest would explode. How could this be? He half-listened as his father moved forward to announce the score. Kenzie charged across the field toward Quade, but he was directed back to the target as Quade stated, "Round four to the Buchans. Score two to two. Last arrow determines the winner. Ramsay, your shot."

Kenzie tried again to race across the field, yelling to Torrian's father.

This time, Quade bent down to listen to Kenzie.

Ranulf hurried back into the trees, hoping to get there before he was noticed. Hell, but his plan had worked to perfection. There was naught wrong with his leg. And though he was the best archer on the field, he did not mind allowing Dugald to win. This was all about teaching the Ramsays a lesson.

He wished to show them not who had the best talent, but who was best at taking control of a situation. The MacNivens and Buchans would be the best clans in the Highlands. All would be talking about them someday, well, more specifically, talking about *him*, Ranulf, the chief of the MacNivens, soon to be the greatest power in the Highlands.

He rotated in a circle, searching for the quiver they'd set here, but he couldn't find it. He was sure he had left it hidden by the bushes at his feet.

A whizzing flew by his ear, and he ducked, knowing

instinctively what it was. A loud thwack followed and he saw an arrow in the tree with the Ramsay fletching.

"Looking for something, my lord?"

A female voice echoed through the trees. He turned to find an arrow aimed directly at his chest, held by that bitch who liked to think herself the best archer in the land—Gwyneth Ramsay.

He'd kill the wench with his bare hands. How dare she get involved with men's affairs. He took one step forward, only for an arrow to land at his feet.

"Are you that daft?" she said with a grin. "Have you not heard my reputation? My favorite thing to do is to shoot rotten bastards in the ballocks. And at present, I think this quiver full of tampered arrows qualifies you for the rotten bastard award. What think you? Do you still wish to take another step?" She lowered the direction of her arrow so it was level with his groin.

He stood still, glaring at her, hoping his most evil look would do its work, but she only laughed. Hell, but if he ever got his hands on that neck of hers....

She made a bird call and then said, "I think my husband would love to see these arrows."

CHAPTER SEVENTEEN

Torrian stood rooted to the ground, watching as Kenzie whispered to his father. Still stunned that he'd missed a target twice, he was frozen in place, unable to speak, unable to nock another arrow.

Logan, who was standing behind him, pushed him forward enough so he could hear the conversation between his sire and Kenzie.

"Kenzie, we must continue this," Quade was saying. "The competition is almost finished. It can wait, whatever it is."

"Begging your pardon, Chief, but nay, it cannot wait. 'Tis about the arrows."

"What about them? I know Torrian missed the target." Quade crossed his arms in front of him as he awaited Kenzie's answer.

The wee laddie handed two arrows to the chief. "See for yourself. I've seen this before in Ayr. 'Tis how they cheat…"

"Who's saying someone cheated?" The Buchan bellowed loud enough to call everyone's attention to himself and then ran toward Quade, Dugald following fast behind him.

Torrian moved close enough to see the arrow in Kenzie's hands.

"See these two Ramsay arrows?" Kenzie asked, shaking them in front of Quade's face. "They are not the same. Someone tampered with the spine of this one, throwing off the path of the arrow. If you hold both of them at the spine, you'll see the difference. The strong one was the first one Torrian used, and this weak one was the one he just shot. Do you not see and feel the difference?" He peered up at the Ramsay chief, hope blooming bright in his face.

Quade picked up the two arrows to examine them before

glancing at Kenzie again.

"I promise, Chief Ramsay. I seen it happen twice in Ayr. If they are too soft or too hard, they fishtail."

Torrian stared at him in surprise. The lad was correct. His last one had fishtailed quite a bit, but how had they managed to tamper with his arrows? There was no question they were *his* arrows; they had the right colors and came from *his* quiver. Then it dawned on him. He turned to the Buchan, the fury inside him growing. "That explains it. 'Twas you. You came up from behind me, you on one side, Ranulf on the other. You both clasped my shoulder. One of you threw the tampered arrows into my quiver."

"Here now," Buchan said, chuckling nervously, "there's no truth to any of this. I did naught. My son is winning and you do not like it. Admit it, Ramsay. You set this lad up to cause trouble. I say 'tis all a lie. Back to the contest. 'Tis one more round until the end."

The crowd began to stir, though, and their unsettled mutterings turning louder.

Just then, Torrian heard a familiar bird-like call. Looking about, he realized Ranulf was missing. "Where the hell is MacNiven?"

The Buchan said, "His leg was bothering him. He returned to the keep."

Torrian recalled seeing the two of them wander off into the trees. "You were in the trees together. Did you stash your arrows there?"

Logan's eyes lit up. "That was Gwynie's call to me. Quade and Buchan, I think you both need to follow me into that patch of trees."

Quade, the two competitors, and Buchan all followed Logan. As soon as they found Gwyneth, she held out the quiver full of Ramsay arrows. "My laird, I watched as Buchan and this fool—" she gestured to Ranulf, "—hid this behind those bushes a short time ago. The blackguard just now came back for the rest of them."

Quade said, "Put your bow down, Gwyneth. I'll deal with the situation."

"What in hell are you doing, MacNiven?" Buchan bellowed with an almost convincing scowl.

Quade pulled three arrows out of the quiver. They were the same as Torrian's two arrows that had missed—weak spines and bearing the Ramsay colors. He rubbed his thumb along each one, testing the strength, and then passed them around to everyone there. "You are correct, Gwyneth. These are not our arrows, though they do bear our colors."

"Do not blame this all on me, Buchan," Ranulf snarled. "'Twas you who wanted your son to win. I only did your bidding." He turned to Quade. "Aye, 'tis true. We tried to fix the contest. What of it? It means naught to me."

"Your reputation as a cheater means naught to you, lad?" Quade said with raised brows.

"Aye, it means naught. Do what you will. The marriage shall take place on the morrow and then we'll be on our way. Now, I must attend to more important matters."

After casting one final threatening glare at Gwyneth, Ranulf moved past everyone and made to leave the area, but Logan Ramsay stopped him. He seized him by the throat and held him in the air, threatening to collapse his windpipe. "I think you need to apologize to my wife for your rudeness. I did not approve of that look you just gave her."

"My apologies," Ranulf rasped. He just barely managed to catch himself when Logan dropped him. Striding away, one hand rubbing his neck, he tried his best to yell over his shoulder, "This is not over."

They headed back out to the field, and Quade took his son's arm and held it up in front of the crowd. "I declare the winner of the contest to be Torrian Ramsay and the entire Ramsay team. The Buchans lose by default for cheating."

Torrian relaxed, grateful they'd found one more reason for him to refuse his marriage. But would it be enough to satisfy his king?

Heather had returned while most of the clan was gathered in at the archery field. Fortunately, she came in from the opposite direction and took the back way to escape being seen. Once inside the portcullis, wee Nellie had already put her finger up to her mouth on three separate occasions to shush her mother, demonstrating to her mother that she would comply with her request to be quiet until they were inside. She had to admit, Nellie had found some wonderful friends at the Ramsay keep. But then, so had she.

She came around the path behind the keep to the kitchens and the back stairway, then settled Nellie in the chamber with the wee lassies, who were thrilled to have her back. They needed a new patient and Nellie was quick to oblige by saying she was almost dead and could not talk—a clever way of following with her mother's rules.

Brenna had not attended the archery contest, so she was there to tell Heather about it, and about how the family had banded together to investigate and observe the Buchans. She'd stayed behind to keep an eye on the littlest members of the family, as she did not trust the Buchans any more than Heather did.

They fussed with herbs, cutting and sorting them into jars. Brenna said, "You know I do believe Torrian has verra strong feelings for you. I've not seen him stand up to his sire the way he did over this proposed match. I hope you know that."

Heather's eyes misted. "Aye, I know he does. I consider myself to be quite fortunate. He's the finest man I've ever met."

"What about your sire?"

"I never knew him. My grandsire was a good man, but Torrian, well, he's different."

"I understand. 'Tis a different kind of love." Brenna smiled, then turned away.

She opened her mouth to deny it was love she felt for Torrian, but she could not lie. She loved him with all her heart. She hoped her heart was not about to be broken.

Brenna said over her shoulder, "I did not expect to see you. I thought you'd gone back to your cave."

"I did." Heather hesitated, but since Brenna was Torrian's stepmother and they were alone, she decided to confess her intentions. "I decided to come back. Torrian is worth fighting for. I could not sit back and watch him marry another without doing whatever I could to stop it. Though I must admit, I am lost as to how to do aught about it."

"Would you like to go to the archery fields? 'Tis where everyone is."

"Nay!" She answered a bit too vehemently.

Brenna quirked a brow at her, but said naught.

"I cannot go for two reasons. One is that I have a fear of crowds." She wiped her hands on a linen towel.

"And the other reason?"

Heather took a deep breath. "Nellie's sire is there and he's threatened to take her away if I tell anyone about her. I'll stay hidden, but I'd still prefer to see if there's aught I could do."

Lady Brenna thought a moment before she responded, "We do not judge people for their past here, Heather. Do not worry. I'll support you in any way I can. If you need help, please come to me."

"Many thanks. I will remember that." Heather recognized what a special woman Lady Brenna was, and understood part of the reason Torrian was so special. He'd been raised to be strong.

A short time later, the noise returned to the great hall, enough for Brenna and Heather to hear them. Heather asked, "Would you mind if I went out the back door? I'm capable of eavesdropping to find the truth at this point." She was determined to hide and watch for any unusual behavior on the part of the Buchans.

Brenna patted her hand. "Go ahead. I'll keep an eye on Nellie. Be careful. I do not trust the Buchans."

It was not long before she saw a couple head toward the stables, looking as if they wished to be unobserved. The sun was setting and the air was misting, so she wasn't quite sure who it was, but it looked to be Davina. She followed behind only to find them heading to the outer bailey, but then they split.

She lost them, but was surprised to run into Lily, following the puppies. She gave Lily a questioning look, and Lily's face lit up.

"I gave Bram and Birk something that Davina dropped, and they are following her scent. I want to know everything that witch does. Did you hear how the Buchans cheated in the archery?"

Heather shook her head, a slow smile crossing her face. "Truly?"

Lily picked up the dogs and paused. "Aye. Heather, please forgive me, but I'm not usually this negative, but I love my brother so. I try to see the goodness in everyone, but this situation is frightening me. Please do not believe the worst of me. Though 'twould be hard for you. You've only seen me at my worst." She hung her head, tears misting in her eyes.

"Lily, I do not think the worst of you. You love your brother and 'tis clear. I love him, too. Unfortunately, he is always being watched since he is the betrothed and the chief's son. He needs someone to help him."

Lily hugged her. "Aye. My thanks for coming along."

"Tell me more about the cheating? They were caught?"

"Aye, I'll tell you about it later. Come, we must follow the dogs." She set the Deerhounds down and gestured to Heather.

The dogs almost caught up with the couple, so Lily and Heather picked them up to stop them from being heard. "Who is it?" Lily asked.

"Davina and someone I do not recognize."

"You cannot see him?" Lily whispered.

"Nay, I only saw his back. Let's wait until they go inside, then we'll get closer and see if we can hear them." She crouched down in her spot, and Lily followed.

"What do you think this is about?"

Heather rolled her eyes. "Probably a lovers' tryst."

Lily shook her fist. "And if 'tis true, we'll catch them right in the act. She'll not marry my brother."

Heather whispered, "Please do not include me. I'll stay in the background or run for help, if you'd like, but I do not want them to see me. I must think of my daughter."

"I'll go on my own," Lily said with a nod. "I'm not afraid of that witch. You watch the pups and I'll handle it."

They waited in silence until they heard faint sounds of kissing and whispering from inside the cottage. They both tried different vantage points in order to hear everything, and finally, Lily motioned for Heather to join her in a spot near the window.

Davina said, "You know I do this for you. 'Twill be a sore hardship for me."

"I know, love. I will not make you wait long." They could hear sounds of kissing begin anew.

Lily quirked her brow at Heather, but she just shrugged. They would have to keep listening to get the information they sought.

A few moments later, voices began again.

"Do you swear not to make me wait too long, Ranulf?"

"I swear," Ranulf answered.

The next part Heather could not make out, but apparently Lily did because she gave Heather a shocked look before she handed

Bram to her and tore over to the door, which she immediately flung open. "How dare you!"

Heather kept herself hidden in the bushes. She could not be seen. How she wished to help Lily, but she needed to think of Nellie. She listened outside the window, knowing she could at least run for help if Lily was threatened in any way.

"You, sir, are scum, and you, my lady, are just what I knew you were. Oh! Cover yourselves!"

Ranulf's voice carried out the door. "Why do you not join us? I love threesomes. Davina and I will make it quite pleasurable for you."

"How dare you make threats against my brother. I said cover yourself. I do not care to look at you…at your…"

His laughter echoed out to Heather, and to her alarm, she could hear someone's steps cross the floor of the cottage. "You're covering your eyes, lass? Do you not like what you see?"

"Nay, I want no part of this, but I do know someone who will be quite interested."

Heather couldn't tell what had transpired, but Lily's voice changed. "Leave me be. You are hurting me."

"Swear you'll not tell what you've seen or heard, and I'll release you." The venom in Ranulf's voice was quite clear.

"I'll do no such thing. Everyone needs to know what a blackguard you are."

Another low voice sounded from behind Heather…Torrian's second, Kyle. "What is going on here, Heather? We heard you were here and Torrian sent me out after you."

Heather pointed to the door. "Lily is inside. Seems we've caught Davina and Ranulf together in a less than desirable situation. I think Ranulf has grabbed Lily."

Kyle's eyes widened and a fury crossed his face. "He's dared to touch Lily?" He flew past her, barging inside just as Lily came barreling out of the entrance, headed back toward the keep. Heather peeked in the door and saw Kyle punch Ranulf, so she decided to follow Lily to see if she was injured, leaving the pups to scamper behind her. She tried to reach her, but the only things she caught were Lily's words drifting back to her.

"Never, never, never, never…"

Torrian stood in the middle of the forest, a place he'd once feared as a youth. Someone, though he could not recall who, had told him that his clan wanted to leave him in the forest to die because of his sickness. The oddest part of it was that Torrian hadn't known what a forest looked like at the time. He'd been unable to leave his bed for so long, he had no memory of the world outside his cottage. His sire and mother had told him they would keep him hidden to keep him safe.

His mother had died just after Lily was born. He still thought of her occasionally, but his memories of that time centered around his father. He would never forget his sire's dedication to making him well.

The pain had been so excruciating then that despite his fear of the forest he had actually asked his sire to leave him there. Aye, he would have rather died. He glanced at the intertwining boughs over his head, sunlight peeking through the branches—the place he'd once feared was so beautiful. His request had been refused, of course, and he'd decided to live the best life available to him. It was then he'd learned to read and write.

All the while, his sire had continued to assure him, day in and day out, that it would get better. If he had to walk to all the green land to find the best healer, even steal that person, he would do it to give his son hope.

Brenna had brought him that hope back then, and someone else had brought hope into his life now. If he wanted to keep that hope—that desire for a bright future—he needed to marry Heather, not Davina.

Kyle had told him all, and now he knew what to do.

He spun around and walked toward the keep, confident in his decision. The forest had given him his answer. He headed into the great hall, speaking to no one because he was too lost in thought. One thing he'd learned from his childhood was how to live within himself.

Once inside, he realized he'd missed the evening meal. He located his sire at the dais and asked to speak with him in private. Uncle Logan joined them at his father's request. Everyone was watching the traveling minstrels perform, so they were able to leave without causing much notice.

Once they were sequestered in the solar, Quade said, "We need to be conscious of our absence. Please do not make this too long."

Torrian nodded to his father, his palms now damp. "I've made my decision, but I need to make you aware of something first."

"We're listening," Uncle Logan responded, a wary expression on his face.

"Lily and Heather followed Ranulf and Davina to a cottage in the outer bailey after the archery contest. They were caught in a lovers' tryst."

Uncle Logan smirked. "While your sister and Heather may conjecture what they were doing, they can hardly make accusations—"

Torrian interrupted him. "Lily walked in and caught them in the act. Ranulf threatened to hurt her if she talked, at which point Kyle entered and witnessed everything. He punched Ranulf and Lily ran off."

His uncle threw his head back and guffawed, but his father's expression was one of shock. "Lily saw—"

"Saw everything, according to Kyle. And there's one other thing you must know. Ranulf plans to kill me within two years."

Logan jumped out of his chair. "I'll kill the whoreson first."

Quade held a restraining hand out toward his brother before returning his gaze to his son. "You have more to say?"

"Aye, I'll be announcing my decision not to marry Davina. I would like to ask you for your support in my marriage to Heather, but I'll announce that at a later time."

Silence settled in the room. Torrian flexed his fists as he waited to see if he had his sire's support or not.

"Torrian, you've clearly made your decision, and we'll all deal with the ramifications. When exactly do you plan to make this announcement?"

"As soon as I walk out of this room. I will not make mention of the lovers, if that is what you are wondering. If they do not press me, I need not give any reason beyond that we are unsuitable. Clearly, Davina agrees with me or she would not be consorting with another."

"Do as you must."

His sire's expression was one of resignation. He could have stayed to argue for his support, but he knew it was the right decision. He could only hope his sire would respect his choice.

When he stepped back into the great hall, the tension was overpowering. Torrian reviewed his plan again in his mind, making sure he'd chosen the right words. He would take complete responsibility for his actions, but he fully expected to have to explain himself to his king in another day or two. He hadn't made his final decision as to what he would say, but he had time to consider his words carefully.

It was time to put an end to this ridiculous farce.

He moved to his place at the dais about the same time his father and uncle returned to the hall.

According to Kyle, the pair had left without an apology, without any guilt for their obvious transgression. Ranulf's parting words as they left the cottage had been, "She's not married yet, lad. We did naught wrong."

Davina had said naught.

Glenn Buchan and his two sons were sitting on the other end of the table on the dais, while Torrian and Davina and Ranulf were seated near Jake and Jamie Grant.

Torrian waited until the timing seemed appropriate, then stood up at his place. The surprised looks on everyone's faces did not deter him. In fact, he was more determined than ever to see this matter settled.

"Your pardon, but I'd like everyone's attention."

While he waited, Davina tugged on his hand, trying to get him to sit back down. "What are you doing?"

He ignored her.

"Please do not do this," she whispered, a harsh edge to her voice.

In a few minutes, the entire great hall had fallen silent, all eyes on him. Intent on doing this as respectfully as possible, he said, "My laird," tipping his head toward his sire, "Chief Buchan," tipping his head toward the cheater. "I make this announcement after much thought and consideration." It was so quiet that if a mouse had run across the room, all present would have been able to hear its tiny feet skitter across the stone. "Certain circumstances have prompted this decision, and I will not share what those circumstances are, but Davina Buchan and I will not be wed on the morrow." He turned to her at his side. "She is a most beautiful woman, and I believe she will find her happiness elsewhere."

With that, Torrian stepped down from the dais and strode out the front door without stopping.

It was not until he was out the door that applause erupted behind him.

CHAPTER EIGHTEEN

Heather sat in her chamber listening to all the ruckus in the great hall. She wasn't directly over the balcony, but the din traveled well enough that the moment it stopped, the dead silence carried through to her. Something was amiss, and her heart sped with fear.

She paced her chamber, afraid to leave. Nellie was already in the lassies' chamber, all of them ready for bed. She loved sleeping with Jennet, Brigid, and Sorcha. Heather had naught to do but pace and wait, hoping Torrian would come to her soon. She could not risk wandering around, so she waited.

A subtle rap sounded on her door. She leaned against it, afraid to open it, afraid it might be *him*, but then she heard Torrian's voice.

"'Tis me, Heather."

She opened the door and he shoved his way inside, quickly closing and barring the door behind him. Then his hands wrapped around her waist and he tugged her close, kissing her until her knees buckled. He lifted her legs in the air, encouraging her to wrap them around his waist.

He ended the kiss only long enough to say, "I'm free. I ended the betrothal."

Heather's heart almost burst with excitement. She threw her arms around his neck and kissed him again. She pulled back long enough to say, "Torrian, I'm so happy."

He kissed her, leaning her against the wall, rucking her skirts up until he could run his hand down her thigh.

"Torrian, we have a bed behind you."

He growled, sucking on her lower lip, "I know, but I want you like this. Do you mind?"

"Nay."

He ravaged her mouth, their tongues mating, dancing until they were both short of breath. His hands burned hot on the bare skin of her bottom. She groaned at how good it felt to be in his arms again. Desire built inside her until she wished to scream his name, her breathing ragged.

He stuttered between his gasps. "Never mind. I prefer to touch you everywhere."

He placed her on the bed and undid his brooch to drop his plaid and then his leine to the floor. When he held his hand out to her, she knew exactly what he wanted—mayhap because she wanted it even more. She loosened her ribbons and handed him the gown that he quickly flung over his shoulder.

He froze. "My sweet Heather, you are so beautiful." He stood near her thighs and leaned down to look at her, placing a gentle hand on each of her legs and sliding them up over her pelvis in a slow sensual assault that left her gasping. When his hands reached her breasts, she grasped his forearms, closing her eyes so she could savor the sweetness of touching and being touched by this man.

He leaned down to take her nipple in his mouth and she moaned, doing her best to quiet her sounds, though she would not be embarrassed by them. They were her way of telling him how much his love meant to her. He stood and tugged her to the side of the bed, his hands caressing her bottom as he settled her onto the edge of the mattress. Then he lowered his fingers to tease her clit and plunge his finger inside her. She reached for him because she could wait no longer. As soon as she felt him at the entrance to her sheath, he took over and thrust inside her, groaning, pulling out of her slick sheath and driving into her again and again, their pace increasing to a frenzy like she'd never known.

Her gaze locked on his and he touched her in just the right place, enough to send her catapulting over the edge into a sweet bliss. She opened for him and he groaned in surrender too as her contractions took everything from him.

He leaned over her ear and panted, "I love you, Heather. You're finally mine."

Torrian left Heather's chamber, sneaking down the back

stairway, only to discover that his sire had sent a search party to find him. Kyle ran into him first.

"Could you not have waited for that? I know where you were."

"Nay, I could not wait. We'll marry as soon as we are able." Torrian made his way outside and headed to the middle of the courtyard.

Kyle chased after him. "Where in hell are you going?"

"I'd like to clear my head, 'tis all. May I not have some peace?"

"Nay," Kyle barked. "Everyone is looking for you. Your father wants to see you in the solar."

"Again? But I already spoke to him." Torrian's hands settled on his hips in confusion. What now? Had they not settled this? He was on his own, and he was more convinced than ever he had made the right decision.

Kyle lowered the tone of his voice. "Your sire said to go along with it."

Lily and Bethia came running toward them with Jake. "The elders are all looking for you."

"You should have stayed," Jake said. "I've never seen such a blast of bellowing before. We'll have lots to tell when we return home."

Jamie, Sorcha, and Braden caught up with them.

"I am glad I am not in your place," Braden said. "They are searching the entire castle for you. They even sent a group out on horseback. My sire said he's never seen your sire so upset."

Torrian sighed, glancing from cousin to cousin. "They are all in the solar?" Suddenly, it all made sense. His sire did what the Buchans would expect him to do. He did not want them thinking he was aware of Torrian's plan. Fine, he'd go along.

"Aye. Your sire, your uncles, and the Buchans await you," Kyle answered.

He headed back to the keep, stopping for no one, intent on convincing the rest of his family this was the right thing to do, especially after what Lily had overheard. He knocked on the door and it was flung open by Uncle Logan.

"Hmph. Nice of you to join us, lad, after that spectacle. Come inside and explain yourself."

It was a standoff for show, of that he was sure. The Buchan team—Dugald, Cormag, Glenn and Ranulf MacNiven—stood on one side while Logan, Gwyneth (with her arms crossed, glaring at Ranulf), Brodie, and Brenna on the opposite side. His sire was seated behind the desk. Davina was notably missing.

"Explain yourself, son, and make sure your reasons are good enough," his sire said. "If not, the Buchans have threatened to go home and return with their warriors in full force."

Torrian took his time. There was no doubt in his mind that he'd made the right decision. How to convince the Buchans? He would do what he could not to embarrass Davina too much, but if it came to that before his king, he would tell all.

"In view of all that took place on the archery field, I think 'tis best not to join the two clans." He stood in the center, his hands behind his back. He spoke as if speaking to his sire only. It was proper for his laird to hear him first.

Buchan jumped forward, waving his left arm in the air. "That had naught to do with Davina. How can you use the contest of men to justify not marrying an innocent lass?"

Torrian turned slowly for effect. "Innocent?"

"Aye, innocent. And let's not forget you defiled her. You were ordered to marry and you will marry her on the morrow or we'll head straight to the king to report the injustice, then gather our forces to attack you outright. You have no right to go against the King of the Scots." Spittle sprayed from his mouth he spoke so fast.

Logan stepped forward. "Buchan, now that the king is gone and you got what you wanted, do you truly expect us to believe you did not plan that mockery the other night?"

"I did no such thing. I discovered them after the deed was done. And I'm glad I did. Davina was upset all night." He crossed his arms, the disgruntled look on his face telling all.

Torrian took the opportunity while Buchan ranted to observe Ranulf and Dugald. Though they were controlling their expressions for the most part, he saw each of them smirk more than once. Ranulf had more of a cold, calculating demeanor than Dugald. His guess would be that Dugald struggled to keep up with the two conniving chieftains.

Which of them had defiled his wife-to-be? He would find out.

Quade held up both his hands. Silence fell on the room. "Son, I understand this is less than ideal, but you understand your actions could be considered treason? Only the king can determine your fate if your actions go against the crown."

Torrian did not answer.

"Torrian, you must consider your words carefully. This could have grave consequences."

Torrian was still loathe to disgrace Davina. "My apologies, my laird, but my decision is made. I will not marry Davina Buchan."

Glenn of Buchan's shouts could be heard above all. "You've not seen the last of the Buchans. Our king will set this right. He will force this marriage. How dare you insult my daughter this way! 'Tis treason, for certes."

The door flew open with a bang.

Lily stood there, tears streaming down her face. "No more. Please stop this, Da."

She rushed up next to Torrian, his tall frame towering over her. All voices cut off in a moment.

"Papa, forgive me. I must confess to something I overheard. I am not proud of myself for eavesdropping, but I must be certain that a huge mistake is not made."

Quade gave no hint of his awareness of the situation, but clasped his hands in his lap and said, "Continue, daughter."

"Yesterday, I followed Davina and Ranulf out to a cottage. They entered and I stayed outside to listen. I'm verra suspicious of them."

Ranulf interrupted, his face contorted with frustration. "Aye, we had a tryst. 'Tis of no import." He pointed toward Torrian. "He defiled her, not me."

"The tryst is not of as much import as the promise you made to Davina to kill my brother in two years so you two can marry."

Torrian could have kissed his sister. A look of shock registered on every face in the room except for Ranulf's and his sire's. It was rare for Torrian to catch any emotion in his sire's face, and Logan was a fine actor.

Ranulf glowered at her, his head tipped down as if to gore her like a bull. "You made that up, you bitch."

Torrian flew across the room and grabbed Ranulf, managing to punch him in the face before his sire and uncle pulled him back. He'd kill the bastard for sure.

Lily screamed, and Torrian's sire barked out, "Buchan, take

you and yours off my land. We'll see you in Edinburgh in two days. The king is in residence at his castle there."

Buchan responded in kind. "This isn't over, Ramsay. I demand justice."

They stormed out of the room and Torrian fell into a chair, his rage just now simmering down. That man had dared insult his sister.

He'd also had a difficult time looking at the MacNiven now that he knew of his plans to kill him.

Everyone seemed startled into silence, but after a short while, Quade said, "I'd like to speak with Torrian alone."

As soon as the chamber emptied, Quade motioned for Torrian to take a seat in front of his desk. He did not speak for several moments, obviously measuring his words carefully.

"Son, I know why you are doing this."

"They've lied and been underhanded all along. We must do what's right, and I believe with all the evidence we've gathered, we can convince the king to see our side."

Quade leaned back in his chair and smiled at him, something Torrian hadn't anticipated. "Is that why you're doing it?"

"Aye." He gave him a puzzled look, unsure of his intent.

"Nay, you're doing it because you truly have fallen for a lass, and you wish to marry her and only her. Is that not correct?"

Torrian stared at his sire. "Da, I'm sorry to disappoint you. You know I've vowed to always make you proud of me, but I *am* trying to do what's right."

"Are you not in love with Heather Preston?" His sire sat up and rested his elbows on the desk, leaning toward his son.

Torrian whispered. "Aye. I know that disappoints you. I know you believe in following the king's orders. After all the years I lived with little happiness, I must choose different."

"I do not believe in the king arranging marriages at all. I just do what the king decrees, and sometimes, 'tis marriage to someone you do not choose."

"I know you married Brenna for other reasons, and I thank you for that."

"What?" Quade jerked his head back. "Why do you think I married Brenna?"

"Because you stole her from the Grants and because she fixed

Lily and me. You wanted her around forever in case something else happened to us."

"You're wrong. Completely wrong, though 'twould probably sound better if you were correct."

Torrian stared at his sire, suddenly recalling the many times he'd seen his father with his arms wrapped around Brenna. Or the time he'd caught them kissing when he was younger. "I am? But I thought…"

"Here's the truth. I married your mother because it was arranged by our sires, and I did grow to love her, but I married your stepmother because I wanted to. I loved Brenna so much it frightened me, and that love has only grown. I could not imagine my life without her."

"I never realized, Da."

"So no one realizes more than I do why you made the decision you did." His voice lowered. "But I needed you to make that decision. I was not going to make it for you."

Torrian was stunned. He had no idea what to say to his father's declaration. And it was just like his father to think about his response before he delivered it. He finally understood why he waited until now. It was his sire's way, and one he'd be wise to follow. How many times had he advised him to think about his actions first?

"We all support you completely, son, and I am grateful I will not need to call the Buchans family." He moved from around the desk, pulled Torrian out of the chair and hugged him. "Nicely done."

"But I thought…" Torrian found himself speechless.

"Now get yourself ready to travel. We're headed to Edinburgh to speak to our king, and I think it would be best if we leave Heather behind. We'll depart on the morrow."

"But you are not angry that I may have possibly caused a battle?"

"Your aunt and uncle have worked for the king for years. I doubt he'd accuse you of treason. Now, I do not doubt that the Buchans may choose to attack us in some underhanded way nor do I doubt that the marriage was clearly a power ploy for them anyway, but I also expect the mere prospect of an attack will bring a score or more Grant warriors out of the deep Highlands. There's naught they love more. Brodie, Jake, Jamie, and Kenzie are already headed home, and my guess is they wish to bring the details to Alex Grant. Your uncle Alex does not favor unrest."

"Why not send a messenger?"

"No one knows the Highlands better than the Grant brothers. Uncle Brodie will be on Grant land before I get my group to Edinburgh. I promise you that they will be back."

Nothing could have surprised Torrian more.

CHAPTER NINETEEN

Heather waited in her chamber until later in the night. She was pacing the small space when Torrian finally returned.

"What happened?" She was so afraid for him, for them.

"The Buchans have left, headed to Edinburgh to report to our king, then they will head home to gather their forces and return."

"And your family?" How she prayed they would eventually support their union. She knew Lily, Brenna, and Gwyneth did, for they'd all told her so. But she knew how important it was to Torrian for his sire to stand behind him.

"We have my sire's complete support."

"We do?"

He laughed, "Aye, we do, my sire and all my family. They all hated the Buchans. However, my sire has ordered me to go to Edinburgh with him, and he's asked that we leave you here."

"I think that is wise. I'll stay with Nellie. If all I have to do is wait until you return from Edinburgh, I am happy to do that." She leaned in to kiss him, devouring his lips and wrapping her arms around his neck.

He ended the kiss and leaned his forehead against hers. "Why wait?"

Torrian had a gleam in his eyes she'd learned to love already. "What? What are you suggesting?"

He knelt down in front of her and took her hand in his. "Heather Preston, would you do me the honor of marrying me and becoming my wife this night?"

She hopped in place twice and blurted, "Aye, Aye. Torrian, I love you. Wait, what? Tonight? How could we possibly do it tonight? Does your sire not want the king's blessing for our marriage?"

He stood up, kissed her, and took her hands in his. "Aye, probably, but I was thinking we could visit Father Rab tonight. I'd prefer to marry you before I leave on the morrow. Come, follow me. We'll talk to Father Rab. Have you met him yet?"

"Nay, I have not."

He took her hand and led her through the courtyard, which was basically deserted at this hour. It was late, but he knew Father Rab stayed up late. They'd built him a beautiful chapel after he came to live with them, his grandmama had insisted.

Once inside the charming stone building, they crept up the aisle to the front of the chapel, and Torrian held his hand out to Heather, inviting her to kneel with him. "I said many prayers as a bairn, and they were answered, and now He's brought you to me, so I'd like to thank Him for a moment."

Heather was astounded at the depth of this man who was to be her husband. She knelt beside him onto the soft cushions sewn by the clan, noting the beauty of the carefully tended altar—the chalices, the thick leather-bound book, the cloths sewn with dainty hands, and the exquisite wooden cross above the altar.

A few moments later, a voice echoed beside them. "You've come at an unusual time, nephew. Is there aught I can do to help you?"

Torrian smiled at his uncle, pulling him into a hug, and then introduced him to Heather. Father Rab was a small man, but he did look like Gwyneth. The kindness in his eyes was so inviting. "I do not mean to interrupt your time of prayer, lad. Please come to my chamber when you've finished."

Torrian said, "I'm finished. We've come to talk to you, Father. We'd like to marry."

"Och, I expected that was to come soon. Please follow me and we'll sit at my table."

Father Rab led them through a doorway to his chambers in the back. The first chamber held a table in the center, and shelving along either side of the large hearth. Heather could see that his bed sat in the back chamber with another hearth along the back wall. It was a well-kept space, with fresh rushes on the floor.

"Sit down, please. I'll get some mead." He grabbed three goblets and set them on the table.

He moved slowly, for the stiffness of the joints common for

elders had already settled in his joints, but that lively glitter in his eyes seemed ever present.

"Torrian, you've chosen a fine lass to be your wife, I see, and I'm honored that you've asked me to marry you. I would like to comply, but…"

"Aye, Father?" Torrian leaned toward his uncle.

Heather held her breath, so afraid they were about to be refused. How could this sweet priest turn them down? Was their love not evident? Was it because the others in the family were not present?

"Please, lad, I prefer the title uncle in these chambers." He turned to Heather. "The title uncle is one of my most cherished titles. Torrian honors me by using it, though I'm not his blood uncle. Gwyneth is my only sibling, and I have been blessed by her bairns, and I count myself grateful that Brenna and Quade's bairns call me uncle as well."

"Uncle Rab? You were saying?"

Heather squeezed Torrian's hand under the table, gripping him too tight, she was certain.

"Aye. Allow me to continue. 'Twould be my honor to marry you once you return from Edinburgh, but I must deny you now."

Torrian's brow furrowed as he glanced at Heather. "But why must we wait? My sire? Uncle Logan? Who has told you to refuse us?"

"Torrian, aye, your father and uncle have both spoken with me about waiting. You know I would risk my place here as priest if I were to go against the king's orders. As you know, the laird speaks for the king."

"Torrian." Heather peeked at him. "We cannot ask him to risk his assignment here. 'Twould not be right."

He nodded his agreement. "Mayhap you are correct. Uncle, I accept your provisions. But please promise to marry us on my return?"

"Aye, I would be honored, lad."

"There's more, is there not? Someone else has requested for us to wait?"

Father Rab sighed, his hands moving into prayer form in front of his face. "There is a reason I am not at liberty to explain. This person's concern is for Heather, not you. My belief is that it is in both of your best interests to wait. I have prayed for guidance in this matter, and I believe I am doing what the Lord would want me to do. The Lord tells me you will marry and live a wonderful life together, but it must wait."

Silence settled between them. Heather could not imagine who else had asked him to postpone their marriage. There could only be one person, and the thought made her stomach turn.

Nellie's father.

The Ramsay contingency met in Edinburgh two days later, and quite a contingency it was. Quade and Logan had both acquiesced to their wives, who had feared leaving their bairns at home in case the Buchans posed an attack while they were away. Of course, Quade prided himself in having enough warriors to leave his home well-guarded in his absence, so he gave in only because he suspected they all wished to attend the royal castle.

So Quade and Brenna brought Torrian, Lily, Bethia, Gregor, and Jennet, while Logan and Gwyneth brought Maggie, Molly, Sorcha, Gavin, and Brigid. The wee ones were excited to be traveling together to the royal castle, and had promised to be on their best behavior.

Edinburgh castle was one of the most regal of all, sitting atop a huge hill. From a distance, the top of the towers appeared to touch the sky. They arrived near dusk, and the torches lighting up the parapets and the path to the castle made the place appear magical.

As they made their way from the courtyard to the stables, a booming voice sounded from outside the gates. "Greetings, Ramsays. How do you all fare?"

A chorus of "Uncle Micheil!" rang out and the bairns rushed him all at once, causing him to explode into laughter as he dismounted his horse. His eldest son David was traveling with him.

"How are Diana and Daniel?" Brenna asked Micheil.

"They are well, though Diana does have her breathing problems that set her abed occasionally. 'Twas a rough winter, but she is better every day."

Quade said, "Why do we not go inside? 'Tis late, and I'd like to get the bairns settled. Then we'll have an ale and talk."

Micheil grasped both of Torrian's shoulders from behind. "Will you ever stop growing taller, lad? You started slow, but it seems you have caught up."

Torrian replied, "I have not grown any taller."

"Still, it does my heart good to see the size of you after the tough start you had in life. And now you wish to marry, but not before you stir up a wee bit of trouble, aye?" he teased him.

"If the Buchans are already here, then you'll see tomorrow 'tis not just a wee bit."

They headed into the great hall, and the king came down from his dais, his guards surrounding him, to greet them. They noticed the Buchans sat at the far end of the hall, but the king ordered the guards to keep the groups separated.

King Alexander said, "While I'd like to say I'm pleased to see you all, I admit I'm discouraged by everything I've been told. For the young ones here, we have some minstrels coming to entertain you. For the rest of you, I'll be speaking to you in my chambers before I make my final decision." He held his hand up to beckon to one of the servants. A woman rushed over. "Ena, please see the lassies and the lads settled in the bairns' wing for the night while I speak with my chieftains."

"Of course, my king. Come this way, wee ones."

Jennet ran up to the king. "Wait, please." She held her hand up to him. "My king, may I see your hand?"

Quade said, "Jennet, do not bother King Alexander."

The king chuckled and waved his hand in dismissal before he held it down to the wee lassie. "Nay, she is no trouble, Chief Ramsay. I'm quite curious to see what the healer's daughter wishes." He held his hand down for her inspection.

Jennet studied his hand closely, turning it one way and then the other, flexing his fingers. Torrian noticed that Brenna was holding her hand in front of her mouth to hide a wee smile. "My king, on the morrow, if 'twould please you, I'd like to apply some ointment for the stiffness you have in your hand. I also have some salve to place on that cut. We cannot afford to have the leader of the Scots turn feverish from such a wee cut." She stepped back, her usual serious expression in place, and awaited his answer.

The king's eyes danced in delight, but then his gaze fell to his hand. "You have an ointment that can help the soreness in my hand?" He flexed his fingers as if to test their ease of movement.

"Aye, I believe the soreness will ease after a few applications."

"Verra well. 'Twould please me if you and your mother would tend to my hand in the morning. I will send for you. Now go enjoy your chamber. I have goat's milk and berry tarts for you."

Jennet's eyes lit up, and she did a deep curtsy before strolling off to follow Ena.

Brenna mouthed, "My thanks." Brenna and Gwyneth slipped off with Ena to get the bairns settled.

"Gentlemen, as you can see, the Buchans are here and have told me much. I'd like to see you all in my solar to allow Torrian to give me his reasons for defying my order, and I will make my final decree on the morrow. I prefer to sleep before passing judgments, especially one of such magnitude."

Torrian followed the others into the solar, suddenly realizing the full ramifications of his decision. He had one chance to convince his king he was correct in his assessment of the Buchans. He prayed the man had an open mind.

Quade, Logan, and Micheil stood at the periphery of the room while Torrian stood directly in front of the king. The king's solar was rich with tapestries on the wall, and a threaded rug covered the area under their feet. A large hearth sat on the outside wall, decorated on both sides with gold candlestick holders. The chamber was brighter at night than the outdoors in day. The desk was twice the size of Quade's and had ornate scrolls around the edges.

Torrian was so impressed with his surroundings that he did not quite know where to look.

The king took a seat and held out his arms. "Please begin, son. I'd like to hear your reasons for defying my decree before I have you tossed in chains."

An unsettled feeling coursed through him, something that felt a lot like doubt. How he wished his father or his Uncle Logan would speak for him, but he knew what was expected of him.

"Your pardon, my king." He linked his hands behind his back and stood with his feet planted slightly apart. "I have refused Davina Buchan because of the deceit she committed the last night you were at the Ramsay keep. I did not defile the lass, nor have I ever defiled a lass. My heritage is that I am expected to take over as chieftain of the Ramsays when my father is no longer able. That also means that my sons will be chieftains for the Scottish crown. I feel 'tis not in the Scots' best interest to have such trickery in our bloodlines."

The king steepled his fingers, his elbows planted on the desk in front of him. "Have you not forgotten that I was there when that transpired? I have already passed my judgment on that incident, in fact, 'twas a major factor in my decision to order you to marry. Davina is a beautiful lass. Lads tend to be randy, and I do not fault you for being a wee bit excited about taking what was to be your right, but you cannot back out of the agreement now."

"But it did not happen." Torrian's chest tightened in fear, his thoughts muddled in his brain. There had to be something else he could say to convince the man.

"Lad, I saw the blood, still damp, on the linens. You cannot deny that."

Torrian opened his mouth, then closed it. He hung his head in shame, not because he was guilty, but because he was failing to defend himself properly. His brain had simply stopped functioning.

Quade came over to stand by his side. "My king, I wish to share with you my main concern with this match."

"Go ahead, though I'll not listen to these same arguments for long, Ramsay. I'm tired and need to find my chamber."

"Davina was found in a compromising situation with Ranulf MacNiven. My daughter heard MacNiven promise to kill my son so they could marry and gain control of our land."

The king tipped his head to one side. "Ramsay, I cannot blame someone for coupling before the lass is married. As for the other, the Buchans have already informed me of this accusation that they claim to be completely false." He sighed, holding his head. "Seems to me I'm going to have to decide which of my subjects is lying and which is being honest. How I detest these decisions. Verra well. I'll consider your arguments and will announce my final decision on the morrow.

Logan stepped forward, "May I add, my king, that Gwyneth discovered deceit over an archery contest. MacNiven tampered with Torrian's arrows, causing them to fishtail."

The king mopped his brow with a linen square. "I understand

the Buchans may have questionable tactics. But do you not recall how desperately I need this match to keep my kingdom in peace? Does all that has transpired not convince you, Logan Ramsay, that I need this family to keep watch over the Buchans even more? Peace is more important than the desires of two young ones. Please remember that. Son, you marry for the Scots and for your clan." He moved around his desk and headed toward the door. "I've heard all I care to hear. I do promise to give this matter careful consideration. Good eve, gentlemen."

Torrian stared at his sire and his uncles. He could tell from the expressions on their faces that their session with the king could not have gone any worse.

CHAPTER TWENTY

When the king proclaimed he was ready to announce his decision, the great hall quickly filled to capacity. The king sat at the dais with his advisors, the Buchans stood on one side glaring at the Ramsays on the opposite side. Torrian feared that if the regent did not make his announcement soon, the warriors would launch themselves across the room at one another.

The king leaned over to speak to the head of his guards, and the man whistled. Another line of guards came in and stood beside each of the groups. Torrian stared at his feet so as not to laugh. Apparently, the king had the same thought. This could turn violent if the looks on the Buchans' faces were any indication.

Several others from the burgh entered to stand at the back of the room, interested in any important proceedings at Edinburgh Castle. Quiet whisperings could be heard until the king held up his hand in a demand for silence. He waved to Quade and to Glenn of Buchan and the two groups stepped forward. Torrian stood directly in front of the king, and Quade, Brenna, Logan, Gwyneth, and Micheil were behind him. The bairns stood gathered behind their parents.

On the other side, Davina of Buchan sauntered over, swaying her hips as she moved, much to the delight of the lads in the chamber, but Torrian ignored her. Behind her stood her sire, her brothers Dugald and Cormag, and Ranulf.

The only one who did not seem in control of her emotions was Lily, whose cheeks were already flooded with tears. Her sniffling was the only sound to be heard.

A guard stepped forward. "The king will make his

pronouncement now. All subjects are to be quiet until he leaves the chamber."

The king stood, rubbing the bandage on his left hand. Torrian could only guess Jennet had tended his hand as promised. Torrian glanced over his shoulder and noticed Molly had a firm hand on Jennet while Maggie held Brigid.

Torrian's gut clenched as he waited. Sweat broke out on his brow, but he forced himself to think about Heather's beautiful face, her warm smile, and her shimmering eyes, one blue and one green.

The king began. "I have given both sides careful consideration, and I have not found any reason compelling enough to change my original decision. I believe it to be in the best interest of this kingdom for Davina Buchan to marry Torrian Ramsay and make an alliance between the two clans. The marriage will take place here on the morrow. If either of you refuse, you'll be in chains in my dungeon."

The Buchan contingency erupted into cheers, along with many of the spectators. Torrian glanced at his sire to see his reaction. There was unmistakable disappointment in Quade's eyes, and Brenna seemed close to tears. Torrian's sire wrapped his arm around Brenna's waist to pull her close, and she buried her face in his leine.

That was why none of them noticed when a wee lass with brown hair and intent brown eyes strode to the front of the dais and then marched over to Ranulf MacNiven. She stood in front of him with her arm outstretched, but he ignored her.

The rest of the crowd was still reacting to the king's decree, talking amongst themselves, comforting one another, and some were even crying, but Jennet stood firm in front of Ranulf and the rest of the Buchans.

Torrian watched as Ranulf tried to push her hand away, but Jennet held firm. Scowling, she proceeded to push something toward him. Then he showed his true nature.

"Enough, you wee witch. Go back to your own." His shout echoed across the hall.

She dropped her arm, but the wee lass was too strong natured to be frightened by a bellowing voice. Rather than back away, she continued to stare at him in confusion. Torrian almost moved to her side, but something in his gut told him to wait.

The chamber quieted at Ranulf's bellow, but he continued to lambaste her because she had not yet moved. Finally he grabbed her, spun her around, and shoved her back toward the Ramsays. "Get away from me, you bitch!"

The entire room froze. Brenna and Quade finally noticed Jennet had left the group, and they ushered her over to them. "My apologies, my king," Brenna said.

The king stood and raised his arms. "Silence!"

The only one who made a peep was Jennet, who stared up at her mother with wide eyes. "But Mama, I must give him another."

"Lady Brenna, bring the lass forward," the king said. He stepped down from the dais so as to be closer to her height. "She did such a fine job tending me this morn that I wish to hear what she has to say."

"This is preposterous, my king," Ranulf shouted. "Why are you wasting your time with a wee bairn?"

King Alexander glowered at him. "I said silence to all, and that includes you, MacNiven. Sometimes, 'tis only the wee bairns that speak the truth."

Jennet still held on to some mystery object as she stared up at the king.

The king returned his attention to Jennet. "Now, my wee lassie, what is that in your hand?"

Jennet replied, "First, my king, I must ask after your hand. Has the ointment helped at all?"

Ranulf made to move toward Jennet, but two guards grabbed him and held him in his place.

The king threw his head back and laughed. "Aye, but you'll make the Scots a fine healer, just like your mama and Aunt Jennie before you. My hand is much better, and my thanks to you. Now tell me why you wish to speak to Ranulf here." He waved his hand toward the Buchans.

"I was just doing as he asked. When he was at our castle, he came upon Brigid and me as we were practicing surgery on a dead chicken. He requested two vials of blood, but I only had enough blood to give him one vial." She held the glass vial in her hand up for him to inspect. "Do you not see? I have brought him his second vial as he requested. He said he needed it right away, so I gave him my sincerest apologies. He does not seem verra happy that it took so long."

Torrian couldn't believe what he'd heard. So that explained where Davina had gotten the blood. He knew it had not come from her, unless she'd pricked herself, but that would have been too easily seen. He glanced at Uncle Logan, Uncle Micheil, and Aunt Gwyneth, and their grins made the hope in his heart blossom. Was his luck truly about to change?

The king took the vial from Jennet and said, "I'll take care of it, my dear. You may return to your family."

He held the glass up to the light coming in through the window, and Torrian could tell from the dark red cast and the way it stuck to the glass that it was indeed a vial of blood. His king marched over to Davina and whispered, "Is this true, lass? Did you use a vial of chicken's blood to deceive me into believing this lad stole your maidenhead?"

Davina stared up at the king, her lower lip trembling. She burst into tears and flung her arm out, pointing her finger toward her father. "He made me do it; they both did. I just wished to marry him to make my sire happy." Her tears turned into sobs and she dropped her head into her hands in embarrassment.

The king returned to his dais, his eyes blazing. No one spoke a word, but the sounds of Davina's tears echoed throughout the chamber. As soon as he reached his spot, he declared, "The wedding is off due to this trickery! Ramsays, you are all free to go. Buchans and the MacNiven, I shall see you in my solar...*now*!

Lily jumped a foot in the air and ran to Torrian, hugging him and crying on his shoulder. Then she turned to her wee sister, lifted her into the air, and kissed both her cheeks. "You are different, Jennet, but I do love you so."

Jennet frowned as her family fussed over her. "I do not understand all this fuss over the vial of blood, but clearly 'tis a good thing."

One of the king's advisors came over to them and said, "The king has ordered a feast for your clan in the East Hall. Please join us there."

As the hugs and well wishes continued, Torrian watched the Buchans leave and said a quick prayer of thanks. Glenn of Buchan made his way over to Micheil, standing on the edge of the chamber, and Torrian heard him say, "This is not over. We will finish it."

Micheil drawled, "I look forward to it."

As soon as the family was alone in the East Hall, many of them already seated at the massive trestle table, Brenna and Quade called wee Jennet to them. Everyone ceased talking to listen to Brenna. "Now, I know you all wish to thank Jennet and pat her on her back," she said, "but I have something else to say to her."

Jennet hung her head. "I know, Mama. My apologies. 'Twas wrong to go against your wishes."

Brigid burst into tears in her seat next to Logan. He picked her up and hugged her. "Now tell your Aunt Brenna what you have to say." Logan set her down next to Jennet. The wee lassies almost appeared to be twins, they looked so much alike. Their hair was almost the same color, a chestnut brown, and both had worn it tied back in buns in a manner that Aunt Avelina had taught them. They wore light-colored matching gowns decorated with wide ribbons, but Jennet's eyes were brown while Brigid's were green, and Brigid was a wee bit shorter than her older cousin.

Gwyneth prompted, "Go on, Brigid. Speak up."

"I'm sorry, Aunt Brenna, for doing surgery without you."

Jennet added, "Do not be mad at her, Mama. 'Twas my idea. I do not know why the king wished to keep the vial, though. 'Twas the other who requested it."

Torrian came up behind the two of them, scooped one up in each arm and lifted them high in the air. "I must say my thanks to you, wee troublemakers. You've saved the day for me." He kissed both of their cheeks with loud smacks until they giggled.

Brenna stepped next to him and said, "Hell, but I must agree with him this time, lassies. Still, you must never do to it again!" She kissed each of the girls, causing them to giggle even more.

"Mama, you said a bad word," Jennet peered at her.

"Aye, 'tis true, but 'twas an especially unnerving day. Do not think you may repeat it, either. I'll forgive you for doing the surgery this time, but you must be wiser about your decisions."

They all resumed their seats at the table, and soon servants entered with trays full of pheasant, pork, and meat pies, along with a huge bowl of peas and another overflowing with carrots and turnips, Lily's favorite. There were several loaves of crusty breads warm from the ovens, though of course Torrian and Lily could not touch those.

A dish of blackberries and walnuts came next, along with plum pudding and an apple pie, but the last dish was set in front of Jennet.

Ena said, "This is special from the king just for you, lass."

Jennet's eyes lit up at the bowl of orange slices that had been set in front of her. They'd never seen them before. She bit into one and sprayed juice everywhere, then shared her slices with everyone at the table.

Once everyone filled their plates, Logan held his hand up, silencing everyone. "I still have one question. It does not add up for me. Brenna, do not take offense, your daughter is bright, but I have to wonder. Jennet, why did you bring that vial with you today? Why did you not wait until later?"

Torrian had wondered the same thing. It was difficult to believe a lass of that age, particularly one who did not seem to understand the significance of her action, could have timed her move so well.

Jennet picked her head up and pointed to someone sitting nearby.

A head full of dark curls tipped down to stare at her hands in her lap, her blush a deep pink.

"Molly?" Logan said.

She picked her head up, straightened her shoulders, and replied. "I found the vial in her satchel last night and asked her about it. When she explained it to me, I kept it in my pocket until I thought the time was right, then I handed it to her and told her to take it to that man."

Gwyneth, who was seated next to her daughter, leaned over and kissed her on the cheek. "Perfect, just perfect you are, and you always have been."

Molly grinned with pleasure.

"You're right, Gwynie," Logan added. "She'll make a great spy for the crown."

CHAPTER TWENTY-ONE

"Shut up, did you not hear me? Just stop the drivel that pours from your mouth." Ranulf had heard enough. "Do you not recall the idea of using chicken blood 'twas your idea, old man?"

Glenn Buchan was relentless. "Forget all that has happened. Where do we go from here?"

Ranulf spat off to the side as he galloped beside the Buchan chieftain. "We attack the whoresons, that's where we go from here. We return to your castle, gather our guards, and go after them. They've insulted you, me, and your daughter."

Glenn said, "Mayhap 'tis time to rest the issue for a while and think on our strategy. Build our forces. What say you, Dugald?"

Dugald replied, "I'm with the MacNiven. We attack. They've embarrassed my beloved sister, and someone needs to pay."

Ranulf muttered, "And we'll do it so fast they'll never see us coming."

∞

Heather was so pleased to see Torrian and the rest of his clan return that she almost cried with relief. She'd squinted and squinted over the valley to see if Davina was with them on horseback, but there was no sign of her.

Fearing there was still a chance all had not gone according to plan, she stayed inside until they arrived, Nellie at her side. Once the group reached the portcullis, though, the Ramsay war whoop was so loud that she knew they had won. Huddling in the corner near the hearth, she waited, her heart full of anxiety, until the first person came through the door—Torrian. His gaze searched the hall until he found hers and the smile on his face shot straight to her core. Could it be?

"Torrian?" she whispered.

He held his arms out to her and she raced into them until he picked her up and swung her around in a circle. Kyle came in directly behind him, overflowing with questions. He'd stayed behind to guard the castle, and apparently heard tales already.

When Torrian set Heather down, he greeted Kyle and waved for Nellie to join them.

"I cannot believe what I've heard. Is it true wee Jennet saved your arse?" Kyle whispered as Torrian picked Nellie up for a hug.

The door opened, and Jennet and Brigid rushed into the great room. Torrian picked up first Jennet and then Brigid, swinging them up over his head in glee. "You heard correctly, Kyle. Wee Jennet had Ranulf MacNiven shaking in his boots with fury. 'Twas something to see. This lassie brought that scum to his knees in front of the King of the Scots." He set both lassies down.

Jennet peered up at him with a frown. "I did not see Ranulf kneel to the King. When did that transpire?"

"Och, Jennet, 'tis an expression."

Kyle choked on the laugh he was holding back.

Jennet headed up the stairs to her chamber. "I am of the hope he will not ask me for another vial of blood again. I had to make a promise to my mama." Brigid giggled into her hand and followed her cousin up the stairs, then said, "Nellie, would you like to come with us?"

Nellie looked at her mother, then scampered up the stairs as soon as Heather nodded.

Once the wee ones were out of hearing distance, Torrian led Kyle and Heather over to the hearth to explain all to them. All while he spoke, he held tight to Heather's hand, and when he finished, he shrugged his shoulders and stared at Heather. "I'm free to marry as I wish. We have some planning to do, wife-to be."

Heather threw her arms around his neck and kissed him.

⤫⤬

Two days later, they had not gotten much further in their planning and they slept apart, though Torrian loved to sneak kisses from her. He'd told her they would marry when he'd return, but each time she'd mentioned their wedding, he'd changed the subject. She did not understand why, but she believed the wedding had taken on some form of secrecy. Her only concern was marrying in front of a crowd. She was definitely more comfortable around his family, but would she be able to marry him in front of his entire clan?

Some of the Grants arrived that day, though she was unsure if it was expected or not, but she was too busy trying to sew herself a new gown for her wedding to pay much attention. The garment was a pale green color similar to the buds on the trees in early spring. Nellie was off with her new friends. A knock sounded at her door, and she beckoned the caller inside.

Brenna stood in her doorway. "If you are not too busy, lass, we'd like to invite you to a special gathering."

Heather had no idea what Brenna was about, but she adored her mother-to-be and would never turn her down. Having never had a mother or father, she treasured Torrian's parents and hoped to have a strong relationship with them. So far, they had been wonderful. "Of course," she said.

Though she followed Brenna down the passageway without question, she could not imagine where she was being led or why. There were many Grants chatting in the great hall, but Brenna led her past them, to where Torrian was standing beside the door to his sire's solar. He held his hand out to her, and she gladly took it. She wished to ask him what to expect, but she found she could not.

Brenna kissed her on the cheek and walked away, which puzzled her even more. "I know this will be a shock to you," Torrian said, reaching up to stroke her face, "but I think you'll be pleased."

He must have seen the confusion on her face because he kissed her cheek and said, "Trust me, lass. I have chosen to do this in this manner because I love you so."

With a sudden whoosh inside her belly, her fear took over.

She clutched his hand with a death grip, and she could feel her heartbeat speed up. Glancing at him, she tried to speak but naught came out. The laughter of the group echoed behind her, reminding her how many were now in the hall. Could she handle this?

Torrian stopped, placed his finger under her chin, and locked his gaze on hers. "Sweeting, 'twill be all right. I'm with you. Trust in me."

The entire hall seemed to close in on her as her breathing increased. How would she ever learn to get past her fears? She closed her eyes for a moment to breathe in Torrian's scent in an attempt to relax her body.

"Aye, take another deep breath. I'll not leave your side. Do you trust me?"

She nodded, opening her eyes again slowly, focusing on him.

"Follow me. There are not many inside."

Heather stepped cautiously inside the solar. Father Rab was facing her, talking with another priest who had his back to her. Wee Kenzie was there too, along with another lad speaking to Quade and Brodie.

She took another deep breath and was pleased to feel her insides calm.

Kenzie ran to her side and tugged on her arm. "Please come closer."

He pulled her over to the lad with the tousled, sun-colored hair, and the lad turned to her. At the same time, the priest who was with Father Rab gave her his full attention.

"Heather, this is my adopted cousin, Loki," Torrian said, "and this is his sire, Father Francis Prestwick."

"Greetings," Heather did a small curtsy, but she froze the instant she lifted her gaze to the two in front of her.

Looking at the lad called Loki was like seeing her reflection in the loch, only he was male. She stood a distance away yet, but the pressure of a small pair of hands against her back propelled her forward until she stood almost nose-to-nose with Loki.

A giggle erupted behind her and Kenzie said, "Look closer, lass." Kenzie moved to her side and held his head tilted as if waiting for something.

Then she understood. She stared into Loki's one blue eye and one green eye, and her heart burst open. Then she glanced at his sire, only to gasp again and take a step back.

Torrian squeezed her hand and pulled her to a nearby chair. "I think we should all sit."

Loki took the chair opposite Heather and his sire—could he be *their* sire?—sat next to him. She heard Quade leave the room, and Brodie followed, tugging wee Kenzie by the hand. "You've seen your favorite part, Kenzie."

"I ken, but 'twas it not the best, grandsire? It gets better each time."

Soon the only ones left in the room with her besides Torrian were Loki and the two priests.

Her voice cracked and she whispered, "I do not understand."

"Please, allow me to explain," Father Francis said.

She nodded and folded her hands into her lap while Torrian sat in the chair next to hers and wrapped an arm around her shoulder.

Father Francis said, "Many years ago, I fell in love with the sweetest woman in the world, and I believe she is your mother."

Heather tried to stop her breath from hitching, but she could not.

"Your mother, Ciara Blackett, was married to an evil man. A long time before I became a priest, I lived in a cottage not far from her. I fell in love with your mother, and I am ashamed to say we committed a grave sin. You see, Ciara had two children, Loki, who sits in front of you, and a daughter. I believe both children were mine rather than Blackett's. This daughter was never named, and I was told that both Ciara and her two children died soon after the daughter's birth. I never met you, but I had seen Loki. I know 'tis possible that I'm wrong and you are not my daughter, but your eye color tells me you are."

Heather looked back and forth between the two men in front of her. Could it be true? Her vision flooded with tears as she stared at these men whose eye coloring was identical to hers.

"It must be true," she whispered. "I've not seen another with eyes like ours."

Father said, "Nay, 'tis quite rare."

She turned to Torrian. "You knew?"

"Aye. I suspected many moons ago when I came upon you while I was in the woods with my pups, but you ran away. At the time, I'd just learned that Loki's sire was alive."

Loki added, "Do not fault Torrian. When he told me about you, I asked him not to share the truth with you. I think 'tis something that must be done in person." Then Loki asked, "Would you mind telling us what you know of your parents? Who raised you? That may help us piece everything together."

Heather stuttered, but she continued. "I was raised by my grandparents in Perthshire, not far from the Buchan land. They told me my mother died in childbirth. I recall meeting an aunt on a couple of occasions, but she was a distance away."

"Do you remember aught about a brother?" Loki's gaze settled on her, unwavering.

Tears misted in her eyes as she thought back to a day when she was young. Her grandmama had told her she looked like her brother. "Aye, on one occasion my grandmother mentioned a brother, but my grandsire yelled at her." She stared at her hands in her lap. "They never said another word about a brother. I thought she was mistaken. I had no idea…"

Loki said, "I know exactly how you feel, lass. Kenzie brought me to Father Francis the same way."

Tears spilled over onto her cheeks and she reached for Torrian's hand. "I recall one other thing."

Father Francis whispered, "What is it, lass?"

"The only thing they said about my sire was that they hated him. They said my mother was the sweetest creature ever, and my father was cruel."

"Mayhap we should leave it to you, Heather. I cannot prove you are my daughter, but I can attest that your mother was indeed the sweetest creature ever, and if you believe me to be your sire, I'd be happy to tell you all I know about her."

Heather sobbed into her hands, then stood and leaned toward Loki. Wrapping her arms around him, she said, "I'm so happy to meet you, brother." She turned to Father Francis and fell into his arms sobbing. "Will you tell me about my mother someday?"

"Aye, naught would give me more pleasure."

Loki let out a deep breath. "I believe you're my sister. My mother hated Blackett. I've met him and they had good reason to hate him. He beat her. You were fortunate your…our grandparents took you away. I wish I had known them. You have much to share with me."

She turned to him with a questioning look. "You did not know them?"

"Blackett left me to die in the woods after our mother died. I suffered a head injury that took my memories of my life before that. Though some memories have returned, I have none of grandparents. I may have known them, but I do not recall. I lived on the roads of Ayr for years until I was adopted by the Grants. Father Francis is my true sire, but Brodie Grant is my adopted sire."

"Welcome to the family, Heather Preston," Father Francis said. "I must confess, I am the one who asked Father Rab not to marry you until we met. It was too late for me to marry my son and his wife, but I hoped for the opportunity to be the one to marry you and Torrian, if it proved true that you are my daughter."

"I would be honored to have you marry us, Father." Heather laughed and hugged them both. She turned back to gaze at Torrian. "Do you not agree?"

He rubbed his hand in small circles on her back. "Aye. I would be honored, and it pleases me that your brother is my cousin. I hope you are not angry at me for keeping the secret."

She threw her arms around her husband-to-be. "Nay." She paused to give him a thoughtful look, taking in the kindness and love she saw in his gaze. "I do not think I could ever get angry with you."

Loki added, "I heard my sister say that, cousin." He winked at him. "See if she says the same after you've been married for a few moons."

⁂

They'd all stayed up late into the night, Heather, Loki, and Father Francis getting to know one another. Brodie, Nicol, his guard, and Loki had talked non-stop about the Battle of Largs and all the stunts Loki had pulled. Heather loved listening to these tales of her brother's clever-thinking, but she enjoyed watching Kenzie even more. He loved to hoot and laugh about everything his adopted sire had taught him.

At one point, Kenzie had hopped out of his chair and bolted over to his cousins, shouting, "See, I do have the most aunts and uncles. I'm counting again."

"What are you talking about, Kenzie?" Loki asked.

"I want to have the most kin of all. I'm almost there, you ken. Now I have Heather and Nellie." His chin jutted up in pride. "See, I had none, now I have more than anyone."

They'd laughed at the rascal, but Heather understood how serious he was. She'd started to feel the same.

Nellie had been hesitant around her new uncle and grandsire, but Heather believed she would accept them eventually. She'd had little experience around men, so it was still new for her, though she'd accepted Torrian quickly. Mayhap the same would happen for Nellie's new uncle and grandfather.

Heather and Torrian married the following day with both Father Francis and Father Rab presiding over the ceremony.

Now they had a future full of family and love in front of them. Heather could not stop smiling as Father Rab and Father Francis led them through the service in the chapel. She had Loki to her left while Torrian had Lily to his right, and Nellie stood between them. The rest of the Ramsays and Grants filled the small chapel.

Once they finished exchanging vows, they passed through a wave of congratulatory hugs and kisses and stepped into the courtyard to the waves and cheers of the Ramsay clanspeople. Heather had been concerned about the sheer number of his clan, but with Torrian by her side, she'd had no trouble with the ceremony.

Just as they were about to move the celebration to the great hall, shouts and war whoops sounded from outside the gates.

They were not of the Ramsay kind.

The Buchans had returned.

Screams echoed throughout the courtyard as men, women, and children ran for cover. The Buchans had climbed over the curtain wall using rope ladders, then opened the outside gate, so now men flooded the courtyard, swinging their swords at every Ramsay they saw.

And every Ramsay and Grant warrior pulled their swords out of their sheaths and fought back, going into full battle mode in an instant. Many of the warriors fought their way toward the stables to get on horseback.

Torrian pushed Heather toward the keep, grabbing Nellie and protecting her against his chest as she clutched his plaid.

Once they were safely inside the door, Torrian said, "Bar yourself in your chamber, but I must ask you before I go. Who, lass? I need a name. He could be a part of this."

Heather trusted her husband, she had to, but she did not want Nellie to hear, so she leaned over and whispered the name into Torrian's ear.

"Up the stairs with you. Remember, I love you both."

"Be careful," Heather cried after him as he rushed out the door, "and Loki and Kenzie, too."

He simply nodded and continued on his way.

Though Heather did not think she could stand to stay hidden away inside while they were out there risking their lives, Nellie came first. She ran up the stairs with Nellie in her arms, then followed the passageway until she found the lassies' chamber. She opened the door and pushed Nellie into the room, and followed her in and barred the door behind them. Someone had already brought Bethia, Jennet, Brigid, Sorcha, Molly, and Maggie into the room, and they were all wide-eyed with fear. The guard had his back to her. She knew the Ramsays usually had a guard in with the lassies during times of trouble, so she breathed a sigh of relief at the sight of him.

She ran to the window and pulled back the fur, surprised to see the courtyard was now almost empty except for the men who had already fallen. The meadow outside the curtain wall was a melee of horses, clashing steel, war whoops, and screams of pain. At least that meant the Ramsays had driven them out. The lassies were absolutely silent behind her, probably as terrified as she was.

A hand grabbed her from behind, covering her mouth.

"I told you to stay away from Ramsay castle. Now you'll pay." Nellie's father's voice crawled up her spine, making her freeze in terror. "Do as I say, Heather, and I'll leave all the lassies alone. Understood?"

She nodded. He wrenched her backwards and shoved her toward the door.

"Mama!" was the last sound she heard as he yanked her down the staircase to the kitchens.

CHAPTER TWENTY-TWO

Torrian had never experienced such a battle. Once on horseback outside the gates, he fought between Jake and Loki. He swung at each warrior who passed in his line of vision, slicing into arms and legs, sending blood spurting everywhere.

He'd never seen so much blood. Had he the time, he might be ill over all the gore, but he knew that would cost him his own life, and he suddenly had very much to live for. Five warriors bore down on the three of them. Torrian concentrated on the three in the middle, knowing instinctively that Loki and Jake would take out the other two. The one in the center was Torrian's primary focus, but just before he reached him, a stone flew out of nowhere and caught the man square in the temple, throwing him off his horse.

Kenzie. He'd heard the stories of Loki and his slinger in the Battle of Largs. Loki must have passed his skills on to his adopted son. The man's tumble upset the riders on either side of him, giving Torrian his opening. He swung his sword over his head, connecting with the belly of the bastard on the left and knocking him to the ground. He saw Jake had already unseated his opponent, but couldn't see Loki. He took another swing toward the third rider headed toward him and sliced the man's left side, taking him down.

When Torrian finally caught sight of Loki, he breathed a sigh of relief. His cousin had easily dispatched the man who'd charged him. Torrian surveyed the scene again. Uncle Logan and Kyle battled not far from him, Logan bellowing the Ramsay war whoop after each warrior he felled. He searched the area for the men he wished to find, but he only saw Ranulf fighting in the rear.

Arrows sliced through the air, and from the way each

connected with its targets, it was clearly the handiwork of Aunt Gwyneth. Just as they charged toward another group of warriors, a lass's scream rent the air. It was a moment before it registered that it was his name being yelled. He jerked his head to the left in time to see Heather on a horse with another lad. It was not Ranulf, so it could only be Glenn or Dugald.

He flicked the reins of his horse and charged after the man, but the horse slipped into the woods, and Torrian lost sight of him. Four guards were protecting the blackguard's back. It mattered not—Torrian would take on twice that number to protect his wee wife.

There was the sound of approaching horses behind him, and Torrian glanced over his shoulder to see two horses—Loki, Kenzie riding in front of him, and Jake. He said a quick prayer of thanks, liking his odds much better.

He could not lose her, he just couldn't.

◇◇◇

Heather bounced on the back of the horse, swinging against her captor whenever she had the chance. He grabbed her by the hair, wrenching her head back. "You hit me again, and I'll knock you out. I do not need you awake to have you."

The threat was enough to change her mind about the attack—instead she tried to figure out where they were headed. It was possible he could be heading toward the cave, but that was too far, she guessed. So the wretch wished to rape her again. Well, this time she'd fight him.

In the meantime, she needed to stay alert and be aware. Torrian would follow for certes. Her hands clung to the horse's mane as they galloped through the forest, branches swinging and hitting them as the mount bolted down the path.

She prayed and prayed for wee Nellie, for her husband, for all the Ramsays whose lives were now at stake because of the Buchans. Eventually they came to a stop in a small glade, not far from an abandoned hut. Her captor yanked her off the horse, shoving her ahead of him, twisting her arm behind her.

"Why are you here and not fighting?" she asked.

"Because this is not my battle. If Ranulf wishes to play the fool, he can, but I'll not lose my life over it."

"Over what? What does he hope to accomplish? The king will

not support this."

"Ranulf thinks he can take over the Highlands, slowly, one clan at a time. The Ramsays are first. You can be sure he will not give up on his goal. But I know everyone else means naught to him, myself included, and I will not die for his goal."

"I think mayhap you are too afraid to fight."

He shoved her through the doorway. "You need to close your mouth. I see you've changed from the innocent lass of years ago. I liked you better the other way."

"I'm sure you did. You'll find I'm not so helpless anymore." Heather surveyed the small hut, noticing it hadn't been occupied in a while. There was a pallet in one corner, a table and two chairs in the center, and shelving along the far wall with various tools used for cooking.

"You are still not strong enough to fight me, wee one." He chucked her under her chin. "I mean to have you, and I will. I warned you to stay away from the Ramsays." He grasped her chin and placed his lips on hers, forcing them apart, sticking his tongue inside her mouth until she gagged.

The fury in his gaze frightened her. "I disgust you now, do I?"

"You always disgusted me."

"We shall see how long you dare to look at me in that manner." He shoved her toward the bed, grabbing her bodice just before she fell backward, ripping it open in the front. "Och, but you do have a nice pair. You always did. I am much better suited for loving than for fighting."

Torrian slowed his horse as Loki drew up beside him, and Jake fell in directly behind them.

"You know where they are headed?" Loki asked.

"Not for certes, but there is a deserted hut not far from here. My guess is that's where he's taking her. He has four guards with him."

Jake said, "He'll post the four guards outside while he takes her inside."

Torrian's jaw clenched. He did not want to think about that, but Jake's assessment made sense.

"Who is it?" asked Kenzie. "Who stole her? Ranulf, the whoreson?"

Torrian replied, "'Tis not Ranulf. I saw him fighting at the rear of his warriors." He wasn't ready to reveal the name of Nellie's sire and his suspicions just yet.

Loki snorted. "Somehow, 'tis not a surprise that he hides in the back."

"How should we handle this?" Torrian asked. Loki was well-known for his scheming and trickery while Jake had the most experience in battle since his sire was the infamous Alexander Grant. They would surely know better than he did.

"Your lead. 'Tis your wife," Loki said. "Trust me, when you see her in his hands, your fury will take over. I know."

Torrian recognized the truth in his statement. "We'll take the four guards out first. What's your choice of weapons?"

"Put Kenzie and me in the trees," Loki said. "We'll play with them a bit first. They won't even know what hit them before 'tis too late."

Kenzie giggled. "Aye, my sire taught me how to be really good with my sling, just like he was." He patted Loki's arm.

Jake nodded. "You hide in the trees, and Torrian and I will wait in the bushes until you get rid of two of them. Then we can take out the other two."

A slow smile crept across Loki's face. "Then whoever has your wife is all yours, cousin."

"Just do not be too slow with this. I do not want him touching her."

"Haste will get a knife in your belly, cousin. Be wise," Jake added.

When they got close, they tied up their horses and crept toward the hut. The four guards were outside just as they expected. Jake found a spot to hide and pointed to a place where Torrian could take cover closer to the hut. Loki lifted Kenzie into a tree the perfect distance to shoot from, then found his own tree to climb.

He winked at Torrian just before he climbed his tree. "Do not worry, cuz. We'll get her back."

Heather fell backward onto the bed, stunned when she heard her bodice rip. She grabbed what ribbons she could and attempted to right herself just as the sound of the guards arguing reached them, causing her kidnapper to step outside. She searched the small cottage, anxious to find something, *anything*, to use against the bastard. On a small shelf, she found just what she needed—a small dagger. She hid it under the pillow and waited for her attacker to return.

He came in with a huff, closing and barring the door behind him, and said, "Foolish arses cannot follow orders, but they'll not bother us again. Now I have you all to myself. The first time will be quick, then the next few times I'll take you as many ways as I can."

She stood up across from him, directly in front of the bed and stared him straight in the eyes. Even though her heart was racing and her belly was churning, she would not give in to him completely.

He ripped the front of her bodice more. "Aye, I preferred you as you were before."

Grabbing her arms tight, he hauled her forward and licked a path up her cheek. She cringed, revulsion sickening her.

He slapped her face. "Do not ever look at me like that again. You think you are better than me now that you've been in a Ramsay bed? Well, you are not. I do not know what more I could do to please you. Have I ever hurt you before?"

She nodded, though her jaw ached too much from his last blow for her to speak. "When? I tried my best to be gentle with you. You were so young. I did not mean to get you with child, I just wanted the chance to love you. Was that so difficult? You could have stayed in Buchan land and I would have taken care of you and Nellie."

"You took my maidenhead. That was meant for my husband." A lone tear trickled down her cheek.

"I suppose I was a scoundrel for that, but you were verra sweet. I brought you gifts, if you recall." He brushed his thumb across her cheek.

Heather did not answer. She listened for sounds outside, hoping for some sign that Torrian was on his way, but all was quiet.

He pushed her down onto the bed, then lowered himself on top of her, pinning her to the bed, after he loosened his breeches. As soon as she felt his weight on her, she knew her choices were limited. Much as she hated to lie, she would do anything to get free.

She pulled her breast free of her clothing and offered her nipple up to him. "Please," she whispered, casting her eyes down.

"You see, was that so hard, my sweet? With pleasure." He leaned toward her breast and licked the underside of it.

As soon as he did, she made her move, grabbing the dagger out from under the pillow and plunging it into his back as hard as she could. He bellowed and reached for the dagger, but she had placed it carefully and he could not locate it. He stood up, raging, and pulled his fist back and hit her square in her belly.

Grasping both of her shoulders, he yanked her out of the bed. "You bitch! You wee bitch! You'll pay for this. Take it out." He turned his shoulder to her while he again tried to reach for the dagger.

Heather shook her head and backed away from him, but he grabbed her by the throat and tossed her against the wall.

Her head snapped back against the stones and she crumpled to the ground.

CHAPTER TWENTY-THREE

Torrian watched as Loki wove his own special brand of magic, but this time with a co-conspirator, Kenzie. He heard voices from inside the cottage, but no words were audible. Oh, how he longed to see her.

The door opened and Dugald stepped out, addressing one of his guards before heading back inside. He dropped the bar in place loud enough to echo across the area.

Torrian ran his hand down his face. Somehow, seeing Dugald in front of him made it worse. He'd kill the whoreson with his bare hands. The only thing that kept him from running inside that very moment was the knowledge that Heather was in that bastard's hands. He could do nothing that would endanger her.

"Ow!" Torrian heard the guard on the opposite side of the field slap his face. "Ian, what the hell did you throw at me? That hurt."

The guard closest to Torrian turned to face the fool. "I did not throw aught. Stop your crying and pay attention."

They settled again at their posts, their eyes fixed on the surrounding area. Another loud bellow sounded from a different guard. "Hell. What in blazes was that, Ian? Are you throwing stones or something? You hit me in my forehead. I'll beat the shite out of you if you do it again."

"What?" Ian said, sounding both defensive and confused. "I did not throw aught."

Another shout followed. "Ow." The fourth guard's hand went to the back of his head. "Ian, you son of a bitch. Do that again and I'll kill you."

Torrian held his laughter in check. Loki and Kenzie were having their fun. Still, he was fast losing his patience, and he wished they would speed things up. His wee wife was inside that cottage with an addled fool.

As if they'd heard his thoughts, several stones launched at the same time, hitting all four guards enough for them to start hurling insults at Ian. All three charged the beleaguered guard.

Loki jumped out of the tree and landed on one of the guards, cutting his throat in an instant. Kenzie threw another rock that hit the second guard in the temple, knocking him out. Now the numbers were in their favor. Torrian lunged for Ian, the closest to him, dodging two of his thrusts before delivering a jarring blow to the man's midsection, enough to fell him so Loki could finish it.

Jake took care of the fourth guard as a lass's screams rent the air.

Heather.

Torrian raced to the door and did his best to kick it open, but it was well barred. Loki joined him and between the two of them, they broke the door down. Once inside, Torrian's eyes immediately shot to Heather—she had crumpled to the floor, and her bodice was ripped in two.

Dugald turned to him, his eyes in a fury.

"Back, Loki," Torrian growled.

Loki moved out of the small cottage, standing in the doorway but giving Torrian the space he needed to fight his battle. Torrian's heart thudded in his chest—was Heather alive?—but he needed to finish this. As Dugald dove for his sword, Torrian swung his weapon in a side arc, connecting with flesh. The wound was not deep enough to end it.

Dugald winced, but he managed to grab the hilt of his sword. Whipping his head around to look at Torrian, he gave him an evil grin and said, "So you'd like a piece of her, too? 'Tis true, Ramsay? I'll share with you."

Torrian's gaze locked on Dugald's sword arm. His sire and uncles had always taught him to assess his enemies before acting. He doubted his adversary was much of a swordsman since his grip on his weapon was not strong. That one moment of hesitation cost him a quick nick to his right leg, but he'd gained much from it— the knowledge of Dugald's weakness. The fool was also now gloating as if he had a chance at beating him.

"That lass is now my wife, and daring to touch my wife was

the last mistake you will ever make." His voice came out in a near whisper. He spun around and turned his sword at an odd angle, connecting with Dugald's hand on the hilt of the weapon. The man's sword went flying into the wall.

Dugald's surprise showed for an instant, but then he smiled. "She was good, too."

Torrian tossed his sword to the floor and took two steps toward Dugald before he kicked his foot out, catching the whoreson in his ballocks. "That's for a man who rapes wee lassies."

Dugald groaned and bent at his waist, clutching his injury.

"And this is from her husband. You'll never touch her again." As soon as Dugald's head dropped down, Torrian swung both fists under the man's chin, forcing his head to snap back with a crack. He collided with the stone wall, but before he fell to the ground, Torrian punched him square in the face.

Torrian stood heaving over the body until he was certain Dugald was dead. Loki and Jake rushed into the cottage. "Breathe a word of what you heard and you'll have to deal with me," he said in a harsh whisper. He did not want anyone else to know the truth about Nellie's sire. The knowledge would go to the grave with him.

Torrian rushed over to Heather, his heart pounding in his chest, his hands shaking with fear. Cradling her in his arms, he lifted her and carried her to the bed.

"I did not hear aught," Loki said. "Did you, Jake?"

"Nay, I heard not a word." Jake replied. "I just watched my cousin kill a man with his bare hands for daring to touch his wife. 'Twas all I saw."

Torrian trusted his cousins to stay silent. He held his wee wife in his arms, hoping she would move, but she did not. He kissed her lips, her cheek, her forehead. "Heather, please wake up. Dugald is dead, and he'll never bother you or Nellie again. Please? I promise I'll protect you forever."

Wee Kenzie crept into the hut, but he said naught. He merely watched them with wide eyes. Loki clasped the lad's shoulder.

"Da, look at her bruises," Kenzie whispered.

Torrian rubbed Heather's arms.

"She breathes?" Jake asked.

"Aye, she's a strong lass. She'll come back to me." No other possibility was acceptable. Torrian rocked her in his arms.

A few moments later, Heather's eyes fluttered open. Her hand reached up to cup Torrian's face. "Oh, Torrian. You came for me. Is Dugald gone?"

Torrian had never experienced such profound relief in his life. He kissed her on the lips and said, "He'll never bother you again."

After taking a moment to thank God above for protecting Heather, he gave his cousins his instructions—telling Kenzie to get his horse and Jake and Loki to handle the Buchans.

He carried her outside to his horse, whispering his love into her ears. He had to keep moving, or he was afraid a tear would show on his cheeks, the first time in many, many years.

It was over, and he and his wife were free at last. He was determined no one would ever keep them apart again.

∽∾

After a full day of cleaning up dead bodies and washing the blood from their stones, the Ramsay clan ate a hearty meal and then settled around the large hearth in the main hall. Torrian wrapped a plaid around Heather and carried her from a bench at the trestle table to a chair before the fire. After seeing her so vulnerable, he would do aught to protect her.

"Husband, I am better. You mustn't fuss over me."

Nellie came over and rested her head in her mama's lap. "Mama, I love you. I'm glad you're better."

Heather ran her fingers through her daughter's fine locks and said, "I love you, too. If you'd like, you may sleep in the lassies' chamber tonight."

She gave her mother a doubtful look. "But I must take care of you, just like I've practiced with Jennet and Brigid."

"Nellie, you need not worry about your mama," Brenna said, smiling at her. "I've checked her and she'll be fine. You can sleep with the lassies."

"Are you sure, Mama?"

"Aye, give me a kiss and you may join your friends."

Her face lit up as she leaned in to give her mother a kiss. She raced toward the stairs, but then turned around and ran over to Torrian so she could plant a kiss on his cheek.

Torrian said, "My thanks, Nellie."

She leaned toward him and whispered, "May I call you Papa?

I've never had a papa before."

Torrian glanced at Heather first, and when he caught her slight nod, he said, "That would make me verra happy, lass."

"Good eve to you, Papa." She grinned and spun around, racing up the stairs again.

"Wait. Nellie?"

She pivoted back to face him. "Aye, Papa?"

"I have something for you." He headed to the corner of the hall and said, "Why do you not take one of the pups to your chamber tonight? Wee Bretta likes you."

The excitement on her face told him he'd made the right decision. He didn't want Nellie to start missing her mother in the middle of the night. "May I, Mama?"

Nellie's face lit up with joy when Heather nodded, and the girl and the pup scampered upstairs together, though Bretta stumbled a couple of times on the steps.

"Are we all settled now?" Uncle Logan asked, as Gwyneth settled onto his lap.

"Aye," Quade answered. "Why?"

"Because I want the whole story," Logan replied.

Quade answered, "You know what happened, Dugald is dead, Ranulf was captured and taken back to the king in chains. I expect he will hang for his part in going against the king's will. According to my sources, they were told if they attacked us, the king would consider it an act of treason. 'Twas probably why Glenn did not participate, so naught will come to him. Davina will survive, I'm sure."

Logan replied, "'Tis not what I meant."

"Then what?" Quade asked. "You were in the middle of the battle. What questions do you have?"

"I want to hear about Kenzie and Loki and the slingers."

Kenzie jumped up and hopped from one leg to the other. "You should have seen the first hit I made. I got him square on the side of his head, and…"

Torrian reached for Heather's hand and helped her to stand, then tiptoed lightly toward the staircase.

"…and then Loki hit the big lout in the forehead." Kenzie threw his head back and broke into peals of laughter, laughing so hard tears came to his eyes. "'Twas so funny when he yelled at

Ian." He swiped one eye and said, "and then…and then I slung another and hit the dim-witted one in the back of the head and then they all started yelling at Ian…all crying because they had been hit…All these big guards whining about wee stones." He bounced around the room, sharing his exuberance with everyone. Before long, they were all laughing with him.

Torrian and Heather were halfway up the staircase when a booming voice called out, "Halt!"

As Torrian turned around, standing in front of Heather so she could lean against him, Logan strode over to the base of the staircase and said, "Where are you two going?"

"Truly, Uncle Logan," Loki chortled, "you ask them such a foolish question on their wedding day?"

Logan's brow lifted. "With all the excitement, I had forgotten."

Torrian added, "Aye, 'tis our wedding night, Uncle. May we not slip away in peace? 'Twas a difficult day for us."

Brodie bolted out of his chair. "Nay, 'tis time for the bedding ceremony." Quade got up to stand next to Brodie, a sly grin on his face.

Heather squeezed tight against Torrian's back. He could feel her trembling start. After all she'd been through today, he was not about to allow this ridiculous custom to take place.

Logan glanced from his brother to Brodie, apparently deciding what he wished to do.

Then Jake, Loki, and Jamie pushed the elders aside and took their place at the base of the staircase, facing the hall with the stance of warriors. "You'll not get past us, Uncles," Loki said. He peered over his shoulder at Torrian and said, "No worries, cousin, we'll stand guard for you this night."

The three crossed their arms at the same time, so Torrian gathered his wee wife up in his arms and carried her into his chamber. He carried her across the threshold and closed and barred the door behind him. "The rest of the night is ours, love."

Logan, Quade, and Brodie still stood at the base of the stairs, staring up at the three Grant lads with confused expressions on their faces. They'd never expected this day to come, but here it was. They'd talked about it, even joked about it many times, but not a one of them ever believed it would come to pass.

The bairns ruled.

CHAPTER TWENTY-FOUR

A fortnight later

The hooded figure crept down the staircase, stepping carefully into the dark passageway. The guard met her and said, "All the way to the end."

She crept past cell after cell, ignoring the couple of men who made lewd comments to her, until she reached the last one on the right.

"This is the one you were searching for, my lady. Ranulf MacNiven, scheduled to hang at high noon on the morrow."

Davina Buchan tossed her hood back once the guard left. The man had his back to her, but she could tell he was awake, so she decided to speak her mind. "Ranulf, I shall never forgive you for what you've done. I know I swore to love you forever, and you promised to do the same, but because of you, I've lost my dearest brother. How could you? Why did you insist on returning to the Ramsays after we were instructed not to? Just because of that foolish idea of yours?"

She paced back and forth in front of his cell, not caring to look at him, but she had to speak her mind. After all, she'd loved him once.

"Ranulf, 'struth is we could have been happy together, but you always wished for more, you thought you could rule the Highlands. If you would have just been satisfied with our love. If you had only known when to stop, I would still have my darling Dugald. Do you hear me, Ranulf? Do you? Answer me!"

She stopped her pacing to stare at him, her hands on her ample hips. "It does not matter. You had my love and you lost it. I hate you. Do you hear me, Ranulf?"

She stomped her foot. "You're ignoring me. I hate you!"

He rotated slowly and when he finally faced her, a twisted smirk greeted her. Davina gasped and raced back down the passageway, so frightened she did not know what to do. Tearing up the steps, she gasped for air, and when she reached the outside she halted, taking deep breaths of the fresh air. She glanced behind her, but no one was there.

Nothing could have scared her more than that moment.

The man in the cell was not Ranulf.

EPILOGUE

Torrian strode through the bailey, Kyle by his side, wiping the sweat from his brow.

"Hellfire, you're giving me a tougher workout every day," Torrian said to his friend, casting a sideways glance at him.

"I do my best to prepare you for battle." The response was delivered with a smirk.

"On my cousins' next visit, I'll put you against the toughest one," Torrian snorted. He wondered how long it would be before he saw the Grants again. They usually came in late summer for the Ramsay Festival.

Life had taken a new turn now that he was married. He looked forward to returning to his wife every day, and there was often a smile on his face for no reason. He had worked hard to help Heather adjust to his large clan. Nellie's easy acceptance of their new family life made them both smile.

As they stepped into the great hall, Torrian was surprised to see his sire sitting in front of the hearth, as if awaiting the final meal of the day. His father's knee had been plaguing him more than ever lately, and he hadn't gone to the lists today as he often did.

"Da, are you well?"

Quade grabbed the arms of the chair to help himself stand. Brenna stood on the other side of the hall and Quade nodded to her, signifying something, though Torrian had no idea what.

His father limped toward him. "Son, we'd like to talk to you inside the solar, if you do not mind. Kyle, he'll find you later."

"Aye, my laird." Kyle gave a nod and departed.

"As you wish, Da." Torrian had no idea what the purpose of the meeting might be. They seemed to have accepted Heather as their own daughter, and wee Nellie never caused any problems.

His father grabbed a cane and limped toward his solar. "Your stepmother finally convinced me to use this to help me walk. I have to admit she was right about it easing my pain."

Brenna joined them and opened the door to the solar. "Aye, on occasion your sire does listen to me, Torrian." She winked at him after Quade passed her. Once they were all inside, Brenna shut the door behind them.

Torrian froze as he took in the room's new arrangement. A second desk had been added to the room, and the two desks were arranged at a right angle, allowing the occupants to see each other and freely converse.

Leaning on his cane with one hand, Quade clasped Torrian's shoulder with the other. "I see you've noticed the change." He had a broad smile on his face, a rare thing for his oft-serious father.

"I've made an important decision. I've decided to step down as chieftain of the Ramsay clan. The time has come for you to take over."

Torrian was dumbfounded. He stared in open shock at his father, then at his stepmother. "But…"

"But naught. You are ready, son. You have a good woman at your side, and you'll make a fine chieftain. Brenna helped me reach this decision. She convinced me the transition would probably go easier for you if I were still here to guide you through it. My knee ailment is not improving, and I cannot move around as I once could. The time is right."

Torrian still could not think of a single word to say. A long moment passed, then he said, "Da, I do not know if I'm capable…"

"You are more than capable," Brenna said. "Your father will still take an active role. He will help you with the ledgers, the crops, and the stores; advise you on the training of the guards; and assist you with our clan's dealings with the king."

"But you've already done a great job with the guards," Quade added. "That will not be a challenge for you. I'm convinced you'll step into this role with ease."

Torrian could not think of anything to say. Would this be too much for Heather? He knew she hated crowds, but she already knew he was to be chieftain one day. He needed to discuss the matter with her.

"Torrian," Quade said. "We'd be pleased if you'd embrace this change. You've been preparing for this role for many years, but if you'd prefer to discuss it with your wife before accepting, please do. As your acting second, Kyle will have to take on more duties. I think you'll agree that he is up for the challenge. He's verra loyal. I'll leave my own second in charge of the guard for a short time to train Kyle. But Seamus is agreeable to taking a step back. It'll be as much a relief for him as it will be for me."

Torrian thought for a moment before nodding. "I accept, Da, but I'd like to discuss it with Heather first, if you do not mind."

"Absolutely. If she agrees, we'll hold a celebration on the morrow in the eve for the entire clan to greet their new laird. I think they'll be pleased with our decision. Go talk with your wife." Quade smiled and hugged his son. "You've earned the right, son. You've worked hard, and I could not be more proud of you."

"I agree with everything your sire has said," Brenna added. "You have made me verra proud as well." She gave him a warm hug and said, "Go confer with Heather."

Turning to head out the door, Torrian left his parents behind and headed up the stairs, taking the steps two at a time in his eagerness to find his beautiful wife. While his parents had taken him by surprise, they'd spoken true—this *was* something he'd prepared for forever. He recalled a conversation he'd had with his uncle Micheil's wife, Diana, who was the chief of the Drummonds. She'd told him the most important quality in a chieftain was for him or her to care about the clan. He'd never forgotten that, and it gave him heart. He loved his clanmates. Of that, he had no doubt.

He arrived at their chamber and peeked his head around the corner of the open door. His wee wife sat in a chair in front of the hearth, working diligently on a new gown for Nellie. She glanced over her shoulder as he entered, her face lighting up at the sight of him.

He moved to her side and wrapped her in his arms, nuzzling her neck. "Good eve to you, my sweeting."

Heather giggled and hunched her shoulders up in response to his nuzzling.

He knew his wife was painfully ticklish, so he ended his

torture. "I have an important question for you."

"Aye, I'm listening, husband." She set Nellie's gown on the small table and gave him her complete attention. "What has you so excited this day?"

Torrian led her over to the bed, setting her close to him. He wished to be able to see the expression in her eyes when he told her his news. "You will not believe what just happened. My sire asked me if I would take over as chieftain now. He wants to pass the leadership over so he can assist me with my role. What do you think?" He watched the expression on her face, hoping he would notice if the thought made her uncomfortable.

Her eyes widened and her face lit up. She squeezed his hands, leaning toward him. "Truly? Now? Or is this in the next few moons?"

"Nay, he plans to make the announcement tomorrow, with Kyle as my second. You should see his solar. He has already added a desk for me."

"How do you feel about it?" she asked, tipping her head.

He thought for a moment, then said, "I am ready for this challenge, especially now that I have you by my side."

"Me? How can I possibly assist you? I'm more worried that my lack of social experience might hold you back."

He could see the genuine concern in her gaze, so he put an end to it. "Never. I want you by my side forever. I trust your judgment in all things, so I will always come to you for advice in matters regarding the clan. Will you support this? Does the thought of my becoming chief frighten you at all?"

Her gaze softened. "Nay, Torrian. I knew when I married you that you would be chief one day. You are born to lead, and I will stand by your side with great pride." Her eyes misted. "I'm just grateful for your love. I will always be here for you as you have been for me."

Torrian tugged her onto his lap and kissed her, cradling her face in his hands. "I love you. Promise me that you'll tell me if the lairdship changes me too much?"

"Aye, I promise. You deserve this. I will stand by your side and help you as I might. I look forward to our future."

"Have you finished your new gown?" he asked.

"Aye, I did. Lily will help me with the fitting." She held it up for him to see, a soft green gown with golden threads about the neck.

"Perfect."

"Do you not think it is too formal?"

"Nay, not at all. 'Tis perfect. My sire plans a huge celebration on the morrow."

"On the morrow?" She leaned forward.

"Aye. On the morrow, I will become the new Ramsay chieftain, and you will become the new mistress of the Ramsay castle." He gave her a sound kiss on the lips and whispered, "Naught could possibly make me happier, wife. I hope to make the entire clan proud. With you by my side, I believe I'll be able to do it. 'Tis time to move forward."

They made their way hand-in-hand down the passageway, heading to the solar to share their decision with the older generation.

Lily stood close to the door to the great hall, having made her way around the chamber. She had paid close attention to all of the attendees at her brother's ceremony, noting especially the pride in her sire's gaze as he passed the title of chieftain over to his firstborn son. Torrian had grown into such a tall and handsome man. Lily remembered all they'd gone through when they were young, though Torrian's illness had been far worse than her own.

She was as proud of her brother as their sire seemed to be. It gave her joy to see Torrian so happy with Heather, so satisfied with his role in the clan. Unfortunately, directly behind that thought came another—one that had crept into her mind more and more as the ceremony progressed.

What would become of her now that her dear brother was chieftain? Her closest friend would no longer have time for her.

Suddenly, she had to get out, she just had to leave. Shoving against the door, she rushed headlong into the cool night, running across the cobblestone courtyard as tears blurred her vision. The toe of her slipper caught the edge of a stone. She lost her bearings and tumbled toward the ground, her arms flailing to save her from hitting her head on the hard surface.

A warm pair of strong arms grabbed her, catching her fall, but her instinct was to fight them. She shoved hard against her savior, but he swung her around to face him without letting her loose.

"Lily, stop! I'll not hurt you."

"Kyle?" She froze, and catching her gaze, he did the same. She stared into the bluest eyes she'd ever seen, wondering why she'd never noticed their coloring before. "What are you doing?"

"Protecting you. 'Tis my job as the chief's second to protect his family. You are his sister, so I must protect you, even if I must follow you to do so."

She took in his chiseled jaw, his dark hair, and his lips, lips that held an appeal she hadn't noticed before. His gaze did not waver, and Lily had the sudden impulse to do something so out of character that it shocked even her.

Lily kissed him. Aye, she lost all control of her senses, and did exactly what her heart directed her to do.

Even more shocking was that he returned the kiss. His lips were warm, and he angled his mouth over hers, using a soft pressure that encouraged her to part her lips. Then his tongue swept inside her mouth.

What was she supposed to do about that?

He tasted of ale and something else, something sweeter than anything she'd ever tasted. All she knew for certes was that she wanted more. With one kiss, Kyle had brought to life a soft yearning she'd never experienced before.

Kyle pulled back, his blue eyes widened as he stared at her lips, now plumped from his delicious assault. And he only offered one word.

"Lily?"

THE END

**Please Enjoy An Excerpt from *One Summerhill Day*
by Keira Montclair**

CHAPTER ONE

Caitlyn McCabe's hands gripped the steering wheel of her car as she headed east on the New York State Thruway. Her hands should be shaking due to the icy road conditions, the frequent black ice, and the occasional sliding of her wheels. In truth, it was the scene she'd left behind that had her on edge, not to mention the big question mark that lay ahead of her.

After twenty-five years, she was alone. Her biggest fear had come true. The last conversation between her and her husband played out in her mind again.

"Caitlyn, I'm sorry. I made a mistake. She means nothing to me. Please stay so we can talk about this. Besides, where will you go? You don't have any family." Bruce had done his best to convince her not to leave him, but she was done. Their relationship had deteriorated over the last year. This was the final straw.

"Wrong. I have my Aunt Margie, and as soon as I pack, I'm heading out this door to go stay with her." She stomped up the stairs to make her point, then proceeded to pack everything she couldn't give up. For all she knew, anything she left behind would probably be sold or tossed into the garbage by her cheating husband.

"Fine, do what you need to do," he shouted behind her. "I'll be waiting when you come to your senses. I need you, Caitlyn. You know that, and you need me."

Humph. He needed her. Hadn't looked like it with her best friend from work in his arms. At least he seemed to feel a little remorse for having been caught in the act. Well, he could have

Lynn, along with the house and all the bad memories it held. She had only moved to Philadelphia for him, so there was no reason for her to stay. After packing most of her belongings into her small car, she'd left the house without looking back. She'd spent the night in a hotel room, so she could make initial divorce arrangements with her lawyer, and phone in her resignation. Though she'd normally only leave a job after giving her two week's notice, desperate times called for desperate measures.

There had been one slight hitch in her escape plan. When she finally reached her aunt's house in the south of Buffalo, she'd been shocked to find out her aunt wasn't there. A stranger had answered the door of the house Aunt Margie had owned for over forty years. They had bought the house from an estate sale.

Her only living relative was dead, and no one had thought to tell her.

Tears slid down her cheeks, blurring her vision, something she couldn't afford right now, not in these driving conditions. Why hadn't she spoken to Aunt Margie for so long? She had been so busy taking extra shifts to help out at the hospital that the months had flown by. Had it really been since Thanksgiving? She'd called and left a message at Christmas, but Aunt Margie had never called back. What a terrible niece she was.

She brought her focus back to the present. What the hell was she doing driving in this weather in western New York? Simple, she had been so upset by the disappearance of her dear aunt she hadn't been thinking clearly. Now she realized what a foolish move it had been to leave Buffalo in this state. It didn't help that she had no idea where she was going. She had to pay attention to the weather and stop thinking about the mess she'd made of her life.

The snow flurries had turned into a squall, and the road was now coated in a thin white blanket that hid the black ice she feared so much and covered the white lines on the edge of the highway. She had to make a decision soon, because she couldn't stay out here in this mess. The wind whipped the snow in her headlights in blinding whorls.

She passed one car in the ditch, then another. Though her fleece gloves hid her knuckles, she was sure they were pale white from their grip on the wheel. As she passed over the next bridge, the wheels of her car lost their grip on the pavement, and the car went skating across the crystalline black surface. Just like that, the control of the vehicle was yanked out of her hands and left up to the mechanics of her vehicle and fate.

She held her breath, waiting and praying for the comfort of traction again. A sigh of relief escaped her lips when the tires grabbed the asphalt again on the other side of the bridge. Okay, she had made it through that one, but how many more close brushes could she handle? A car directly in front of her skidded, but managed to regain control.

She had to get off and find a place to spend the night. *Yes*, she thought, *all you need to do is find a hotel, get your most important belongings inside, and make a plan for the rest of your life.*

The black of the night made the snowflakes hypnotizing in her headlights. A few minutes later, she sighed in relief when she caught sight of a distant green sign indicating an exit off the thruway. In the reduced visibility, the text was illegible. She squinted to bring it into focus, hoping it was a place with hotels, not just an exit to another highway. Without realizing it, she pumped the gas slightly and her back tires spun to the right. She squealed, praying the car would keep on the road and she wouldn't miss the exit. There was no alternative in this weather; she had to get off the thruway as soon as possible. She took her foot off the gas pedal and managed to hold onto the spin before straightening her vehicle.

The sign finally came into view: Summerhill—two miles. She relaxed and said a quick prayer of thanks. She *remembered* Summerhill. It had been her father's favorite place to vacation back when they lived in Buffalo. The city of Summerhill sat on the northern end of one of the Finger Lakes—Orenda Lake.

She hit her right turn signal and allowed her car to slow, only lightly touching the brake pedal, since she knew, as did any halfway decent driver in the northern states, that braking too hard or too fast could send her into a tailspin.

The sign at the end of the exit ramp was covered in snow, but it showed an arrow to the right. Though she had no idea what it was advertising, she was convinced it was the correct way to go since all of the Finger Lakes were south of the thruway. She vowed to pull into the first hotel she reached. A few more minutes and she would be safely ensconced in a warm hotel room with a TV and hopefully Wi-Fi so she could use her laptop.

The snow was heavier on the roadway here. The plows hadn't been out yet, but she could follow the tracks of the car in front of her. Besides that car, there were two others coming toward her and one behind her. The crest indicating the City of Summerhill loomed not far in the distance, a beacon in the chilly, dark night.

One of the dark SUVs headed toward her was going way too fast for the road conditions. Foolish SUV drivers thought they were impervious to snow. Right before it came abreast of her, it skidded out of control.

Caitlyn braked her car harder than she should have in the hopes of avoiding the oncoming vehicle, which was now headed straight toward her. She stepped on her anti-lock brakes until they grabbed, but she still skidded. The sound of crunching metal and a small jolt from behind her indicated the car to her rear had collided with her bumper. Her instinctual reaction was to keep her brakes pushed into the floor as far as possible, which sent her careening sideways down the highway, directly into the path of the skidding SUV. The car from behind hit her again, guaranteeing her fate. The SUV crashed into the left side of her car, inflating her airbag on impact and destroying the front end of the vehicle. The ruined remains of her car skidded sideways off the road, and she screamed as cold metal met the skin of her left leg, followed by a rush of warmth.

The clamor of skidding tires and crunching metal drowned out the sound of her screams. As her car spun, she glanced across a field and noticed a young boy dressed in scruffy old clothes. A big Scottish Deerhound stood next to him, and both of them were staring directly at her.

Somehow she heard the urchin when he whispered, "Do no' worry, missy angel."

Blissful darkness took over as she passed out, still clutching the steering wheel.

NOVELS BY KEIRA MONTCLAIR

THE CLAN GRANT SERIES

#1- RESCUED BY A HIGHLANDER-Alex and Maddie
#2- HEALING A HIGHLANDER'S HEART-Brenna and Quade
#3- LOVE LETTERS FROM LARGS-Brodie and Celestina
#4-JOURNEY TO THE HIGHLANDS-Robbie and Caralyn
#5-HIGHLAND SPARKS-Logan and Gwyneth
#6-MY DESPERATE HIGHLANDER-Micheil and Diana
#7-THE BRIGHTEST STAR IN THE HIGHLANDS-Jennie and Aedan
#8- HIGHLAND HARMONY-Avelina and Drew

THE HIGHLAND CLAN

LOKI-Book One
TORRIAN-Book Two
LILY-Book Three
JAKE-Book Four
ASHLYN-Book Five
MOLLY-Book Six
JAMIE AND GRACIE- Book Seven
SORCHA-Book Eight
KYLA-Book Nine
BETHIA-Book Ten
LOKI'S CHRISTMAS STORY-Book Eleven

THE BAND OF COUSINS

HIGHLAND VENGEANCE
HIGHLAND ABDUCTION
HIGHLAND RETRIBUTION

HIGHLAND LIES
HIGHLAND FORTITUDE
HIGHLAND RESILIENCE
HIGHLAND DEVOTION
HIGHLAND BRAWN
HIGHLAND YULETIDE MAGIC

HIGHLAND SWORDS
THE SCOT'S BETRAYAL

THE SOULMATE CHRONICLES
#1 TRUSTING A HIGHLANDER
#2 TRUSTING A SCOT

STAND-ALONE BOOKS
THE BANISHED HIGHLANDER
REFORMING THE DUKE
WOLF AND THE WILD SCOTS
FALLING FOR THE CHIEFTAIN-3RD in a collaborative
trilogy

**THE SUMMERHILL SERIES- CONTEMPORARY
ROMANCE**
#1-ONE SUMMERHILL DAY
#2-A FRESH START FOR TWO
#3-THREE REASONS TO LOVE

Dear Readers,

I hope you enjoyed my second novel in The Highland Clan series. If you enjoyed reading about Torrian, his story began in HEALING A HIGHLANDER'S HEART.

If you haven't guessed yet, Lily's story will be next in the series.

If you want to know more about my novels, here are some places for you to visit.

1. Visit my website at **www.keiramontclair.com** and sign up for my newsletter. I'll keep you updated about my new releases without bothering you often.

2. **Go to my Facebook page and 'like' me:** You will get updates on any new novels, book signings, and giveaways. **https://www.facebook.com/KeiraMontclair**

3. **Stop by my Pinterest page: http://www.pinterest.com/KeiraMontclair/** You'll see how I envision Torrian, Heather, and Nellie, along with wee Jennet and Brigid.

4. **Give a review on Amazon or Goodreads.** Reviews help self-published authors like me and help other readers as well.

Happy reading!

Keira Montclair
www.keiramontclair.com

ABOUT THE AUTHOR

Keira Montclair is the pen name of an author who lives in Florida with her husband. She loves to write fast-paced, emotional romance, especially with children as secondary characters in her stories.

She has worked as a registered nurse in pediatrics and recovery room nursing. Teaching is another of her loves, as she has taught both high school mathematics and practical nursing.

Now she loves to spend her time writing, but there isn't enough time to write everything she wants! Her Highlander Clan Grant Series is a reader favorite and is a series of eight stand-alone novels. Her third series, The Highland Clan, is set twenty years after the Clan Grant Series and will focus on the Grant/Ramsay descendants.

You may contact her through her website at **www.keiramontclair.com**. She also has a Facebook account and a twitter account through Keira Montclair. If you send her an email through her website, she promises to respond.

Printed in Great Britain
by Amazon